PRAISE FOR MEL ODOM AND THE
ROVER NOVELS

"Odom's latest novel, set in the world of the award-winning *The Rover*, combines a triptych of mini-adventures into a larger story of faith in the power of knowledge to overcome ignorance. Juhg is a resourceful, appealing hero, sustained by his love of books and learning."
— *Library Journal* on *The Quest for the Trilogy*

"The halflings are halfers (or dwellers), and they don't dwell in holes, but they have hairy feet and they're stubby little fellows. The goblins are goblinkin, the wizard looks a lot like Gandalf, there's a dread lord in the background, and the dwarves wield mean battle-axes. And if there isn't a ring to dispose of, at least there's a quest. What more do you want?"
— *Analog* on *The Quest for the Trilogy*

"Odom's bouncy, funny, cliff-hanger adventure is perfect for the Potter crowd, with enough puns, wry asides, and satirical send-ups to amuse Tolkien fans."
— *Kirkus Reviews* on *The Destruction of the Books*

"In the familiar tradition of *The Lord of the Rings*."
— *Publishers Weekly* on *The Destruction of the Books*

boneslicer:

the quest
for the
trilogy

THE ROVER SERIES FROM TOR BOOKS

boneslicer:

the quest for the trilogy

mel odom

TOR® fantasy

A Tom Doherty Associates Book
New York

This is a work of fiction. All of the characters, organizations, and events portrayed in this novel are either products of the author's imagination or are used fictitiously.

BONESLICER: THE QUEST FOR THE TRILOGY

Copyright © 2007 by Mel Odom

Boneslicer was originally published by Tor Books in 2007, in Mel Odom's *The Quest for the Trilogy*.

A Tor Book
Published by Tom Doherty Associates, LLC
175 Fifth Avenue
New York, NY 10010

www.tor-forge.com

Tor® is a registered trademark of Tom Doherty Associates, LLC.

ISBN-13: 978-0-7653-5425-9
ISBN-10: 0-7653-5425-X

First Edition: June 2008

Printed in the United States of America

0 9 8 7 6 5 4 3 2 1

To my son, Chandler.
Daddy created this world with you in mind. Enjoy it.

boneslicer:

the quest
for the
trilogy

FOREWORD

"Education Is Overrated, Grandmagister Juhg!"

having second thoughts, Grandmagister?" a deep voice asked from behind Juhg.

Startled, Juhg turned and faced the speaker. He hadn't even heard him approach. But that was usual for the man. Craugh had spent much of the last thousand years skulking in shadows.

He stood on the loose cobblestones of the street. Dressed in dust-stained russet-colored homespun garments, he didn't look like a wizard. Instead, six and a half feet tall and skinny as a rake, he looked like a weary traveler, days from his last meal.

A wide-brimmed, peaked hat shadowed his face from the noonday sun, but it didn't completely smooth out the crags years had left stamped upon him. Scars lay there too, from knife and sword and arrow. Still, his hawk's beak of a nose and his bright green eyes implied power and a relentless nature. He leaned upon the rough staff he carried, hand resting idly on the crook at the end of it. He drew his other hand through the tangled mess of his long gray beard.

In all the years past that Juhg had known the wizard, Craugh had only referred to him as "apprentice," as if he were the only Novice Librarian that Grandmagister

Lamplighter had ever taken on to train at the Vault of All Known Knowledge. Now, with the Grandmagister's departure and Juhg's naming to the position of Grandmagister, Craugh addressed him by his title. Most of the time.

(Sometimes the wizard still referred to Juhg as *idiot* and *buffoon*, and those weren't meant as terms of endearment. They both missed Edgewick Lamplighter, for reasons each their own, but that didn't mean they agreed how to proceed without their friend.)

"I'm long past second thoughts," Juhg muttered. He drew himself to his full height, still only a little more than three and a half feet tall. He was a dweller, much thinner and more wiry than most. Dwellers tended to be short and stout, and fat in their later years when they could afford to succumb to their innate selfishness. Juhg was pale at present, with fair hair and a youthful appearance. Today, instead of Librarian robes, he wore finery that he felt uncomfortable in.

"Eh?" Craugh said, holding a hand to his ear.

Juhg sighed. He hated it when the wizard pretended not to hear him because he couldn't speak *tall* enough.

"I'm long past second thoughts," Juhg said more loudly, curbing at least three—no, *four*—sharp retorts that came to mind to address Craugh's hearing ability as well as his advancing years.

At the moment, though, he didn't wish to lose Craugh's support and—perhaps it would stretch the very nature of the definition to call it such—friendship. As the new Grandmagister negotiating with the important leaders of the dwarves, humans, and elves along the Shattered Coast, Juhg felt inept and very much alone these past few days.

"Good," Craugh said, and smiled grimly. "You should be of a more positive mind."

"I'm probably on forty-sixth or forty-seventh thoughts," Juhg admitted. "And that's just today. After lunch." In truth, he felt sick. Even so, he felt driven to at least attempt to accomplish the goal he'd set for himself. "I just don't want to botch this."

"Nonsense." Craugh gazed up at the town meeting hall. "You'll do fine."

Making himself breathe out so he wouldn't hyperventilate, Juhg checked his journal to make certain it was the right one and he hadn't forgotten his notes. "I'm afraid they don't like me."

"Poppycock," Craugh said.

Juhg felt a little relieved at that.

"They don't know *you* well enough not to like you," Craugh went on. "It's your ideas they hate."

Those are exactly the words of confidence I was looking for to inspire me. But Craugh's assessment of the situation, however true it might be, stung Juhg's pride. He stood a little straighter and looked into the wizard's insolent gaze.

"They don't know my ideas well enough to hate them," Juhg insisted. "I've barely begun speaking."

"Then perhaps," Craugh said, "we should go inside and finish what you have begun." Without another word, he stepped toward the town meeting hall.

Sighing again, taking one last look at the ship in the harbor, Juhg followed the wizard. *Craugh will lead you to your doom*, he warned himself. *How many times did Grandmagister Lamplighter tell you about adventures he went on because of Craugh? Dozens! At least that many. And how many times did those adventures nearly get him killed? At least nearly every time. At one point or another.*

In the main hallway, dwarven and human guards dressed in heavily armored leather stood watch over the door to the meeting room. They held axes and swords naked in their fists. All of them were sworn to provide security for the important people they represented. Atop the building, elven warders stood at the ready, their hawks and falcons skirling high in the sky to keep an eye on the countryside and the sea.

One of the human guards challenged Craugh, swinging the long handle of his axe to block the way. The guard was younger, taller, and broader, and evidently full of himself concerning his fighting prowess.

"Who are you?" the guard demanded.

Drawing himself up to his full height, Craugh fixed the man with his stare. Displeasure and anger clouded the wizard's face. Lambent green sparks jumped and swirled at the end of his staff.

"I am Craugh," he declared. And his voice filled the space in front of the door like a blow.

Immediately, the guard paled and took a step back, clearing the way. He broke eye contact. His hand shook on his axe. "Forgive me. Please don't turn me into a toad."

The reputation the wizard had for turning people into toads when they irritated him was known far and wide around the mainland. It was rumored that he had increased the toad populations in some areas by whole communities.

Craugh passed on without another word.

Juhg started forward as well, but was blocked instantly by the guardsman's axe. Looking up at the guard, who had seen him both days before when he'd gone into the meeting hall, Juhg blinked in disbelief.

"Who are you?" the guard challenged, sounding fiercer than ever. Evidently he felt he had to regain his status with his companions.

"You know me," Juhg said, exasperated.

"Show me your bracelet," the guard ordered. Copper bracelets stamped with trees, ships, and mountains had been issued to those who were allowed into the meeting.

"I'm the Grandmagister," Juhg began, starting to push back his sleeve to reveal the bracelet. His wrist was bare. Feeling stupid, he remembered that he'd left the bracelet in his room aboard the ship.

"Well?" the guard demanded, as if sensing weakness on Juhg's part.

"I'm the *Grandmagister*," Juhg said again. "I don't look any different today than I did yesterday or the day before."

The guard leaned in more closely, obviously wanting to intimidate Juhg with his greater size.

Juhg, who had grown up as a slave in a goblinkin mine, who had carried the left legs of fellow slaves who had died in the mines back to the harsh overseers to prove the hapless individuals had indeed perished, was not intimidated. He had fought wizards (though not because he wished to), battled goblinkin (only because running hadn't been an option at the time), and faced incredible monsters (drat the luck he sometimes had when he thought about it). Juhg was not impressed.

Although Grandmagister Lamplighter had freed Juhg from the goblinkin slaves and taken him back to Grey-dawn Moors during one of his adventures, the Grand-magister hadn't ever been able to free him from his anger. Two days of being largely ignored and sometimes ridiculed hadn't set well with him.

Before Juhg could stop himself, he caught the human's big nose in a Torellian troll nerve pinch and squeezed. Torellian trolls had at one time been known for their tor-ture techniques. Lord Kharrion had made extensive use of them during the Cataclysm.

The guard yelped in stunned and pained surprise. Para-lyzed by the grip the Grandmagister had on his snout, the burly human dropped to his hands and knees and quickly begged for mercy.

Shocked at what he had done, aware that the guard's companions were closing in on him with edged steel, Juhg released his hold and stepped back. "I am the Grandmagister," he said again.

"I don't care who you are, bub," one of the other human

guards growled, "no one lays a finger on one of Lord Zagobar's personal—"

Craugh raised his staff and brought it down sharply. Green lightning flew from the bottom end of the staff and shot along the hallway floor. Several of the armored guards cried out or cursed. Many of them jumped and rattled their armor. A few of them fell—*splat!*—on their backsides.

"He's with me," Craugh declared, glaring at the guards. "Does anyone have a problem with that?"

"Of course not," the guards all replied in quaking voices. "Go right inside. Sorry to be any trouble."

Juhg heaved out a disgusted breath as he trailed in the wizard's wake. *A wizard should not get more respect than a Librarian.* But that was the way it had always been. After all, Librarians couldn't turn malcontents into toads.

Behind him, one of the dwarven guards took off his hat and enthusiastically smacked the fallen human guard with it. "You stupid miscreant! You could have gotten the lot of us turned to toads!"

Juhg had to hurry to keep up with the wizard. They passed through the rows of seats, most of them filled with those who had come to the meeting. They still glared at Juhg with a mixture of awe, disbelief, and resentment. Several were openly hostile. After all, during the thousand years that had followed the Cataclysm, most of them had thought all books were destroyed.

Lord Kharrion's campaign, besides taking over the world, had been directed toward the destruction of every book that had been written. During the war with the goblinkin, none of the elves, dwarves, or humans had known Lord Kharrion was searching for *The Book of Time*, which had been lost. *The Book of Time* was indestructible.

The fact that Kharrion had also been Craugh's only son remained unknown by all except Juhg.

Craugh stopped so suddenly that Juhg nearly tripped

over his own feet while trying to stop. The wizard turned around and gestured Juhg to the front of the great hall.

Juhg stood for a moment. "I thought perhaps," he said quietly, "you might like to say a few words."

"No," Craugh replied.

"But you came such a long way."

"To hear *you*."

After two days of arguing and attempting to justify his existence, Juhg felt hollowed out. *I should have run for the ship*, he told himself.

Impatiently, Craugh waved him to the front of the room. Lamps lit the stage there, filled with lummin juice, which the glimmerworms of Greydawn Moors produced, and which burned more cleanly and efficiently than whale oil or tallow. That fuel had interested several of the merchants among the crowd and lent proof to Juhg's statement that he was from another place.

But a *Library*? When Juhg had first told them that, even though most of them had heard the rumors that had spread when the Vault of All Known Knowledge had been destroyed almost eight years ago, they had looked upon him with derision.

He was a dweller. By their standards, since dwellers couldn't or wouldn't fight, didn't produce anything worthwhile, and on the whole were known for their greedy and selfish ways, he couldn't possibly be in charge of such a great thing as the Vault of All Known Knowledge. In fact, Grandmagister Lamplighter had been the first to ever hold that office who wasn't human.

"Go," Craugh admonished, shooing Juhg along as he would a child.

Reluctantly, Juhg walked to the front of the assembly. He felt the cruel stares boring into his back. His feet felt leaden and everything in him screamed *Run!* But he didn't. He was following in Edgewick Lamplighter's footsteps and forging a path of his own.

Grumbles and curses arose all around him, sounding as unforgiving and throaty as the Lost Sea, which had been trapped in an underground cave in the Krelmayne Jungles. Even though the lake and the surrounding cave systems had been filled with savage predators that had no eyes and hunted by vibration, Juhg thought he would rather be there at Grandmagister Lamplighter's side in the sinking dinghy once more than facing the hostile crowd.

At the stage, Juhg climbed the stairs, then walked over to the lectern, which hadn't been cut to dweller specifications. He had to climb up on two wooden boxes to reach the proper height.

The audience laughed *at* Juhg, not *with* him. A few disparaging comments about short people and dwellers reached his sensitive ears. His face flamed slightly, but it was as much from anger as from embarrassment.

"Greetings," Juhg said bravely. And he smiled just the way Barndal Krunk had suggested in his book, *Oratories of Those Who Would Be Listened To*. It didn't work and he felt stupid standing there grinning like a loon. He also tried imagining the audience was sitting there in their underwear, but that didn't work either. He was fairly certain several of the poor sailors of the nearby Twisted Eel River didn't own underwear. And imagining the fierce Blade Works Forge dwarves in their underwear was just too horrible to contemplate.

Now, for the first time, utter silence filled the great hall.

Juhg tried to find Craugh out in the audience, hoping to find a friendly face to focus on. *If that's the friendliest face you can hope to find*, he told himself, *you might just as well hang yourself on this stage*.

"As many of you have come to know these past two days," Juhg ventured on, knowing that there were some among the assembly now who had only arrived, "I am Grandmagister of the Vault of All Known Knowledge, the Great Library that was built near the end of the

Cataclysm to save the books from Lord Kharrion's goblinkin horde."

"Dwellers is worthless!" someone roared from the back. A chorus of boos followed.

Patiently, Juhg waited for the remonstrations to die away. He gripped the edges of the too-wide lectern. "I sent heralds to gather you all here," he went on, "in the hope of presenting my vision of schools along the Shattered Coast."

"Schools!" someone yelled. "Fish got schools! We ain't fish!"

"Your children and their children need educations," Juhg said. "With Lord Kharrion defeated, with the goblinkin horde in abeyance—"

"They ain't in abeyance!" someone shouted. "They's down to the south! Where they always been! We need to go down there an' burn 'em all out rather than sittin' here on our duffs listenin' to a halfer tryin' to convince us he's important!"

Cheering broke out immediately.

Thoughts of war bring these people together, but peacetime divides them. Juhg couldn't believe it.

"We should all get us an ale down at Keelhauler's Tavern an' head on out down there."

And more wars have started with tankards of foaming ale. Juhg raised his voice. "You'll have your chance at the goblinkin soon enough. But if you aren't ready for them, they'll destroy you."

That declaration set off another wave of hostility.

An elf stood up in the front row. His two great wolves roused with him, growling fiercely as they stood with their forelegs on the arms of his chair and rose nearly to their master's shoulders.

He was an elven warder, marked by his green leathers, bow, and pointed ears as well as the animal companions he kept. His long hair was the color of poplar bark and stood out against the golden skin. Amethyst eyes glinted like stone. Thin and beautiful and arrogant, the elf leaned on his unstrung bow and gazed at the assembly.

"Quiet," he said. "I wish to hear what the halfer has to say."

A group of rough-hewn sailors stood up in the back. "We don't take no orders 'cept from our cap'n, *elf*," one of their number said. He made the word a curse.

The elf smiled lazily. "You'll do well to take orders from me, human. Or at least not feel so emboldened in my presence. Your continued survival could count on that."

A dwarf stood up only a few feet from the elf. His gnarled hand held a battle-axe that was taller than he was. Scars marked his face and arms, offering testimony to a warrior's life and not a miner's. His fierce beard looked like the hide ripped from a bear but was stippled through with gray. "That'll be enough threats, Oryn."

Still smiling casually, the elf turned to face the dwarf. "Really, Faldraak? You should know me well enough to know that I don't make threats. I make promises."

"An' you don't have sense enough to come in from the rain," Faldraak accused. "Are you prepared to fight a crew of humans?"

"I am," Oryn replied. "The only question is whether or not I have to fight a dwarf as well."

Several other elves stood up. "Oryn won't fight alone," one of them promised.

Armor clanking, a dozen dwarves flanked Faldraak.

"Fight!" someone in the back yelled. "There's gonna be a fight between the elves and the dwarves!"

Unable to bear it any longer, Juhg gave in to his anger. "*Stop!*" Amplified by the construction of the stage, his voice rang out over the assembly hall with shocking loudness. Before he knew it, he'd abandoned the lectern and stood at the stage's edge.

The crowd turned on Juhg at once, as if suddenly

realizing their presence and the discomfort between them there was his entire fault.

Too late, Juhg realized that he should have stayed behind the lectern. At least it would have offered some shelter against arrows and throwing knives. Still, his fear wasn't enough to quiet the anger that moved within him.

"Look at you!" he accused. "Ready to fight each other over a few harsh words!" He stood on trembling legs but found he couldn't back away from his own fight with them. "Is this the kind of world you want to give each other? One where you have to fight each other instead of the goblinkin?"

No one said anything. All eyes were upon him.

"Because that's how it was before Lord Kharrion gathered the goblinkin tribes, you know," Juhg said. "Before he came among them, they were wary and distrustful of each other. They preyed on each other, thieving and murdering among themselves because they didn't like fighting humans, dwarves, or elves. But Kharrion taught them to work together. *And they very nearly destroyed the world.*"

The audience stood quietly listening to Juhg for the first time in three days.

"Now that the goblinkin aren't the threat they used to be," Juhg said, "maybe you can go back to killing each other over territory nobody wants or needs. Or to feel secure. Or over harsh words. Or any of the other reasons people have found to go to war over since groups first gathered."

"Make your point, halfer," a human merchant said. He was dressed in finery and accompanied by a dozen armed guards. Age and success had turned him plump and soft. His hair was black but the color looked false. Jeweled rings glinted on his fingers. "For two days, you've stood up there and ranted and raved about the Library's existence, which"—he turned to address the crowd—"I think nobody really cares about."

A few in the audience agreed with him.

"I'd heard the Library existed only a few years ago," the human continued. "There was some mention of a battle against a man named Aldhran Khempus. Supposedly, there are *two* libraries, in fact."

"Yes," Juhg said, "there are." He had discovered the second while rescuing Grandmagister Lamplighter and searching for *The Book of Time*.

"In the past," the merchant said, "simply owning a book was enough to get you killed not only by the goblinkin, but generally by anyone who found you with one."

"The times are changing," Juhg said.

"You're only here," the merchant continued, "because you want the people here to help aid in your defense from the goblinkin. I've heard they've sent raiding parties out to your little island."

"They have," Juhg admitted. "Those goblinkin raiding parties haven't succeeded in reaching Greydawn Moors. They never will. The island's defenders will never allow that to happen."

"How many dwellers are among those defenders?" the human taunted.

"Dwellers," Juhg said, "aren't warriors. We were charged by the Old Ones to become the keepers of the Great Library."

"That's what you do?"

"Yes."

The human held up his hands in fake supplication. "Then why did you call us here, telling us that the fate of the world rested in our hands?"

"Because it does," Juhg said.

"How?"

Leaping from the stage, Juhg opened his backpack, took several books from it, and walked to the elven warder and surveyed him. "You're a Fire Lily elf from the Joksdam Still Waters."

Oryn was unimpressed. "A number of those present know who I am."

Opening the book, Juhg flipped to one of the illustrations that showed the wide river that wound through what had once been Teldane's Bounty but was now the Shattered Coast. "But I know the history of your people. I know what Joksdam Still Waters looked like when it was whole, when it was a place of beauty and not a place of dead trees and cities."

The picture was in color, elaborately inked and designed to catch the eye. It showed an elven warder on a leaf boat sculling the waters and battling a sea troll three times his size.

Reverently, Oryn took the book. "Kaece the Swift," he marveled. The other elven warders crowded in around him to peer over his shoulder.

"Yes." Juhg had deliberately ordered the story of Kaece the Swift copied. "This is his story, Oryn. His *true* story. Before Lord Kharrion came among the Fire Lily elves and destroyed them." He changed his language to the elven tongue. "And it's written in the language of your people."

Cautiously, Oryn flipped through the book, stopping at several other pictures. All of them were in color, which had drawn a lot of complaints from Juhg's overworked Library staff, but he'd wanted to make a good impression.

"You know his story?" Oryn asked.

"I've read it," Juhg said.

"There have been few like him."

"I know."

Oryn looked at Juhg with new respect. "You have read this?"

"Yes."

"Could you"—he hesitated, because elves were haughty beings and didn't like being beholden to another—"read this to me?"

"I will."

Oryn's hands closed tightly around the book. "What do you want for such a book?"

"The book is yours," Juhg said. "It's the Library's gift to you."

"I can't just accept such a gift." Nor did Oryn seem especially desirous of returning the book. "There must be something I can give you in return."

"There is," Juhg said.

Wariness entered the amethyst eyes.

"Give me your promise that you will let me teach you to read this book," Juhg said. "And others like it. Whether at the Vault of All Known Knowledge, your home, or someplace else you might wish to meet. And promise me too that you will teach at least two others to read this book, and that they will each teach two more, and that the teaching will continue."

"I have two sons and a daughter," Oryn said. "I give you my word that I will do as you ask."

"Thank you," Juhg said. He turned to Faldraak and took out another book. "You're of the Ringing Anvil dwarves."

"I am," Faldraak replied proudly. "Ringing Anvil steel is like no other. We're known for it."

"Your people once built armor for kings," Juhg said. "And you constructed iron figureheads and rams for ships that were magically made so they wouldn't rust."

Faldraak shook his shaggy head. "A myth, nothing more."

Dwarves and magic didn't get along well. Everyone knew that. Humans and elves were more open to it, though elves held more with nature and humans tended to be more destructive.

Juhg opened the book. "The secret of that magically imbued iron was the Ringing Anvil clan's alone. They wrested the process from a dragon named Kallenmarsdale who lived long ago and high up in the Boar's Snout Mountains."

The dwarf's eyes widened. "Not many know that tale."

"I know more than the tale," Juhg said quietly. "I know the secret of how magic was put into that iron."

"No," Faldraak whispered hoarsely.

Juhg opened the book to a picture of a dwarf grabbing hold of the toe of a dragon swooping over a mountaintop with the setting sun in the background. "Drathnon the Bold. The Ringing Anvil dwarf who bearded Kallenmarsdale in his lair."

Faldraak snatched the book from Juhg's hands. "The secret of the magical iron lies in here?"

"It does."

"And you would give it to me?"

"It's yours."

"You will read this to me?"

"I will. But only at the same price that Oryn's paying."

Without warning, Faldraak gave a cry of gladness, tossed his battle-axe to one of his companions, and wrapped his arms around Juhg, lifting the dweller from his feet like a puppy. "Ah, now you are a surprise, you are! You done filled this old dwarf's heart with gladness! I'd thought that secret lost an' gone forever!"

Juhg almost couldn't breathe. He felt certain his ribs would be bruised for days. A moment later, Faldraak placed him back upon his feet.

During the next several minutes, Juhg passed out twenty-seven other books to people who had come to the gathering. Only five histories didn't have descendants to give them to, and several others were disappointed that they didn't have anything. Juhg got all their names and promised to get them each books upon his return to the Vault of All Known Knowledge. He could only imagine the protests of his poor staff, who were dividing their time between getting the Library back into shape, teaching Novices, and carrying on their own works and studies.

In the end, he returned to the stage, though he didn't

humiliate himself by crawling up to the lectern again. He spoke to them from the stage's edge.

"These books represent the worlds that existed before the Cataclysm," Juhg said.

Amazingly, the audience was quiet now, hanging onto his words. He couldn't believe how much giving them the books had impressed them.

"They also represent the worlds your children and your children's children can return to," Juhg went on. "As the goblinkin are driven back, and I believe they will be, the world will grow smaller, not larger. Our lives will become larger. We won't exist as little communities. But as we grow, we'll develop the same problems we had that Lord Kharrion was able to take advantage of in the early part of the Cataclysm."

"What are you talking about?" the human merchant demanded.

"Sit down, Dooly!" someone yelled. "I want to hear the halfer speak!"

"Don't you know what he's talking about?" Dooly demanded. "Truly?" He hurried on before anyone answered. "This halfer is intending to pick your pockets! Who do you think is going to pay for these schools he intends to build?"

That started another ripple of speculative conversation. Obviously, the merchant could smell a plea for donations a mile away.

"Tell them," Dooly snarled at Juhg. "Tell them that's why you gathered them here. To fleece them of money."

Honesty is the best policy, Juhg told himself. He tried desperately not to remember how many times he knew of that such a practice had gotten the practitioner killed.

"The establishment of schools will require help," Juhg said.

Immediately some of the goodwill of the book presentation evaporated. No one liked the idea of giving away gold.

"Some of that help," Juhg said, speaking over the noise, "will, of necessity, be of a financial nature. To feed and clothe the students and teachers while they are at their studies for the first year. Then they can garden, hunt, or fish to get what they need or the goods to trade for what they need. But most of the help needed will be only labor to build the schools."

"For what purpose?" Dooly asked. "To deprive farmers of their helpers? Artisans of their apprentices? To make every man and woman work two and three times as hard as he or she should have to, while their sons and daughters sit in some schoolhouse and do nothing?"

"To get an education," Juhg replied, trying to control the damage of the merchant's words. "In order to learn to do things and teach others. In order to better live with one another. We will someday live in one world again. We should live in it better than we have in the past. The children need education to do that."

"Education is overrated, Grandmagister," Dooly accused. "You stand up there today, offering your gifts and your promises, and you want only to make our lives harder. I've had just about enough of this foolishness and your empty words."

A single green spark danced from the back of the room, drawing the attention of several attendees. As Dooly continued haranguing Juhg, the spark sailed over and attached itself to the back of the merchant's head. As Dooly talked, his tongue got longer and longer, and his face broadened and shortened, till he soon showed the wide face of a toad atop human shoulders. His hair became bumps and warts.

Several of the people around Dooly started laughing. Even Juhg couldn't help smiling.

Abruptly, Dooly stopped speaking and glared at the people around him. "What?" he demanded. His tongue flicked out like a whip. Evidently he saw that movement for the first time. Experimentally, he flicked his tongue out several times. Then he raised his hands and felt his head.

"Oh no!" he cried. "Oh no! Oh—*ribbit*!" Holding onto his head, he fled the room. Before he reached the door, his gait changed from a run into bounding hops. The door closed after his retreat.

"Perhaps," a deep voice from the back of the room suggested, "we could do the Grandmagister the courtesy of listening to his plans."

"It'd be better than being a toad," someone grunted irritably.

"Continue, Grandmagister," Oryn said.

And Juhg did.

"Coercion wasn't part of my presentation," Juhg said.

"No, I claim credit for that," Craugh responded. "Once I used it, things seemed to go more smoothly."

Juhg looked around Keelhauler's Tavern, which was a waterfront dive not too far from *Moonsdreamer*, the ship that had brought him from Greydawn Moors. That also meant the ship was only a short distance away if things turned ugly locally and they had to run for it.

Over the years, the tavern's owners had enlarged the building three or possibly four times, simply hauling over other structures and attaching them, then laying in a floor. As a result, the floors were of varying heights and weren't always level. The furniture consisted of a hodgepodge of whatever had showed up at the door.

Although the tavern was filled near to bursting with all the extra people in for the meeting, no one sat close to Craugh and Juhg. It was, under the toad circumstances, understandable.

"They're afraid of you," Juhg said.

Craugh preened in self-satisfaction. "They should be."

Juhg sighed. "It's difficult to get anyone to do anything charitable when they feel threatened."

"I beg to differ. After the possibility of being turned into toads was presented, they sat and listened while you droned on and on about schools and education."

"I didn't drone."

Craugh frowned. "Your elocution lacks. 'We must build for the future. We must ensure our children know about the past before they step into the future.'" The wizard shook his head. "The toad threat? That was eloquent. Short, punchy, attention-getting." He took another cream-filled bitter blueberry tort from the plate he'd ordered and dug in. For all his leanness, the wizard was a bottomless pit when it came to food. "You don't *ask* people for help. You *tell* them to help you."

"Or you turn them into toads."

Craugh shrugged. "If I threatened that, then yes, I turn them into toads. Threats don't carry much weight if you don't occasionally carry them out."

Despair weighed heavily on Juhg. "Toads can't build schools."

"Actually, toads can't do much of anything. Except eat flies." Craugh brushed cookie crumbs from his beard. "I believe that was the point."

"We need these people's goodwill."

"Over the years, Grandmagister, I have found that people demonstrate an overall lack of enthusiastic good-will without being properly motivated. Especially when it comes to public projects. I merely provided the motivation. Had I been here two days ago, doubtless you would have already been finished."

One way or another, Juhg silently agreed.

"Now if Wick had addressed those people today—" Craugh caught himself and shook his head. "Alas, but that's not to be, is it?" He smiled a little, but sadness touched his green eyes.

"I regret that I'm not Grandmagister Lamplighter," Juhg said, feeling the old pain stir inside him as well. Although he understood Grandmagister Lamplighter's decision to explore the realms opened up to him by *The Book of Time*, Juhg hadn't quite forgiven his mentor for leaving.

"No," Craugh said forcefully. "Never regret that. You are you, Grandmagister Juhg, and were it not for you, the possibility of giving back all the lost knowledge to the people of the world would never have come this far."

Pain tightened Juhg's throat. For all that they argued and disagreed, he and Craugh had shared a love and deep respect for Edgewick Lamplighter. They were the only two who knew most of the Grandmagister's life. They had shared his adventures outside Greydawn Moors and had gotten to see him work. None of the Grandmagister's acquaintances on the Shattered Coast had ever come to Greydawn Moors.

"Thank you," Juhg whispered.

"Your friendship these days," the wizard said, "means a lot to me."

That admission from Craugh was both surprising and touching. Juhg didn't know what to say. The silence stretched between them, crowded by the conversations throughout the rest of the tavern.

"You didn't come here today for the presentation, did you?" Juhg asked. He'd asked earlier, but Craugh had never answered him. The wizard didn't answer any questions until he was ready. But that didn't mean he couldn't be asked again.

"No, I didn't." Craugh took another tort and nibbled at the edge. "Something else brought me to you."

Silently, Juhg waited. Only trouble would bring Craugh to him. He didn't want to ask what *that* was. So he didn't.

"Tell me," Craugh said almost conversationally, as if the potential fate of the world didn't hang in his words, "have you ever heard of Lord Kharrion's Wrath?"

Juhg reflected for a moment. "No. Not really. There was some mention of it in Troffin's *Legacy of the Cataclysm*."

"I'm not familiar with that."

"Most people aren't. The Grandmagister had me read it one day, but he never explained why."

"Ah. What did the book say about Lord Kharrion's Wrath?"

"Only that it was a weapon the Goblin Lord had been building toward the end of the Cataclysm. I think the legend was eventually dismissed as a fabrication."

Craugh took out his pipe and filled it. He snapped his fingers and a green flame sprang to life on his thumb. In short order, he had the pipe going merrily and a cloud of smoke wreathed his hat.

"What," the wizard asked, "if I told you the story of Lord Kharrion's Wrath was true?"

Juhg thought about that. "Then I'd say it was over a thousand years too late."

"Perhaps not."

Disturbing images took shape in Craugh's pipe smoke. Wars were fought in those small clouds. Juhg didn't know if the smoke revealed things yet to come or were drawn from the wizard's memory.

"Wick, at one time, was on the trail of Lord Kharrion's Wrath," Craugh said. "Quite by accident, though. He'd ended up in the Cinder Clouds Islands as a result of an argument between Hallekk and another ship's crew one night in the Yondering Docks."

"The Grandmagister wouldn't get involved in an argument," Juhg said automatically. "Besides, there'd be nothing to argue over. The Grandmagister would know the answers."

"No one believed him."

"And he went to prove them wrong?" Juhg shook his head. "That still doesn't sound like the Grandmagister."

Craugh coughed delicately. "Actually, Wick wasn't given a choice."

Juhg lifted a suspicious eyebrow.

"We waited until Wick was deep into his cups, then we took him back to the ship."

"You shanghaied him? Again?" Juhg couldn't believe it.

"It was Hallekk's idea, actually."

At the time, Hallekk had probably been first mate on *One-Eyed Peggie*, Greydawn Moors' only dwarven pirate ship. The crew had shanghaied Grandmagister Lamplighter from the Yondering Docks all those years ago to fill their crew, so deep in their cups they hadn't realized then that he was a Librarian.

Juhg wondered why the Grandmagister would have gone adventuring again just to satisfy Hallekk's need to win a wager.

"Did the Grandmagister believe in Lord Kharrion's Wrath?" Juhg asked.

"He did. He saw it."

That announcement took Juhg by surprise. "He never mentioned it to me."

"Wick has lived . . . an *adventurous* life. Quite contrary to a normal dweller's desires." Craugh puffed on his pipe and a dreadful dragon sailed in full attack in the clouds dappling the tavern ceiling. Several nearby patrons sat in frozen astonishment, then carefully—quietly—left their seats and departed. "I'm sure he didn't tell you everything."

"I've read everything he wrote."

"Perhaps he didn't write about everything he witnessed."

Juhg shook his head immediately. "That wasn't his way. He taught me the importance of keeping a journal." Reaching into his robes, he took out a journal he'd made himself.

After placing the journal on the table, he flipped through the pages and revealed the images and words he'd wrought over the last few days. Images of Shark's Maw Cove, the meeting hall, the principal attendees he'd met, as well as plants, structures, and animals that had caught his curious eye all filled the pages amid notes and monographs.

"This is just the bare beginning of this book, though," Juhg said. "I've been working on a more finished one on board *Moonsdreamer*." He closed the book and put it away. "The Grandmagister kept a record of *everything*."

"So he did. Which leads us to the conclusion that you *haven't* read everything Wick wrote."

"Impossible."

Saying nothing, the wizard reached inside his traveling cloak, took out a fat book, and dropped it with a *thump* onto the table. "Have you read this?"

Juhg recognized Grandmagister Lamplighter's handiwork immediately. The Grandmagister had always been very exact when he built a journal to record his adventures. This one had a lacquered finish over maple stained deep red that would be proof against impact and water.

Opening the book, Juhg found the Grandmagister's hand upon the pages. Juhg knew his mentor's style instantly from the Qs. Grandmagister Lamplighter had the most beautiful Qs of any Librarian.

Several of the pages, though, showed charring. Other pages showed where pinholes had burned through.

The frontispiece showed an exquisite drawing of *One-Eyed Peggie* sitting at anchor at the Yondering Docks. Dwarves, one of them barrel-chested Hallekk, stood on the deck working at their chores.

"Where did you get this?" Juhg asked, astounded.

"At the Vault. I just came from there."

"Impossible."

"You didn't know where all Wick's hiding places were," Craugh said.

"He would have told me."

"That book that you hold in your hand proves that he didn't."

Juhg couldn't argue that and didn't, though he sorely wanted to. "Why wouldn't he tell me?"

"Maybe he just never got around to it," the wizard gently suggested.

Looking at the opening pages, Juhg discovered that he couldn't read them. "It's written in code."

"Wick was very careful."

Let's only hope the Grandmagister still is, Juhg fervently hoped. *Wherever The Book of Time has taken him.*

"Can you read it?" Craugh asked.

Quickly, Juhg took out his own journal and tried some of the various codes he and the Grandmagister had devised over the years of their adventuring. In short order, the strange symbols became perfectly understandable words.

"Yes. It's written in one of the first codes the Grandmagister taught me." Excitement filled Juhg at the discovery.

"Good. That proves that he intended to let you know about this book at some date," Craugh said.

Relief flooded Juhg. "Why did you bring this book to me?"

Craugh was silent for a moment, contemplating his response. "Because I can't read it. I need it translated."

"You want me to translate this?"

"Can you name another more suited to the task?"

"No," he replied.

"Neither could I."

"Don't you already know what this book contains?"

Hesitantly, Craugh shook his head. "I don't know. Though Wick and I trusted each other and would have laid down our lives for each other—and almost had occasion to do so now and again—we still maintained our own counsel in some areas." He sighed and a lightning storm manifested in the smoke over his peaked hat. Green sparks danced within the storm. "I think it was because Wick knew—*knows*—that I have my own secrets from him."

Chief among those secrets had been Craugh's own early villainy and search for power through *The Book of Time*. And the fact that Craugh had fathered Lord Kharrion. Only Juhg knew that, and it had been the first secret he had kept from Grandmagister Lamplighter.

"But I was with Wick when he found Lord Kharrion's Wrath," Craugh said.

"It *is* a weapon?"

"Yes."

"What kind of weapon?"

"Read the book," Craugh directed. "I don't want to risk influencing translations or interpretations of what you find there. When you have the book decoded, we'll compare what we know."

Suddenly a thump sounded on the tavern's roof. Then more thumps followed, as if a giant were walking across the split wood shingles. Other thumps sounded in different spots, indicating that more than one thing now walked atop the building.

Craugh stood immediately and took up his staff. His eyes narrowed in consternation. "Quickly, Grandmagister. It appears my arrival here hasn't gone unnoticed."

"Unnoticed?" Juhg got to his feet. "You were trying to arrive *unnoticed*?" That could only bode the gravest trouble.

Striding to the center of the big room, Craugh glared up at the ceiling.

"Unnoticed by whom?" Juhg asked, remaining by the table. He peered through the window. Outside, night had come to Shark's Maw Cove. Lanterns lit the crooked boardwalks that led through the boggy marshland to the docks and dilapidated warehouses.

"Those who would prevent me from learning anything further of Lord Kharrion's Wrath, of course." Craugh took his staff in both hands. Green sparks whirled around both ends of it.

The magic was so intense in the room that Juhg felt the hairs on his arms standing to attention. He reached down and slipped out the long fighting knife his friend Raisho had given him years ago when they had entered a trade partnership. That had been when Juhg had tried to leave the Vault of All Known Knowledge because he and Grandmagister Lamplighter had been of different views on how to proceed with the Library.

Juhg said, "Who—"

Then the roof splintered and caved in, scattering shingles in all directions. Three impossible figures dropped to the tavern floor and stood on clawed feet with toes as big as tree roots.

They were vaguely human in shape, possessing two arms and two legs, and had vaguely human features that looked like ridged skulls with flat brown eyes the size of saucers. No nose and a ragged slit for a mouth completed their features. Warped ears twisted like conch shells stuck out on the sides of their heads. They had four fingers and four toes at the ends of their extremities, but those were each as large as a man's wrist. Their skin looked like cypress bark streaked with moss. When they stood, Juhg realized they very nearly reached the ceiling beams, making them at least thirteen or fourteen feet tall. Pungent and strong, the stink of a fecund swamp clung to them.

As one, they turned their gazes on Craugh.

"Get behind me," the wizard ordered.

Juhg did as he was bade, but he was thinking that since the creatures seemed interested in Craugh, maybe that was the *last* place he wanted to be. Still, he couldn't desert the wizard and leave him to face his foes alone. He shoved Grandmagister Lamplighter's coded book into his backpack, took a fresh grip on his fighting knife, and peered around Craugh's leg.

"Dark magic!" someone cried in warning.

"Bog beasts!" another shouted.

The Keelhauler's Tavern emptied in short order. Several of the patrons simply threw chairs through the windows and followed them outside. Only a few elven, dwarven, and human warriors remained. Most of those who had been bending their elbows were sailors and merchants, not versed in the arts of combat.

"Wizard," one of the bog beasts growled in a deep voice that seemed to erupt from within him. It threw a hand forward and a vine leaped from it like a fisherman's line. Thick and fibrous, the vine streaked straight for Craugh.

Hardly moving, the wizard attempted to block the vine with his staff. The vine reacted like a live thing, curling around the staff and tightening. The bog beast fisted the vine and yanked.

Incredibly, Craugh stood against the creature's immense strength, once again demonstrating that he was more than human. He spoke a Word in a harsh tongue. With a *bamf!* green flames spread along the staff. The vine crackled, burning to ash in the space of a heartbeat.

The bog beast screamed in pain and drew back its hand.

"Get back, foul swamp spawn!" Craugh commanded.

The bog beasts surged forward. Their feet hammered against the wooden floor, shattering thick planks that had withstood the test of time till that night.

"Axes!" one of the dwarves yelled. "Don't let them black-hearted beasties tear up *our* tavern!"

At once, the dwarves broke up into three groups of four, standing one by two by one deep. As needed, they rotated the leader in case he grew tired from attacking their enemies or was wounded, moving into the defensive anvil formation—two by two, with shields raised—to wear through an opponent's attack, then back into the axe formation.

The elven warders had nocked their bows. Arrows sped across the short distance of the room and feathered the bog beasts. The creatures roared in anger and pain but showed no sign of turning from Craugh.

Roaring, unleashing Words of power, Craugh raised his flaming staff and brought it crashing down on the floor. In response, Juhg thought the earth had shivered free of its moorings. He toppled and fell, striving desperately to push himself back to his feet.

Everyone in the tavern fell, including the elves, dwarves, and humans. Even the bog beasts toppled. Then what was left of the roof dropped as well, crashing down around Juhg. None of it hit him. When he peered fearfully up from under his folded arm, he saw that a green bubble surrounded Craugh and him. Sparks shimmered along the surface of the bubble. Then it disappeared.

Juhg stood. Tremors continued through the ground and he felt certain the earth would open up and swallow them at any moment.

Bellowing angrily, the bog beasts surged up from under the debris that had fallen on them. One of them threw a vine at Craugh, catching the wizard around the lower right leg. Obviously drained by the spell he had cast, Craugh was slow to react. The bog beast yanked, pulling the wizard from his feet.

Moving by instinct, Juhg scrambled after Craugh, leaping to the top of a broken table and slashing his knife across the vine. The fibrous length parted with only passing resistance. Another bog beast cast its line, but Juhg stomped on an abandoned serving platter and caused it to leap into the air. The vine pierced the platter and was deflected from its target enough to miss, though it was only a matter of inches.

Craugh regained his feet and clapped his hat back on. He took a firmer grip on his staff.

"Scribbler!" a familiar voice yelled.

Turning, Juhg saw Raisho standing in the crooked doorway. The young sailor had become Juhg's best friend during recent years. They had become trading partners when Juhg had been determined to abandon the Vault of All Known Knowledge eight years ago; Raisho had only been twenty.

(Eight years meant a lot to a human. Now Raisho had found his true family, married a mermaid, and had one child and another on the way, and captained *Moonsdreamer*, the ship he'd named after his daughter. At six feet two inches tall, he had filled out over the years, becoming thicker and more powerful, but still went smooth-shaven because his wife preferred him that way.)

Blue tattoos showed on his ebony skin, marred here and there by scars from men and beasts he'd battled while sailing the Blood-Soaked Sea and adventuring with Juhg. A headband of fire opals, made by his beautiful wife, held his thick, unruly black hair back from his handsome face. Silver hoops dangled in his ears. He carried a dwarven-smithed cutlass in his hard right hand. He wore only sailor's breeches, soft leather boots, and a chain mail shirt over his bare chest.

"Scribbler!" Concern etched on his face, eyes straining against the darkness inside the tavern, Raisho strode into the tavern.

"I'm here," Juhg called.

"Thank the Old Ones," Raisho said, striding over to join him and Craugh. "I thought ye'd 'ad yer gullet slit for sure this time. Especially after I'd 'eard Craugh was about an' I saw the dragon flyin' around."

"Dragon?" Juhg echoed.

Raisho nodded. "I was told it was the dragon what dropped them creatures onto the tavern. Didn't know what they was lookin' for. Till I 'eard Craugh was 'ere with ye."

"Dragon?" Juhg repeated, stuck on the possibility that one of those monsters might even now be lurking about outside awaiting them.

"Of course there's a dragon," Craugh growled. "I was going to tell you about the dragon."

"You might have mentioned it before now," Juhg grumbled.

Roaring war cries, the dwarves and humans took up the attack once more, chopping into the backsides of the bog beasts with unrelenting zeal. Shooting with their incredible skill, the elven warders put more arrows into their targets around their fellow combatants. The two back bog beasts had to turn to deal with their opponents.

The bog beast facing Craugh rushed forward, flinging both hands out so that vines shot toward him.

The wizard ducked, whipped his hat off with one hand, spoke a Word, and sent his hat spinning toward the bog beast. Inches from the creature, the hat turned into a flaming fireball nearly two feet in diameter that slammed into the bog beast's chest with a *boom!* louder than thunder.

The creature rocked back on its tree root toes. Dry cracks spread across its chest where the fireball had struck. Craugh pressed his advantage, ducking in and driving the end of his staff into his opponent's chest. Startled, the bog beast glanced down and started to close a hand around Craugh's staff, then the dryness spread through the creature and it fell to pieces.

One of the dwarves grabbed an unbroken lantern from one of the wall sconces. The wick remained aflame inside the glass. Yelling a warning to his fellow warriors, the dwarf heaved the lantern at the bog beast. The lantern shattered against the creature, spreading oil that quickly caught fire. Dry patches showed on the bog beast and it began struggling to move. A moment later, spreading fires throughout the wreckage of the bar, the bog beast broke into pieces.

Taking note of what was going on, the elven warders dipped their arrows in oil and loosed flaming shafts into the remaining bog beast, quickly reducing it to chunks of dry earth that tumbled across the shattered tavern floor. The combatants cheered at once, no longer divided in their goals while facing a common foe.

"Go," Craugh said, "quickly. We may yet face more opposition." He waved his arms to usher Juhg and Raisho into motion.

"Mayhap if we were to split up," Raisho suggested to the wizard. "Ye can go one way. Me an' Juhg, we'll go another."

"No," Craugh said.

Raisho gave a disappointed frown. "I thought not. But I'm tellin' ye now, if'n ye get me ship busted up somewheres, ye're gonna be responsible for replacin' 'er."

Together, they ran out of the building as the flames leaped higher.

"Too bad about your hat," Juhg told Craugh.

"Eh?" the wizard said. Then nodded. "Right. My hat." He snapped his fingers and suddenly the hat was sailing through the air toward them. Effortlessly, Craugh caught the hat and clapped it onto his head. He smiled and wiggled his eyebrows. "This hat has gotten me out of several tight spots over the years. One day, mayhap, I'll tell you the story of how I acquired it."

Intrigued as he was by the story of the wizard's hat, Juhg glanced overhead, spotting the two moons that circled the world. Bright red and speeding on the first of his trips across the night sky, Jhurjan the Swift and Bold was full and close now, occupying fully a tenth of the sky. Farther to the south, glowing a demure pale blue, Gesa the Fair made her way more sedately, with grace and self-control.

There were, thankfully, no dragons in sight.

They ran on, racing down the hill toward the harbor, then down the steep, crooked steps, and—finally—across the swaying bridges that connected the decrepit docks. When they reached *Moonsdreamer*, Raisho hailed his crew, who were already crowded at the railing with weapons to hand.

In minutes, they cast off and *Moonsdreamer*'s sails scaled the masts and belled out from the 'yards. Juhg stood in the bow. Before he knew it, his personal journal and a piece of charcoal were in his hands. By Jhurjan's light, he quickly blocked out the shapes of the bog beasts. Despite the danger, it was what Grandmagister Lamplighter had trained him to do. He wrote his questions for Craugh in the margins while Raisho got his ship into the wind with all due haste.

Unfortunately, Craugh didn't intend to answer many questions.

Seated in the galley with a hot cup of spiced choma at the table before him, Juhg looked at the wizard. "Who sent the bog beasts?"

Craugh scowled. "I told you I wouldn't influence your reading of Wick's book. I meant that."

"Those were bog beasts," Juhg said. "I've never seen creatures like them."

"See? Even more reason I shouldn't answer your idle curiosities."

Not believing what he was hearing, Juhg said, "They tried to kill us. I'd say that I'm motivated by more than idle curiosity."

"Still," Craugh said, "your neutrality in the matter of decoding the book is important, Grandmagister. You have a duty to do the best that you can."

Using his title as he did, Juhg knew that Craugh sought

to motivate him. However, knowing the wizard was a manipulator negated that maneuver. Unfortunately, Juhg also saw the truth in Craugh's words, so it may well have been that the pronouncement wasn't a manipulation. Thinking like that made Juhg's head hurt.

In the end, he knew what Grandmagister Lamplighter would have done: seek out the mysteries the book held.

"All right, all right." Juhg sighed. "I understand all that, and mayhap I even agree that you might be correct in your assessment of how things should be handled."

"Thank the Old Ones," Craugh replied with a small smile that he didn't truly mean.

"That said," Juhg went on, "what *can* you tell me?"

Craugh counted off answers on his fingers. "That we are arrayed against a powerful enemy. That Lord Kharrion's Wrath truly exists. That Wick was on the trail of it all these years ago. That there are secrets that no one was meant to know all those years ago that we must surely find out now." He paused for a moment. "Oh, and one other thing: The stakes are high."

Juhg waited.

"What you may find out in that book," Craugh said, "might well affect the futures of three different communities. One or all will prove guilty of some of the vilest villainies perpetrated during the Cataclysm. When others find out, old enmities might well be re-established and result in hundreds or thousands of deaths." He regarded Juhg. "Is that enough?"

More than enough, Juhg thought, suddenly feeling glum and overwhelmed.

"Scribbler."

Juhg looked back to see Raisho standing in the doorway to the stairs that led up to the deck. The familiar roll of the ship across the waves rocked them.

"There's no sign of pursuit," Raisho said. "We escaped clean enough."

"Good." Juhg felt a little relief. He picked up Grandmagister Lamplighter's book and ran a finger along the charred pages. Curiosity nagged at him as it always did.

"Doesn't mean there won't be any," Raisho went on, and the statement was more of a question.

"I've laid enchantments on the ship," Craugh said. "We're protected better than most."

Raisho nodded. "I'll keep double guards posted in any case. But what 'eading should we take?"

"You've stores packed away?" Craugh asked.

"Aye."

"Then stay at sea."

Raisho frowned. "I've got perishable goods aboardship."

"Continue the trade route we planned on," Juhg said. "We don't want to draw any more attention than we have to. A trade ship not trading will trigger prying interests."

"We may need to travel once you have the book deciphered," Craugh pointed out. "It would be better if we knew from where."

"We'll deal with that when—and *if*—it happens," Juhg replied. He looked at the wizard, expecting an argument.

Instead, Craugh quietly agreed.

That let Juhg know how serious the situation was. And how dangerous. He sipped the choma and turned his attention to the book that contained one of Grandmagister Lamplighter's adventures he hadn't known anything about. In a short time, the coded entries turned into words in his mind and he wrote them down in a new book.

1

The Tavern Brawl

Wick."

Placing his finger inside the book to hold his place, Second Level Librarian Edgewick Lamplighter sighed and glanced up at the speaker. He tried not to show his displeasure at being interrupted at his reading, but it was difficult.

"What is it?" Wick asked.

"Your friends," Paunsel whispered. He was a dweller like Wick, only grossly rotund with slicked-back hair and a thin mustache. He wiped his hands nervously on a bar towel.

"What friends?" Wick was immediately interested, for as a Librarian he had few friends among the sailors and merchants that lined the Yondering Docks in Greydawn Moors.

Paunsel jerked a hesitant thumb over his shoulder.

For the first time, Wick heard the raucous laughter and ribald poetry coming from the tavern's main room. Choosing to be alone with his book (and only a nonreader would call it alone because those poor unfortunates couldn't truly trigger the magic captured in the pages of a book!), Wick had retreated to one of the small side rooms and refused to acknowledge the baleful glances the cleaning crews had given him.

Peering cautiously around the tavern owner, keenly aware that one of the back doors out of the buildings was close at hand just as he'd planned, Wick stared into the main room. Of course, since the Wheelhouse Tavern served all who had coin to pay for it, the place was packed with dwarves come to slake their prodigious thirst.

"The dwarven . . . *pirates*," Paunsel whispered.

Glee touched Wick's heart then. There was only one ship that came to the Yondering Docks carrying *dwarven* pirates. Many months had passed since he'd last seen the crew of *One-Eyed Peggie*. He looked forward to seeing Cap'n Farok, Hallekk, Zeddar, Naght, Jurral, Slops, and even Critter, the foul-tempered rhowdor ship's mascot.

But Wick also knew what the ship's crew was like when they were in their cups. He looked at Paunsel. "Are they fighting someone?"

"Not yet."

"But the likelihood is there?"

Paunsel looked aggrieved. "Yes. Otherwise I wouldn't have bothered you at your studies, Librarian." The tavern owner was one of the few in Greydawn Moors who talked respectfully with Librarians.

Over the years, most of the townsfolk had come to resent the Grandmagister and the Librarians, insisting that the food sent up to the Vault of All Known Knowledge was a burden the rest of the population shouldn't have to bear. Of course, it was mostly the dwellers that said that. The elven warders who guarded the island's forests and mountains, the humans who pretended to be pirates out in the Blood-Soaked Sea, and the dwarven guards and craftsmen were more generous.

Hmmm, Wick thought, for roving across to the Shattered Coast and beyond had taught him to always carefully examine his options. *Renewing acquaintances at the cost of becoming embroiled in a battle isn't all that appetizing. Especially on a full stomach.*

Despite Hallekk and Cobner's attempts to turn him into a pirate or a warrior, Wick was very much satisfied with being a Librarian. He preferred to do his adventuring in the stacks of romances in Hralbomm's Wing while avoiding Grandmagister Frollo's wrath. The Grandmagister was of the opinion that Wick should use his personal reading time more wisely.

"Well?" Paunsel prompted.

"I'm thinking," Wick replied. He tried drumming his fingers on the tabletop the way Grandmagister Frollo did, but evidently the task wasn't as easy as he'd believed. Also, the cadence of Taurak Bleiyz's brave war song was stuck in his head from the book and his fingers kept finding that beat.

"They're going to tear up my tavern," Paunsel said.

The angry voices in the next room rose to a new, and even more threatening, level. Wick's ears pricked, listening with more experience than he'd ever intended for the hiss of swords clearing leather.

"Who are they arguing with?" Wick asked. *Perhaps if it's someone Hallekk and the others can easily frighten off, I could go meet them. After all, if they win an argument, their purses will open and the wine will flow.* It was a pleasing prospect. But he longed to get Taurak Bleiyz across the spiderweb and safely away from his enemies.

"Humans," Paunsel sneered. "The crew of *Stormrider*."

Wick knew of the ship and the crew. If ever there were warriors that could evenly meet dwarven warriors, it was *Stormrider*'s crew.

"What are they arguing about?"

Paunsel sighed, obviously on the verge of giving up asking for help. "Something that happened long ago. An alliance or something that met Lord Kharrion's goblinkin army in the Painted Canyon."

"Ah." Although Wick didn't know the story of the battle well, he was a Librarian. A recently promoted *Second* Level Librarian at that. He thought he could settle an

argument between ships' crews and probably earn himself
a few more cups of sparkleberry wine for his troubles. "I
can handle this."

"Thank the Old Ones," Paunsel said, though with far
more sarcasm than Wick would have wanted to hear. The
tavern keeper waved the Librarian to the main room.

Wick placed his bookmark within the romance and
glanced at the page number to memorize it just in case
before putting it into his book bag. The memorization
was a practice he'd made a habit of when he'd first gone
to the Great Library as a Novice. Then he slid out of the
booth, straightened the lines of his Librarian's robe—
now gray with dark blue fringe, changed from white to
denote his promotion—grabbed the straps of his book
bag, and headed for the main room.

The room was packed with sailors and cargo handlers.
Lanterns filled with glimmerworm juice glowed softly blue
in sconces. Several others hung from ships' wheels sus-
pended from the ceiling. A number of patrons gathered
around the fireplace at the other end of the room. Humans
and dwarves sometimes mixed, but the five elven warders
in from the forest to trade for goods they couldn't get on
their own in the wild sat by themselves.

"—'Twas Oskarr what betrayed the alliance at Painted
Canyon," a human at one of the tables declared. He was
easily six and a half feet tall, almost a giant. His shaggy
blond hair trailed down to his shoulders and matched the
full beard he sported.

"No!" Hallekk bellowed, standing at the bar with his
fellow pirates from *One-Eyed Peggie*. He was tall for a
dwarf, and an axe handle would be challenged to span his
shoulders. His dark brown beard was braided with yel-
lowed bone carved into fish shapes. A bright kerchief
bound his head and gold hoops danced in his ears. He
wore a seaman's breeches and shirt, and held his great
battle-axe casually at his side.

In Wick's opinion, *One-Eyed Peggie*'s first mate didn't look like a dwarf anyone would want to rile. *Unless, of course*, he amended, *you're a human giant and you've had too much to drink*. Wick could see at once that the situation could easily get out of control.

"Now I've kept a civil tongue in me head while ye've been blatherin' on about what happened back then," Hallekk roared loud enough to earn the attention of everyone in the tavern, "but I'll not have ye besmirchin' the name of Oskarr."

"Don't let him talk to you like that, Verdin," one of the other human sailors piped up. "Stupid dwarf is thick everywhere else, ye know he's gotta be thick in the head, too."

Hallekk bristled at the insult.

Verdin's eyes narrowed as he strived to look even more fierce and threatening.

"Ye better not be a-glowerin' at me," Hallekk growled in warning. "I don't take kindly to such intimidation."

"Go on, Hallekk!" a shrill voice called out. "Poke him in the eyes! Tweak his nose! Pull his hair! Thump him till he rings like a drum!"

The voice drew everyone's attention to the rafters above the counter, for the moment silencing the verbal sparring between Verdin and Hallekk. A rhowdor stood on the rafter, dressed in bright plumage that began with an explosion of red on its chest and wings with a few scattered patches of yellow. The ends of the wings and the tail feathers turned green that was so dark it looked blue and black. The bird flailed his wings, shadowboxing unsteadily on the rafter and breathing in short gusts through its curved beak.

Little more than a foot tall with twin pink horns jutting from above its hatchet face, the avian peered down with its one good emerald eye. A black leather patch that bore a skull and crossbones made of studs covered the other eye. A golden hoop earring dangled from one ear tuft.

The rhowdor was intelligent, capable of speaking the common language as well as any others it learned. There were few of the creatures in the world these days. This one was named Critter and crewed aboard *One-Eyed Peggie*.

"What are ye a-lookin' at, ye daft idiot?" Critter called out, taking a break from matching skills with its imaginary opponent. "Ain't ye ever seen a talkin' bird before?"

It was obvious that Verdin hadn't.

"Why, ye're a pantywaist, ye are," the rhowdor crowed fiercely. It walked along the rafter, and from the stumbling steps it took, Wick knew the bird had drunk far too much for its own good. "I could take ye with one wing tied behind me an' me tail feathers on fire." The bird held one wing behind its back and fluttered the other one, nearly knocking itself from the rafter. "I'll show ye. Somebody get me a rope an' tie me wing up behind me back."

"Somebody get me a *stewpot*," Verdin replied, and several of the tavern's patrons—including members of *One-Eyed Peggie*'s crew—laughed uproariously.

"I'll keelhaul ye!" Critter swore. "I'll turn ye inside out an' hang ye with yer own tripe!" The rhowdor launched itself from the rafter, spreading its multicolored wings out in a three-foot span that suddenly made it look huge. It flew straight at Verdin, claws raking the air.

The human sailor ducked beneath the claws, eyes wide with surprise.

Critter sailed above the heads of the other patrons, wobbling drunkenly like a floundering ship, and managed to swing around for another pass. It screeched at the top of its voice.

Verdin stood suddenly and snatched a serving platter from a nearby table. The young sailor held the platter up like a shield.

Spotting the obstruction, Critter tried to stop the attack. Instead, all the rhowdor managed was an ungainly and panicked wing flapping. It hit the wooden serving platter with a pronounced *thump!* that scattered feathers in all directions.

The crowd all groaned, "Ooooooooh!" in sympathy.

Even though he didn't especially like the rhowdor, Wick winced a little himself. The bird would be lucky if something wasn't broken by the impact.

Off balance, Critter sailed on, flapping weakly and somehow gliding back toward Hallekk and the dwarven pirate crew. The front row of human sailors had to duck to let the rhowdor go by. It landed on its back, wings spread across the sawdust-covered floor, feathers wafting through the air in its wake, and came to a stop at Hallekk's boots.

"That's gonna leave a mark," someone promised.

"*Awwwwwwwrrrrrkkkkk!*" Critter cried out. The rhowdor lifted its head uncertainly, bobbing at the end of its long neck, and fastened its beady eye on Hallekk. "He sucker-punched me, Hallekk! Struck me while I wasn't lookin'!" Its head wobbled one last time, then thudded against the floor. The rhowdor lay still.

Wick stood in frozen awe. Even though he didn't like Critter, he'd never wished the rhowdor harm. Well, maybe that wasn't quite as truthful as it could have been. He actually *had* wished Critter harm; he'd just never wanted to be there when it happened.

The silence held for a moment as everyone stared at the fallen rhowdor.

Finally, someone asked, "Is it dead?"

"We should be so lucky," someone else (and Wick truly believed it was one of *One-Eyed Peggie*'s crew that said this) unkindly added.

Hallekk knelt down and picked up the rhowdor by the feet. The bird dangled limply, a scrawny shadow of its former self. The dwarf squinted at it and smelled its beak.

"Oh, it's dead all right," the big dwarf growled. "Dead *drunk*." He shook his shaggy head. "It's still breathin'."

"Be careful with him!" Slops shouldered his way out of the crowd of dwarven pirates. Old and flinty-eyed, he was the ship's cook. When Wick had been shanghaied and first crewed aboard *One-Eyed Peggie*, Slops had been a cruel taskmaster in the galley.

Twisting slightly and flipping his wrist, Hallekk tossed the unconscious rhowdor to Slops. The cook caught Critter tenderly, and held the bird in his arms like a newborn babe.

"Ye gonna let that loudmouth get away with harmin' the ship's mascot?" Slops demanded. "If'n ye ask me, if'n ye do, why ye ain't much of a—"

Hallekk shoved his big face into the cook's, stopping Slops's tirade at once.

Slops backed away meekly. For all his bluster and loud voice, the ship's cook knew the first mate would pound him into a Lantessian pretzel. "I'm just gonna take Critter back to the ship. Tend to him a little."

"Good," Hallekk said, "'cause I've had me fill of him tonight, I have." Then he shifted his attention back to Verdin, who still held the serving platter. "Now ye, ye're gonna take back everythin' ye said about Master Blacksmith Oskarr."

"Over me dead body," Verdin said. "Or do ye let yer ship's mascot fight all yer battles for ye?"

Grim-faced, Hallekk started forward, lifting his battle-axe easily in one hand. *One-Eyed Peggie*'s crew fell in behind him.

Verdin and his crew stood up as well and advanced a line.

That was when Wick decided that discretion was once again the better part of valor. He started to turn to head back for the exit in the other room. At that same time, though, Paunsel acted in the only way he knew to prevent damage to his tavern: He shoved Wick in between the two groups.

Stumbling and flailing, realizing that he very probably looked like a good imitation of Critter flying through the air after he'd struck the serving platter, Wick caught himself against a table and managed to stay upright. Unfortunately, he was between the two groups of combatants, both of whom had braced with drawn weapons against the unexpected attack.

Cowering, Wick closed his eyes, dropped to his knees, and covered his head with his arms. He waited to be pierced and smited.

"Wick," Hallekk growled.

Cautiously, Wick opened one eye, marveling at his survival. The humans and dwarves still stood poised. *I'm not dead.* Then he looked at the weapons ringing him, some of them only inches away, and decided that his present predicament hadn't appreciably improved. He swallowed hard and his Adam's apple bobbed past a sailor's cutlass blade both ways, though hanging slightly on the way up.

"What're ye a-doin' here, little feller?" Hallekk asked. There was some sincere warmth in his eyes. He even had a trace of a smile.

"I'm attempting to keep you from killing these sailors," Wick said, still on his knees and both hands wrapped around his head, though he had managed to open both eyes now.

The humans snorted and addressed him with threats regarding their skill and his assumption of who would lose the coming fight.

Sensing the sudden shifting of the tide of animosity in the room, Wick quickly added, "These *brave, brave* sailors without whom Greydawn Moors would never have enough trade goods." *Surely that will appease them,* the little Librarian hoped. He stopped himself from swallowing again because he didn't think his Adam's apple would survive a second trip.

"Get yer hands off him," Hallekk ordered. "He's a Librarian. Ain't no one a-gonna harm ye." He knotted a big fist in Wick's robes and yanked him into a fierce hug that left his feet dangling. "I've missed ye somethin' awful, little man. No one tells a story quite the way ye do."

"Hallekk?" Wick wheezed, certain he'd never draw another breath through the cracked rib cage he must have.

"Aye," the big dwarf said, his ugly face only inches from Wick's.

"Could you put me down?"

"Well, sure." Hallekk did with surprising gentleness.

Straightening himself with as much aplomb as he could muster on knees that rattled with fear, Wick nodded at the dwarf. "It's good to see you again, Hallekk."

"I wish it were under better circumstances," Hallekk replied. Straightening his kerchief, he waved at Wick. "An' if'n ye'll shove off for a bit, it'll get better really soon. We got some business here needs tendin', a bar what needs a-clearin' of the riff-raff."

"Ha!" Verdin exclaimed. "Ye ain't dwarf enough to get that job done!"

"About that business," Wick began, trying to interrupt before they closed ranks with him in the middle, "I really think we should talk."

"Ain't no time for talkin'." Hallekk glared fiercely across the top of Wick's head. "Gotta smash the knobs of these here bilge rats."

"Gonna *be* smashed, ye mean," Verdin said.

"Maybe I can help," Wick said.

The human and the dwarf looked at him.

And maybe I can die right here, Wick thought, shrinking inside like new-fallen snow under a gentle rain.

"How can ye help?" Verdin asked.

Hoping that his weak knees didn't desert him entirely, Wick stood erect as Grandmagister Frollo always told him to when he addressed assemblies at the Vault of All

Known Knowledge. "I'm a Second Level Librarian at the Great Library," he said. "You're obviously in a war of wits."

"An' they didn't come armed," Hallekk said.

Verdin scowled at the big dwarf. "Mayhap he's come to take yer final words." He turned to Wick. "That'd be somethin' along the lines of 'Ow! Ouch! By the Old Ones, he was too fast an' too strong fer me!' "

"Why you—" Hallekk began, starting forward.

Wick shoved his hand against the big dwarf's chest, but he might as well have been seeking to stop a warship under full sail with a good wind behind her. In seconds, he was smashed between the bodies of the two combatants.

"Enough!" Wick cried in a voice too shrill to be his. But it was the best he could manage under the circumstances with the wind left to him. "Don't make me tell Grandmagister Frollo!"

Surprisingly, that threat stopped the two crews in their tracks. Hallekk and Verdin separated and Wick plopped to the ground.

"Ye'd do that, ye little halfer?" Verdin asked, eyes round with surprise.

"Over a tavern brawl?" Hallekk asked, surprised as well.

Then Wick remembered the power the Grandmagister had over the ships' crews. They all operated by charter with the Vault of All Known Knowledge. Although Grandmagister Frollo hadn't taken much of an interest in the affairs of Greydawn Moors, the previous Grandmagister, Ludaan, had spent a lot of time among the Greydawn Moors townsfolk, including the elven warders, dwarven guards, and human sailors. Ludaan was even friends with Craugh the wizard, which seemed a most unlikely and unthankful task.

At any time, the Grandmagister could revoke a ship's charter and order the crew landlocked. With as much anger and consternation as he'd drawn, Wick was certain he'd threatened far beyond his intentions. He stuck out a foot and started to ease away.

Paunsel blocked the path, folding his arms and shaking his head.

"Well," Wick tried in a less threatening tone, "perhaps it needn't come to anything as dire as that."

"C'mon, little man," Hallekk beseeched. "A good fight clears the air an' invigorates the blood. I'm just gonna thump him a little. Teach him the wrongness of his arrogant ways. It's a lesson his da shoulda taught him."

"Gonna get thumped, ye mean," Verdin replied.

Sensing that everything was about to get out of hand once more, Wick said, "Maybe I could help."

"Who?" Hallekk and Verdin demanded at once, shoving their faces into his.

"Eeep!" Wick cried, suddenly startled again. Embarrassed, cheeks burning, he clapped his hands over his mouth.

Verdin turned to Hallekk. "Seems a mite sheepish."

Hallekk shrugged. "Ol' Wick's better at adventurin' when things gets impossible."

"Humph!" the sailor snorted. "Sounds about as threatening as a hissing Kardalvian dung beetle!"

"Still," Hallekk sighed, "he does have the ear of the Grandmagister. Perhaps 'twould be better if'n we heard him out. Then we can get back to the thumpin'."

Wick stood on shaking knees. *I faced the dragon Shengharck in his lair in the Broken Forge Mountains. I slew him there. Well, perhaps that was by accident, but I did it.* He made himself take a breath because he'd suddenly realized he wasn't breathing, and turning blue while trying to make a point didn't seem very inspiring.

"You're arguing over the events of the Painted Canyon," Wick said in what he hoped was a reasonable and not fearful tone of voice.

"Aye," both potential combatants replied.

"Everybody knows they was betrayed there," Hallekk said. "Thousands of warriors lost their lives in that battle."

"By Oskarr the dwarven leader," Verdin said. "He was the one what sold out the human an' the elven warriors what was gathered there against Lord Kharrion's armies."

Instantly a quiet fell over the crowd. No one spoke the Goblin Lord's name out loud for fear it might trigger ill luck. Only a few years ago, on the night when Wick had first been shanghaied by *One-Eyed Peggie*'s crew, Boneblights had descended upon Greydawn Moors and very nearly been the end of him. But they had been after the book Warder Kestin had taken to Craugh.

"Master Blacksmith Oskarr of the Cinder Clouds Islands was a good an' fair dwarf," Hallekk insisted.

"No one," Wick said, before he had time to truly think about what he was saying or remember why he should keep his mouth shut, "knows who betrayed those warriors. I've studied the Battle of Fell's Keep, which is what that engagement in the Cataclysm was called."

Verdin fixed Wick with a glaring eye. "Ye know about that battle?"

"I do," Wick said. It had been mentioned in one of the books he'd read. He didn't forget anything he read, which was partly due to his training and partly because that's just the way he was.

"Then who was the traitor?" Hallekk asked.

And the whole tavern leaned in closer to listen to the tale.

2

A Tale of Betrayal

The Battle of Fell's Keep took place near the end of the Cataclysm," Wick said in a good strong voice that he used for training Novices at the Vault of All Known Knowledge. He sat on the counter in front of the tavern, which didn't please Paunsel, but at least none of the crockery seemed at risk. "At that time, as you may recall, the Goblin Lord—"

"Was thumpin' melons an' takin' names," Hallekk scowled. "Aye, we know all of that. 'Twas a hard time for the Unity."

"Goblinkin tribes had laid aside their old rivalries," Wick said, "and they'd gathered beneath the Goblin Lord's banner. Everywhere an honest dwarf, human, or elf looked in those days, they saw the banner bearing the crimson mailed fist clenched on a field of sky blue. Those were the Days of Darkness."

Enamored of the attention he was getting from the previously raucous crowd—and perhaps a little emboldened by the sparkleberry wine and the tale of Taurak Bleiyz he'd been enjoying, Wick pushed himself to his feet. Although he often spoke in front of groups within the walls of the Vault of All Known Knowledge, those instances paled in comparison to how he'd felt while speaking in front of *One-Eyed Peggie*'s crew or the Brandt's Circle of Thieves.

They'd been audiences who had appreciated his skills as a raconteur. He'd come alive then in ways he knew Grandmagister Frollo would never have approved of.

"Teldane's Bounty had fallen by that time," Wick continued. "Lord Kharrion's evil spell had wreaked havoc on the mainland. He'd sent a plague of locusts, followed by a killing blight that stripped the orchards and farms that grew there. Ships had gone down to watery graves with thousands of men, women, and children aboard, most of them freezing in the wintry waters of the Gentlewind Sea after Lord Kharrion had summoned mountains up from the sea to break apart the land."

A sad quietness held sway over the tavern crowd. Wick knew that Paunsel would hold him accountable for slowing the flow of wine and ale in the tavern. But Wick was consumed by the tale, as were his listeners.

"Those deaths were not in vain," Wick said. "For the first time since the beginning of the Cataclysm, dwarves, humans, and elves set aside their differences and came together for one purpose. Though there had been talk of working together to make the world a better place, that course had never taken root. But they could agree to save the world. And they set about that task."

"But it was almost too late," someone said.

"Silverleaves Glen fell in the next year," Wick said, remembering the poor, cursed creature he had met on his first voyage aboard *One-Eyed Peggie*. "Lord Kharrion destroyed the elven tree village, Cloud Heights, and killed King Amalryn and his beautiful queen, N'riya."

The elven warders in the back room lowered their proud heads in sympathy. All the elves had known about Silverleaves Glen.

"Furthermore," Wick said, "the Goblin Lord put to death the three princes. He reserved a far harsher fate for the nine princesses, breaking them and warping them into creatures he could use. They became Embyrs, beings of flame who lived only to destroy, and who had no memory of what they had been or what they had done."

"Aye," a human sailor said. "I've heard tell of 'em, all right. They're still out there, still killin' an' destroyin'. Made all of fire, they are, an' terrible vengeful. They find a ship at sea, like as not they'll burn her to the waterline just outta spite."

The crew of *One-Eyed Peggie* said nothing. They had seen an Embyr up close and been some of those fortunate enough to have survived such an encounter. Wick had managed to save them all by touching, if only briefly, the Embyr's angry heart.

Wick strode along the countertop, knowing that he held captive every eye in the room. "The goblinkin came roaring up out of the Western Empire, destroying everything in their path. Lord Kharrion designed a pincer movement, one that would trap those retreating overland from the south in the narrow confines of the Painted Canyon as it passed through the Unmerciful Shards, that range of the Misty Mountains where the dragonkind spawn."

Hallekk handed Wick a tankard of sparkleberry wine and he quaffed it down, warming to the story.

"For those of you who don't know, the goblinkin first took over the south," Wick continued. "They came up from Gaheral's Wastelands, where vile things were said to run rampant after the wizard unwittingly unleashed bloodthirsty creatures from other worlds." He shrugged. "Or mayhap they were created when Gaheral's Wild Magic finally turned on him as everyone believed would happen."

"They had driven them goblinkin there over the years," Hallekk said. "Beat 'em back until they had no place to go but the Wastelands."

"Before Lord Kharrion showed up in their midst, yes,"

Wick agreed. "But the Wastelands turned out to be a boon to the goblinkin. The harsh territory killed off all the weaker ones, leaving only those strong enough to survive the unforgiving climate and the bloodthirsty predators. When the Goblin Lord gathered them to his cause, they were ready to kill everything in their path."

"An' they did," Verdin said.

"Yes," Wick echoed as he watched Hallekk pour him another tankard of wine. He drank it down gratefully, surprised at the way his head felt as if it were floating. "They did. After Teldane's Bounty was destroyed and the ships dragged down to the bottom of the Gentlewind Sea, after Cloud Heights was ripped asunder and torn from the trees at Silverleaves Glen, humans, dwarves, and elves began a mass exodus from the south, driven unmercifully by the combined might of the goblinkin tribes."

Despite the time spent in the Wastelands, the goblinkin population hadn't dwindled. They had no equal when it came to bearing offspring then, and still didn't. Even the humans came in at a distant second, followed by the dwarves and elves, but the goblinkin far outlived the humans.

Unless they were killed, Wick remembered. And that had been an accepted solution to the goblinkin problem for a long time.

Moving quickly, Wick lined up several tankards on the countertop, fashioning a replica of the Painted Canyon to better illustrate his story. He tiptoed through the tankards as he continued.

"The fugitives from the south were desperate," Wick said. "The number of warriors among them had drastically been cut, split off in the effort to hold Teldane's Bounty, and falling to goblinkin weapons. They needed an escape route. But the Goblin Lord was determined not to let them have it."

"He was waitin' on 'em in the Painted Canyon," someone said.

"He was," Wick agreed. "He harried the escapees from behind with one army, while he worked around to their flank with another. He planned to ambush them there in the Unmerciful Shards."

"How did Lord Kharrion get through the dragons?" someone asked.

Wick paced along the countertop. "Foul being that he was, the Goblin Lord had established a treaty with the dragons through the Dragon King Shengharck. Several of those the goblinkin captured were delivered to the spawning dragons in the Unmerciful Shards. And other places. The dragons didn't have to hunt anymore, and they didn't have to worry about being destroyed. All they had to do was not attack the goblinkin."

The horror of the thing washed over the crowd. Wick doubted that any among them had ever seen a great dragon feed on bound prisoners, but he had while in Shengharck's lair in the Broken Forge Mountains. It was a terrible sight and sound that he would never forget.

"Fortunately, the Unity found out about Lord Kharrion's ambush," Wick said. "They were able to muster three armies, though none of them at full strength, and get them to the Painted Canyon. Each of those armies represented the humans, dwarves, and elves who had taken up arms against Lord Kharrion."

"But there wasn't a dweller army, was there?" someone asked snidely. "Noooooo. The halfers were hidin' out here in Greydawn Moors, puttin' their little Library together, protectin' the books."

"Quiet!" a voice thundered.

Every head in the tavern snapped in the direction of the voice. Hands reached for swords and axes. Then, when they recognized Craugh standing in the doorway, the dwarves and humans quickly looked away and were silent.

The wizard walked into the room and a threatening chill seemed to follow him. "Continue your tale, Second Level Librarian Lamplighter." He paused and looked around the room. "And just for clarification, there'll be no fighting here tonight."

"Thank the Old Ones." Paunsel sighed.

Wick was grateful to see that Craugh had put in an appearance, but he was worried as well. Since the very first time he'd gone with the wizard to the mainland on one journey or another, his life had been at risk constantly. He didn't think Craugh had shown up at Paunsel's for the sparkleberry wine.

"Okay," Wick said. But some of the drama had gone out of the presentation. Craugh was the only person he'd known who had actually lived through the Cataclysm and knew many of the key events firsthand. "Where was I?"

"The Unity forces sent three armies to the Painted Canyon to head off Lord Kharrion's forces." Craugh sat at a table near the front whose previous tenants had rapidly evacuated at his approach. He placed his staff across the table and stretched his long legs under it. "One of dwarves, one of elves, and one of humans. Carry on."

"Right." Wick tried to marshal his thoughts, but the sparkleberry wine was interfering almost as much as his nerves. "So there they were. Three armies headed for Painted Canyon and the goblinkin hordes. Master Blacksmith Oskarr of the Cinder Clouds Islands led the dwarves. The elves were marshaled by King Faeyn of the Tangletree Glen. And General Crisstun of Promise Wharf commanded the humans. They reached the pass at the Unmerciful Shards under the cover of night before the fugitives and were able to set up defensive positions at Fell's Keep, an old human trading post that had been abandoned after the dragons had started nesting there."

The tavern crowd hung on every word. Although none of them had experienced war on quite the level of the

Cataclysm, all of them had probably fought for their lives against men or beasts at one time or another. They knew what those armies faced.

"The defenders let the fugitives through," Wick said, "and settled in to fight. Then came the goblinkin, marching in double-time, their ranks swelled with monsters and dire creatures Lord Kharrion had lured to their dark cause. Confronted with so many goblinkin, the three armies knew they were fated to die. If they tried to fall back, their resistance would fall apart and they would leave the rearguard of the fugitives open to attack."

Silence rang throughout the tavern.

"They'd already lost so much at Teldane's Bounty," Wick said, "that no one could bear to lose women and children again. So it was decided among the warriors of those three armies that they would sell their lives as dearly as possible and hope to slow the encroaching goblinkin horde enough that the fugitives might be able to escape."

"'Twas a brave an' selfless thing they did," Hallekk stated.

"'Twas," Verdin agreed. "Too bad they had to go an' get betrayed the way they was. Mayhap more of 'em might have survived."

"For nine days," Wick went on, hurrying so the argument wouldn't begin again, "the defenders of Fell's Keep kept the goblinkin at bay. They fought till the Painted Canyon ran red with blood. At night, when the goblinkin made camp and slept, elven warders went quietly among them and stole supplies and arrows, and killed goblinkin where they found them—strung up the bodies from the cliff sides, tossed their ugly heads into the campfires, and put horse droppings into the soup the goblinkin had made of fallen enemies—as testimony to the fate that awaited those who continued to fight."

The crowd listened in rapt attention.

"Goblins know of the Battle of Fell's Keep," Wick whispered, pitching his voice to roll over the crowd. "Stories of those days are still told around goblinkin campfires, and they're whispered among the young to scare each other." He knew that because he'd sat captive around those campfires a time or two.

"Who betrayed them?" someone asked.

"No one knows," Wick said. "Although many tried to guess afterward." He sat heavily, no longer as sure-footed as he'd been. He didn't know if it was the sadness of the story or the potent sparkleberry wine that did him in. "On the morning of the tenth day, nearly all of the Unity army took sick and couldn't even stand to defend themselves. The goblinkin came among them like butchers in the slaughterhouse. No one was spared."

"It was the dwarven leader," Verdin insisted. "He spread the sickness among the surviving troops so that his own life might be spared."

"Watch yer blasphemous tongue there, swab," Hallekk growled.

"Then ye explain to me how it was Oskarr managed to escape the sickness an' make it back to the Cinder Clouds Islands."

"He were a warrior!" Hallekk roared. "He managed to evade that sickness, an' he got what he could of his troops outta the Painted Canyon an' retreated."

"After they'd made a pact to stay an' die together."

"Doesn't make no sense to die when it ain't gonna help nothin'. They knew if they'd bolted from Fell's Keep that most of 'em woulda died. The sickness did 'em in afore that. The only thing Oskarr could do was lead them what was healthy enough to run for their lives an' take 'em outta that death trap. He did it."

"He went back home and stayed away from the fighting."

"But Oskarr didn't leave the war," Wick said. "Oskarr returned to the Cinder Clouds Islands and worked on the side of the Unity until Lord Kharrion was finally killed."

"Hammerin' out swords an' armor from the safety of his forge," Verdin accused.

"It's powerful hard for an army to fight when it ain't got the tools it needs to see the job finished," Hallekk said. "When it come to a-buildin' them tools, wasn't none finer than Master Blacksmith Oskarr. He hammered out a lot of armor an' weapons them Unity troops needed over them years."

"Faugh!" Verdin said. "'Twas fightin' that were needed! An' after that, Oskarr lived himself out a life that was fat an' happy."

"No," Wick said. "Oskarr died there in the Cinder Clouds Islands. For six years, Master Blacksmith Oskarr and his chief armorers supplied the Unity army. The forges never ran cold and the dwarves worked in shifts every hour of the day, hammering out swords and armor and arrowheads. During that time, it is said, the Cinder Clouds Islands were never silent, and the ringing of hammers filled all of the forges. In time, their work there drew the ire of the Goblin Lord because the supplies Master Blacksmith Oskarr and his people made started to turn the tide of the war."

"Lord Kharrion attacked the Cinder Clouds Islands," a dwarf said.

"He did," Wick agreed. "The Goblin Lord's spies discovered that Oskarr was preparing another large shipment of equipment in one month. Lord Kharrion put goblinkin ships in the water and went on the attack. He lay siege to Oskarr's city and waited to starve them out. As everyone knows, there wasn't much else in the Cinder Clouds Islands but veins of iron ore. It was a hardscrabble place even then. Only lizards and scrub brush lived there. Oskarr and his people depended on trade to keep food on the table."

"There was fish," someone suggested.

"The water was fouled by the forges," Craugh said. "The Cinder Clouds Islands dwarves used forges tapped directly into the volcanoes that spewed forth the island archipelago. Sulfur, soot, and ash clouded the waters around the island and chased away all living things on land and in the sea. It's impressive that the dwarves were strong enough to survive there. Volcanoes are very hard to tame."

Wick felt certain the wizard spoke from experience.

"There's no truer heat than that of a volcano," a dwarf stated. "Makes metal easy to work with, then leaves it hard as can be. The Cinder Clouds Islands dwarves weren't the only ones who learned that trick."

"And they could have only fished out to sea if they had access to the harbor," Wick said. "With Lord Kharrion's forces sitting in the Rusting Sea, that wasn't going to happen. But the Goblin Lord was too impatient to simply wait Oskarr and his people out. Instead, he worked his evil magic and turned the volcanoes the Cinder Clouds Islands dwarves had tapped into against them." He paused to let the dramatic tension increase. "The Goblin Lord's spell struck deeply into the heart of the volcano and wreaked havoc with the forges. In seconds, several of the islands— including the one where Oskarr and his hand-picked blacksmiths worked—sank beneath the waves of the Rusting Sea."

"Oskarr died?" Verdin asked.

Wick nodded. "He did. And nearly every man, woman, and child of his village died with him." Shuddering at the memory, he tried to forget about the accounts he'd read of the horrifying incident. It was no use. His imagination, in addition to being wild and vivid, also knew no rest. "Throughout the rest of the war against Lord Kharrion, no weapons or armor came from the Cinder Clouds Islands forges."

"Pity he didn't die before he betrayed the others at Painted Canyon," Verdin said.

"Why do you think Oskarr betrayed them forces?" Hallekk demanded.

"He was the only one of the leaders that didn't succumb to the sickness," Verdin said.

"That's because he was a dwarf!" Hallekk exploded. "Dwarves don't get overly sick!"

"Plenty of other dwarves got sick durin' that time." Verdin stuck out his jaw defiantly.

"Is that true?" one of the other humans asked Wick.

The little Librarian hesitated, but he knew he couldn't lie to those gathered there. "Many of the dwarves did get sick," he answered.

"But not Oskarr?"

"Not Oskarr."

"Why not?"

"No one knows." Wick listened anxiously as silence created a pall over the room. *Perhaps that telling lacked something*, he told himself. At least they weren't threatening to kill each other anymore.

Later, when the tavern had cleared out and most of the patrons had returned to their ships, Wick sat drinking quietly at a table with Craugh and Hallekk. Paunsel didn't dare chase the wizard off because he had no designs on becoming a toad.

Talk was small, generally anecdotes about things they'd seen or done, bits and pieces Wick had read of late, and a few choice comments about the ongoing chess game the Librarian and the wizard conducted through a series of letters through shipboard mail.

Wick could see that Hallekk was mightily disturbed

over the argument that had cropped up during the night. He hated to see his friend so troubled.

"For what it's worth," Wick said, "I don't think Oskarr betrayed those men at the Battle of Fell's Keep."

Hallekk sighed, and the candle flame on the table between them danced between life and death, then finally stood tall once more. "I know, little man."

"I tried the best I could to express the situation."

"I saw that." Hallekk frowned. "The problem is that that battle is still talked about, even a thousand years later." He waved at the tavern. "Not just here. But all along the mainland as well. Ever'where ye go, sooner or later, the talk'll turn to the Battle of Fell's Keep."

Wick knew that was true. He'd been in taverns along the Shattered Coast that had turned into great battles themselves between humans, dwarves, and elves over what had transpired in the Painted Canyon at the end of those ten days of siege.

"What happened there," Hallekk said, "it's a sore spot that most just can't keep from pickin' at. Ye don't see it come up so much here on Greydawn Moors, but out in the rest of the world?" He shook his big head.

"It's a serious problem," Craugh said. "One that will have to be dealt with sooner or later."

Wick studied the wizard. Although he hadn't yet said what had drawn him to Greydawn Moors, Craugh had come in looking slightly bedraggled, with half-healed cuts on his face and hands. Obviously he'd been somewhere dangerous doing something dangerous against someone who had been . . . dangerous.

Wick was unhappy with his limited mental word choice. Finding new words was somehow beyond him. *You've got to slow down on the sparkleberry wine*, he told himself. *It's making your head as thick as Slops's mashed potatoes. And they could be used for mortar.*

Cleaning the mess those potatoes made on plates after they'd gotten cold had been one of Wick's greatest struggles while he served as dishwasher aboard *One-Eyed Peggie*. He hadn't known how the dwarven pirates had gotten it through their systems. It had to have been a gastronomical feat.

But he didn't say a word when Hallekk filled his tankard again. Trying to match a dwarf in drinking was usually a strategy bound for painful failure and serious regret, but Wick thought himself equal to the task that night. If only the room would occasionally stop spinning.

"Even with Lord Kharrion out of the way," Craugh said, "the goblinkin have continued to hold sway in the south, and they look to be turning an avaricious eye to the north. Their numbers are on the increase again, and they'll soon be back up to fighting strength."

Hallekk looked at the wizard. "Do ye think they'll take another run at her? Killin' out all the other races, I mean?"

Wick hadn't thought about that. He'd been to the mainland a few times, and he'd seen how the goblinkin empire had fragmented somewhat, but they'd remained particularly strong in the south. Thinking that they might someday unite and take up the genocidal war once more was frightening. Even the magical fog and enchanted sea monsters in the Blood-Soaked Sea couldn't protect the Vault of All Known Knowledge forever.

"If they do, humans, dwarves, and elves will have to find the strength to once more stand united," Craugh said. "If they don't, they will all fall." He sipped his wine. "It would be better if they were able to put the Battle of Fell's Keep behind them."

"They're still different races," Wick pointed out. "There's some natural discord between them anyway."

"Yes, but it's been my experience that those dislikes can be worked through. Prejudice is an ugly thing that feeds on its own energies. It doesn't bring anything with it; the perceived hatred of others that are different drains and limits." Craugh tugged at his beard. "But it would be better if the questions over the Battle of Fell's Keep were resolved."

"There has to be an answer somewheres." Hallekk fixed Wick with a curious look. "Mayhap in them books of yers."

"They're not mine." Wick had to work a little harder to make the words come out.

"Haven't ye got someplace where ye can look up the battle?"

Wick shook his head and felt it sway sickeningly, thinking just for a moment that it had somehow come loose from his shoulders. "We're still sorting out all the journals, memoirs, and histories. If anything was written by anyone who was there, it hasn't turned up yet."

"Perhaps," Craugh suggested, "those manuscripts never made it to the Vault of All Known Knowledge."

"But why wouldn't they?" Wick asked.

"Perhaps," Craugh said slowly, as if warming to the possibility himself, "those memoirs weren't yet written at the time the different cities and towns surrendered their libraries." He took out his pipe and lit up. "It is something to think about."

Personally, Wick thought he'd be better off thinking about it in the morning. For the moment, he was sleepier than he'd ever been.

When he felt himself swaying, Wick believed at first that he was still asleep. During the night, he'd dreamed of being Taurak Bleiyz rescuing the fair Princess Lissamae from the evil clutches of the cunning wolf's head, Mamjor Dornthoth in the Gulches of Fiery Doom. He thought the swaying was just his imagination taking him out over the spiderweb spanning the Rushing River.

The dream had been an enjoyable time spent in slumber. In fact, he was already thinking of how he'd like to render a second, fresher version of the tale with color illustrations.

Opening his eyes, something he wasn't always able to do while held captive in a dream, Wick stared at the low ceiling overhead and the end of the hammock he was lying in.

"No!" he croaked.

Panicked, he tried to turn over in the hammock to take in the small room and promptly fell out onto the hardwood floor. His head slammed into the solid surface. Stars spun behind his eyes. That was further proof he wasn't dreaming: He never hit bottom when he fell in his dreams.

The impact ignited a headache that seemed on the verge of shattering his skull. A nasty, bitter taste filled his mouth. That definitely wasn't normal. Suspicion darkened his thoughts.

Moaning a little with the effort, Wick levered himself up and stumbled to the porthole. He peered out at the curling waves of plum-colored ocean.

I'm on the Blood-Soaked Sea! he thought in disbelief. *I've been shanghaied! Again!*

3

"We Have a Mission for You, Librarian Lamplighter"

Angry and hurting, Wick headed for the door. Then he noticed the small hammock hanging above the one he'd fallen out of. Inside the hammock, Critter slept with its wings flared out to its sides.

Remembering how Critter had unmercifully awakened him the first time he'd been taken aboard *One-Eyed Peggie*, Wick yelled, "Wake up, ye goldbrickin' feather duster!" and gave the small hammock a spin, looping it over and over from its ties.

The rhowdor spun in the hammock, then fell out and tumbled toward the ground. Critter fluttered and landed on its bottom on the floor with its legs flared out. For a moment, its head bobbed like a yo-yo on a string. It blinked its eye quickly, then focused on Wick with a narrowed, baleful gaze.

"Why ye sawed-off sorry excuse fer a pirate!" Critter exploded. It kicked its claws and got its legs under it. "Ye slime-suckin' bilge rat! Ye're gonna pay fer that, ye are!" It came at Wick, barely weaving as its sticklike legs churned.

Still, Wick moved quickly and let himself out the door. He closed it behind him just in time to hear a satisfying *thud!* that warmed his heart and alleviated some of the misery he felt.

Critter cursed Wick thoroughly through the door and kicked it.

Ignoring the rhowdor, knowing the bird couldn't open the door and trusting that it would be some time before Critter could fly through the porthole, Wick turned his attention to the ship's deck. If waking up in a hammock in the same room as Critter wasn't proof enough, all the familiar faces of the crew told him immediately he was on *One-Eyed Peggie*.

They all called out to him in greeting, but most of them were moving slowly after shore leave. Sail filled the 'yards and popped in the strong breeze. The sun hung high in the eastern sky, and he noticed they were headed toward it. The mainland lay in that direction, but he judged that they were headed too far south to be making for the Shattered Coast. Somewhere south of there then, but he hadn't yet been in that direction.

Why? Wick wondered. But he knew asking himself that question wouldn't do any good. So he went looking for Hallekk, going up the stairs to the stern castle.

The big first mate was on the stern deck, just as Wick thought he would be. Surprisingly, Cap'n Farok was there as well. Even Craugh stood there with them, brimmed hat shadowing his eyes as he gazed out to sea.

That can't be good, Wick thought, but his anger grew inside him. He strode over to them and they all looked at him.

"A fair mornin' to ye, Librarian," Cap'n Farok greeted in his creaky voice.

Cap'n Farok was the oldest dwarf Wick had ever seen outside of an illustration in one of the books in Hralbomm's Wing in the vault. Almost a head shorter than Hallekk, Farok had silvery gray hair so aged that it was turning alabaster. The years had robbed his face of its firmness, so wrinkled that it looked like it had been hollowed out and was falling in on itself. He wore a fine suit and a decorated hat that set him apart from his crew.

Some of Wick's anger evaporated at seeing the old ship's captain. Farok's health hadn't been good for the last few years. Much of the time he was bedridden. On occasion, he'd talked of stepping down from his post and letting Hallekk take over as captain, but his crew had refused. Everyone knew that the only family Farok had was aboard *One-Eyed Peggie*. If he returned to Greydawn Moors, or any other place, for that matter, he'd only die among strangers.

"A fair morning to you, too, Cap'n," Wick said respectfully. "I—"

"I 'spect ye got questions," Farok interrupted.

"Aye, I do. Also, I need to ask you to turn around and take me back to Greydawn Moors. I've work to do at the Vault of All Known Knowledge. I don't know whose grand idea it was to kidnap me—" Here he glared at Craugh and Hallekk, both of whom he knew well enough to trust that they wouldn't turn him into a toad or beat him to a pulp respectively. Although the kidnapping had been a total surprise. "—but someone here deserves a swift—"

Farok held up a quavering hand. "It were me idea, Librarian."

Over Farok's shoulder, Craugh and Hallekk grinned at Wick and raised their eyebrows, waiting to see how he was going to finish the threat he'd started.

"—*chance* to let me know what's going on," Wick fumbled. He couldn't believe Farok had given the order to take him from Greydawn Moors. They traveled well aboard the ship when Wick was about tracking books down on the mainland, often playing chess and talking over nautical stories—which were a treasure trove for Wick because he took notes in his journals, but both of them knew he wasn't exactly pirate material.

"Over the mornin' meal then," Farok agreed. "I 'spect ye've got an appetite?"

Wick's stomach rumbled for all to hear.

"Well then," Farok said, laughing, "that's answer enough." He turned to the first mate. "Hallekk, the table if ye please. We'll be after takin' our meal here on the stern deck."

Hallekk went to the stern railing and bawled out the orders.

"An' when we finish the morning meal," Farok went on, "then we'll talk about why ye're here."

In short order, ship's crew brought out the captain's table and covered it with food. The sea was calm enough for them to eat, and being outside in the open was better than being closed up in the captain's cramped quarters or sharing mess with the crew down in the galley.

"Tuck in, Librarian, tuck in," Farok invited as he shoved a napkin down the front of his blouse. "We've just come from shore leave, an' them good people of Greydawn Moors has been mightily generous."

Hallekk passed plates around.

They were fired pottery, robin's-egg blue with gold-leaf trim showing beautifully rendered images of fantastic forest beasts. The luster of the plates was so shiny Wick could see himself in it.

"Oh my," he gasped. "Have you seen this?"

Farok leaned over and peered at the plate. "What is it? Did Slops not get them plates clean again? I've already had a talk to him about that."

"No. The plates are fine. But it's the plates themselves." Wick turned the plate to face the dwarven captain. "Do you know what they are?"

"Why, they's plates," Farok said.

"I believe Wick is referring to the fact that these plates are Delothian warder plates." Craugh sawed through a plump sausage with a knife, then forked up a chunk and popped it into his mouth.

Wick gazed at the wizard in disbelief. "You knew that?"

"Yes. I'm not uneducated."

"But you're eating off them!"

"That's what they were made for." Craugh sectioned a firepear and forked a bit of it as well. "To be eaten off of."

"But not by a bunch of dwarven pirates!" Wick was suddenly aware of how quiet the stern deck had gotten. Had the wind died down? He tried to recover. "Dwarven pirates who are actually heroes in disguise." *There. That sounds better, doesn't it?*

Hallekk looked grudgingly at his plate, then a little ashamed. "I ain't fit to be eatin' off this plate, is that what ye're a-sayin'?"

"No," Wick replied, feeling bad and wishing he had a way out of the hole he'd dug for himself. "What I'm saying is that these plates have a unique history." He turned the plate in his hands, finding the beginning of the story rendered there in the images. "This tale is about Noosif, the beaver companion of Warder Riantap, who was a great champion and cared for the Cealoch River from the Sparkling Falls to the Moons-kissed Deltalands where the Haidon lumberjack settlement lived."

Leaning close to his plate, scraping away a piece of egg from the edge, Hallekk said, "This one's about an eagle."

"That's probably an owl," Wick said automatically. "The Band of Fur, Feather, and Fin didn't include an eagle. There were twelve animals in all, creatures of the Delothian warders—humans, not elves—who fought the Mad Empress Maligna during the Zenoffran Troll War."

"I weren't aware there were any trolls in Zenoffra," Hallekk said.

"There weren't," Wick agreed, "after the Delothian warders finished with them. Until that time, the Mad

Empress had employed them to build engines of destruction in the Skytrees Forest. Then the Haidon lumberjacks were able to move in and start harvesting trees for the ships made down in Cogsdale, where so many cargo ships were built. That war was important to the human sailors because it gave them resources to build fleets of trading and war vessels." He shrugged. "Of course, they immediately started competitions for trade goods and sank many of those ships."

"Are ye a-gonna eat, Librarian?" Farok asked. "While it's still hot? Would ye rather have another plate if that one doesn't suit ye?"

Wick sighed. None of them understood. "These were built for the Delothian warders, to commemorate their victory over the Mad Empress. Most of them died or lost their animal companions. They're works of art."

Craugh scooped up a big spoonful of hash browns fried with sweet onions, and plopped it into the center of the plate Wick held. "And today they hold food provided by generous hosts." His eyebrows arched in mild rebuke over his green eyes.

Giving up, Wick quickly filled his plate with sausages, fresh baked biscuits, firepears, corn pancakes that he covered in sweet sparkleberry syrup and tart limemelon wedges.

"Well," Hallekk said, eyeing Wick's burgeoning plate, "one thing ye got to say for them potters what made these plates: They certainly made big ones. Ye ought to be grateful 'bout that."

Wick was, but he ate carefully and didn't drag his fork over the plate.

After the table and the remnants were packed away, Farok and Craugh filled their pipes and lounged in their chairs to smoke. Hallekk went to see to his rounds.

One-Eyed Peggie continued to slice through the Blood-Soaked Sea. The eternal fogs, kept in place through the magical glamours that protected Greydawn Moors, ghosted across the deck and limited vision in all directions. But the sun felt warm.

"Awwwwwwrrrrrrrrkkkkk!" Critter moaned below. The rhowdor sounded as if it were dying.

For a moment, Wick felt sorry for the bird. But not too much. Critter would live; it just wouldn't enjoy the experience for a while.

"Awwwwwwrrrrrrrrkkkkk!" Critter cried again. A moment later, it stumbled across the deck. Its pinkish horned face looked decidedly green. Its brilliant tail feathers, now tangled and some of them broken, trailed on the deck after it.

Struggling mightily, the rhowdor climbed the side, hooked its claws in under the top rail, and hung its head over. It used its wings to steady itself, then heaved again and again, sounding like it was strangling.

Mercilessly, the crew guffawed and hurled insults at the poor bird, making fun of his condition. "That'll teach ye to drink that rotgut, ye bone-headed bird!" someone yelled.

"Just keep throwin' up," someone else said. "When ye see yer claws an' tail feathers comin' up, ye'll know ye're almost done."

Critter tried to hurl an insult back, but ended up hurling over the side halfway through. Trapped with no way to respond, the bird had no choice but to take every scathing insult the crew could think of. And they could think of a lot because they spent a lot of time at sea with nothing to do.

Wick chuckled at the rhowdor's plight in spite of his mood. No one aboard the ship would see any true harm come to the rhowdor, but the bird was not well liked by anyone.

"I'd come to Greydawn Moors on another matter," Craugh said, "when I found you lecturing in Paunsel's."

"I wasn't lecturing," Wick said. "I was merely trying to forestall a brawl. If I'd had any sense, I'd have left out the back way."

"It's probably a good thing you didn't. Tempers seemed high last night." Craugh puffed on his pipe.

"What other matter brought you to Greydawn Moors?" Unable to simply sit and listen, used to having his hands busy all day, Wick reached down into his rucksack and took out one of the journals he kept on hand. A brief check inside assured him that it was blank.

He had a habit of carrying several different journals with him at all times because his attention constantly jumped from subject to subject. Grandmagister Frollo faulted him for that on a regular basis. Wick just had a hard time staying still—unless he had a truly good book in his hands. Thankfully, the Taurak Bleiyz book was in the rucksack as well, though he didn't know when he would ever get the dweller hero across the spiderweb above the Rushing River.

"The Cryptkeeper of Houngal," Craugh said.

Wick glanced sharply at the wizard. "I thought the Cryptkeeper was a myth."

Craugh puffed solemnly on his pipe. "I'd hoped." Something dark and dreadful flickered in his eyes. "But I think I met it."

"Where?" Unbidden, Wick's hands removed a stick of charcoal from the rolled leather pouch that held his writing utensils. Quickly, he sketched out the tall, lean frame of the Cryptkeeper, shrouding the crocodile's skull he reportedly wore in the hood of a tattered cloak.

"Near Moiturl," Craugh answered. "There are ruins there—"

"Tumbledown City," Wick said, nodding, watching with growing interest as the Cryptkeeper took shape on the blank page. "It wasn't always called Tumbledown City. From the geographic references I've been able to piece together, Tumbledown City was once a human settlement called Arrod. It was a meeting place for the humans of Northern Javisham."

"Correct," Craugh said, looking more than slightly impressed. "Truly, Second Level Librarian Wick, your knowledge of the world before the Cataclysm sometimes astounds me."

"You have to remember that all the books I read are pre-Cataclysm," Wick said. "But I listen to the travelers' tales down at the Yondering Docks, and I can sometimes put today's places with what they were all those years ago. During that time, Arrod was a large town—for a human settlement, which wasn't common given that humans tend to wander—and the center of three different trade routes." He started to name them, but Craugh held up his hand in irritation.

I guess, at the moment, he isn't prepared to be astounded anymore, Wick thought.

"We need to talk about why you're aboard *One-Eyed Peggie*," Craugh said.

"What happened to the Cryptkeeper of Houngar?" Wick asked. He hated mysteries. Well, truth to tell, he actually enjoyed them. But not if they weren't properly finished.

"All those years ago? Or when I met him?"

"Both."

"All those years ago, he was a graveyard attendant who stole from the dead. As a result, he was cursed to eternally guard the dead but he couldn't leave the graveyard."

"And if he did?"

"He turned to dust."

"Oh. So you lured him away from the graveyard."

"No," Craugh said, frowning, "I turned him into a toad. When I left, he was hopping around the crypt. If he didn't hop away from the graveyard, he's still there." He smiled a little. "It's a rather fascinating experiment, actually, to see if my spell or the curse gives out first."

"You turned him into a toad. Haven't you ever thought about turning those who vex you into . . . I don't know, *something* else?"

"No," Craugh said flatly. "It works. Why fix it?"

"It's not very creative."

Craugh shifted irritably in his seat and came close to glaring. "Do you think I stole you away from Greydawn Moors to critique my choice of transformations?"

Wick was suddenly aware that he was out on thin ice. "Uh . . . *noooo*?"

"I did not."

Then, before he could stop himself, Wick said, "I thought Cap'n Farok made the decision to shanghai me."

Craugh's face colored darkly with anger.

"I did," Farok said. "After Craugh put the sleeping powder in yer drink an' Hallekk carried ye back to the ship."

"You?" Wick exploded. "Put sleeping powder in my drink?"

"You wouldn't have agreed to come if I'd asked," Craugh said.

"Of course not!" Wick couldn't believe it. The wizard had betrayed him in the past, but nothing like— Then he stopped himself. *Actually, this is exactly like that time in Cormorthal.* He groaned. He couldn't believe he'd been made the fool. *Again.*

"I made the decision for ye," Farok said. "So if'n yer after a-placin' blame, let it be on me head."

Wick gazed at the captain's rheumy old eyes. Even though he struggled valiantly to hang onto his anger, he couldn't. Farok had never betrayed him, never once deserted him to deal with razor-tusked melanoths in a dead-end alley, never abandoned him to explain the theft of an ensorcelled skull in a temple of Thurdamon the Cursed, never—well, all things considered, there was a lot Craugh had to answer for over the years.

Sighing, Wick said, "I'm not going to blame you, Cap'n Farok."

"Good," Craugh said. "Then we can be about this bit of business."

"I *am* going to blame you," Wick declared fiercely.

With an acutely threatening air, Craugh leaned forward and gave Wick the hairy eyeball. "Are you auditioning to be a toad, Librarian?" the wizard asked in a cold, hard voice.

Striving to control his bladder, hoping his voice didn't squeak when he spoke, knowing his first clue would be when the chair he was sitting in suddenly seemed too big, Wick leaned back at the wizard. "I don't know. Can a t-t-toad do whatever it is y-y-you've set your c-c-cap for me to d-d-do?"

For a moment longer, Craugh glared at him. Then he started laughing. "By the Old Ones! Do you know when the last time was that someone stood toe-to-toe with me?"

No, Wick thought.

"Well, actually," Craugh went on, "it was more like toe-to-toad, but there you have it." He looked away and swirled his staff through the air, scattering green embers upon the wind. "We have a mission for you, Librarian Lamplighter. Captain Farok and I."

"I didn't volunteer for this," Wick said.

"Ain't no one more suited to the task," Cap'n Farok said. "I knowed that after Craugh laid it out afore me." He looked at Wick. "We need ye to do it, lad. *I* need ye to do it."

If it had been anyone else who asked me, or threatened *me*, Wick thought, *I wouldn't do it*. But over the years and the journeys to the mainland, he'd developed a strong affection for the crusty old dwarven sea captain. He took a deep breath and let it out.

"What is it?" Wick asked.

"We need ye to go among the Cinder Clouds dwarves an' find Master Blacksmith Oskarr's magic battle-axe, Boneslicer."

"But the Cinder Clouds Islands *sank*!"

"Mayhap not," Cap'n Farok said. " 'Tis true them islands got mightily shaken up, but some of 'em's still there."

"If the battle-axe was still there, someone would have found it."

"Not necessarily," Craugh said. "There were many things lost during the Cataclysm." A great scowl darkened his face. "The problem with lost things is that they don't always stay so."

Wick silently agreed. Cursed objects had a habit of turning up again and again to cause new problems. "Okay, let's assume it's still there. Wonder of wonders, let's assume I even find it. What good will it do?" Though he didn't want to admit it, he was intrigued.

"Magical items, especially ones forged for their bearer, as Boneslicer was for Master Blacksmith Oskarr, have a tendency to absorb something of their respective owners," Craugh said.

"What good will that do?"

"One day, Librarian," Cap'n Farok said, "not in my lifetime, of course, but perhaps in yours, the world will become closer. Dwarves, humans, an' elves will need to know how to live with each other again. If there's to be any peace at all betwixt 'em, them questions about the Battle of Fell's Keep need to be answered. Mayhap, the Old Ones willin', we can get some of them answers ready."

"By going to the Cinder Clouds Islands and finding Master Blacksmith Oskarr's battle-axe?" Wick asked.

"Aye." The old captain nodded.

Wick sighed. "How are we going to do it?"

" 'We'?" Craugh shook his head. "There's no 'we' to this, Librarian Lamplighter. There's only you."

"*Me?*" Wick couldn't believe it. "You're going to plunk me down on an island and expect me to survive? *And* find a mystical battle-axe no one has seen in a thousand years in an island group that was disrupted by volcanoes?"

Craugh looked at him. "No one said this was going to be easy." He was silent for a moment. "But there is an added attraction."

To getting killed and eaten by goblinkin? To being put to death by suspicious dwarves who don't take to strangers? To getting burned to a crisp by a sudden volcanic eruption? Wick couldn't wait to hear how the wizard was going to *attempt* to entice him. If he wasn't sure they'd put him ashore anyway, he'd have argued and demanded, maybe even begged and—

"Master Blacksmith Oskarr believed in the power of books," Craugh said. "The rumor goes that he kept a few personal favorites—and his journals—with him even after he sent everything else he had with Unity ships."

Wick knew they had him then. No one else aboard *One-Eyed Peggie* would lay his life on the line for books. Not the way he would.

He sighed. "All right. But I'm not going to like it."

4

Marooned in the Cinder Clouds Islands

*O*ne-Eyed Peggie sailed slowly through the islands, most of her sails furled and crew lining the railing with weighted lines to call out the depths as they went forward. There were hundreds of islands scattered over the Rusting Sea, which got its name—Wick discovered—from the tiny flecks of oxidized iron ore that fluttered through the depths. As a result, the sea looked dark orange and murky. He doubted anything could live in those waters, but every now and again he saw something huge and monstrous slide through the sea.

Or maybe it was only the churning of the sea, caused by underwater volcanic vents.

The islands came in all sizes. Some of them were no bigger than a foot or two across, looking like a flagstone footpath that had been scattered across the sea. But they were attached to spires of rock firmly attached to the ocean bottom that could rip out an unwary ship's hull. Several others were scarcely large enough for a hut.

Then there were some that soared three and four hundred feet straight up, broken and craggy things devoid of vegetation except for a few gnarly trees and ugly brush that had peculiar reddish-gold blossoms Wick had never before seen.

"What are those blossoms?" Diligently, Wick captured the shape and relative size of the blossoms in his journal. He mixed the color with the pigments he brought with him, but only put a dab of the color on the page to extend his supply. Although, with the ore seemingly in goodly supply on the islands, it was possible he could make more paint by mixing ore in powder form with animal fat. He'd been working quickly, blocking out first impressions of the Cinder Clouds Islands.

Hallekk stood only a short distance away. He looked alert and ready, but he was uneasy about sailing into waters that were unknown to them. Especially a sea that presented such dangers to ships' crews new to the area.

"Them are goldengreed weeds," the big dwarf answered. "Ye'll want to stay away from 'em."

"Why?"

" 'Cause they bite."

" 'Bite'? Like with teeth?" Wick had seen flesh-eating plants before, but they didn't bite. They usually had a tendency to swallow prey whole, asphyxiate it or poison it, then digest it at their leisure. Brandt had once cut him out of a crest-hearted gulper they'd found in a wizard's enchanted greenhouse up in the Thundering Hills while looking for a treasure.

"They bite," Hallekk said, "but not with teeth. Don't know how they do it, an' I've no wish to find out. They got a workin' relationship with a uniquely loathsome weevil what feeds on human flesh."

"You mean they're symbiotic?"

Hallekk glanced at him for a moment. " 'Course I do. How could I mean anything else? Once a goldengreed bites ye, they deposit a weevil what's about to lay eggs—"

"You mean she's gravid," Wick said automatically.

"If'n ye say so. Anyways, the weevil burrows up in yer skin, then digs in deep an' tight. After a few days, she ups an' lays her eggs in ye an' she dies. Only a short while later, them little weevils hatches an' eats ye from the inside out."

"That's disgusting," Wick said. He thought the whole process unnatural and needlessly morbid.

"Aye. Goblinkin in these parts use goldengreed as torture sometimes. Stake a prisoner out, then make bets on how much of him gets eaten afore he croaks." Hallekk looked at Wick with concern in his eyes. "I've heard tell that if'n them newborn weevils are left to their own business, they can eat a man down to skin an' bones in a few weeks. Usually he dies somewheres in there, but it ain't an easy way to go."

"No," Wick agreed, his throat tight and dry. *And they're going to put me off in the middle of that?* "So . . . if I get bitten, what should I do?"

"Burn it out if'n ye can. Dig it out with a knife." Hallekk shrugged. "If'n ye think ye're still infested an' ye can live without that part of yerself, if'n it's only a finger or a toe—or even a hand or a foot—cut it off."

"Oh."

"It's best if ye doesn't get bitten."

"I'll keep that in mind."

"Oh, an' don't go to sleep within driftin' distance of a goldengreed plant. Sometimes them blasted things gets desperate an' takes their chances by jumpin' out of the plant in hopes of landin' on something close by. They get the chance to crawl into yer ear, they'll do it. Then ye'll be keepin' a weevil in mind." Hallekk showed him a callous grin.

Never sleep with your ears open. Wick wrote that in his journal and underlined it. In case he forgot. But he didn't see how that would happen.

"Are you afraid, Wick?"

Startled, Wick looked up from his journal. Actually,

while he'd been working, he didn't feel anything at all. But now that the thought of dying was suddenly thrust into his mind again, he was terrified.

Craugh stood at his side, gazing out at the sea. With the sun setting in the west behind him, Wick could only see the wizard mostly in silhouette. As a result, Craugh looked almost insubstantial, while at the same time shot through with darkness.

"More than I've ever been," Wick said, hoping that Craugh might relent. He knew if he could get the wizard to change his mind, Cap'n Farok would change his, too.

"Well," Craugh said, looking out over the Rusting Sea, "it's always good to be a little afraid, but don't let that fear rule your thinking. Use it to keep you alive."

"Why don't you go," Wick asked, "and I'll stay on the ship and give *you* advice?"

"Do you think the Cinder Clouds dwarves would talk to a wizard?"

No. Nobody wants to talk to a wizard. But Wick didn't say that. Instead, he pointed out, "You don't have to tell them you're a wizard."

Craugh frowned at Wick. "Do I have to ever tell anyone I'm a wizard?"

Wick thought long and hard about that, seeking any avenue of escape. No matter where they went, no one made the mistake of thinking Craugh was just an old human. When someone looked at him, they just saw . . . *wizardly*.

"No," Wick grumped. Then in a lower voice, he mumbled, "But a lot of people think you're an *evil* wizard."

"I heard that."

"You were meant to."

"I know you're not happy about this, Wick," Craugh said, "but it's for the best." He pointed.

Following the bony finger, Wick spotted a seagull flying low over the water on *One-Eyed Peggie*'s port side.

The bird cruised easily, no more than ten feet above the placid, orange-tinted surface.

"Let's say that seagull represents the present," Craugh said. "It sails through life blithely, but one day the past will rear up its ugly snout—"

The water under the seagull suddenly erupted and a wart-covered red snout led a reptilian body up from the sea. Massive jaws opened and closed swiftly with a *snap!* of teeth that sounded like a tree trunk splitting. In the next instant, the seagull was gone and only a few white feathers drifted on the air.

"—and the present will be ripped away," Craugh said.

Listening to the wizard, Wick detected a deeper level of meaning to Craugh's words. The warning scraped against something personal inside Craugh.

"You have to pay attention to the past, Wick," Craugh said quietly. "You read books and look for the old science and history that has been lost or forgotten. But you have to understand that people—humans, dwarves, and elves, and even dwellers—lived in that science and history. They had lives in addition to discoveries and explorations, and some of those lives weren't quite as heroic as the authors of those books would have readers believe. People—" The wizard took a deep breath. "—well, they have a tendency to fail and disappoint. Especially when you view them as strong figures."

The anger and fear drained from Wick when he regarded the wizard. For the first time after all the adventures they had been through, Wick thought Craugh looked somehow vulnerable and lost.

How can you go through a thousand years of living? he wondered. *How many friends, how much family, did you lose over those centuries, Craugh?*

But he knew he dared not ask.

"Those warriors that died at the Battle of Fell's Keep need to be remembered," Craugh said. "But they need to be remembered as a whole, not disparate groups." He looked at the islands before them. "If we can find Oskarr's battle-axe—"

"Boneslicer," Wick put in.

"Just so," the wizard said. "Once you find Boneslicer, we can begin healing that old wound."

Wick thought that all sounded well and good, but he kept remembering how easily the snouted beast—*a giant crocodile?*—leaped from the water and snatched the unsuspecting seagull. How could Craugh and Cap'n Farok possibly believe he was going to succeed at this insane quest?

At dusk, *One-Eyed Peggie* dropped anchor less than a hundred paces from one of the islands. The lookouts had kept careful watch and didn't think any goblins were in the area, but they had heard the clangor of dwarven hammers in the distance and knew they had to be close to a dwarven village.

Dressed in a modest traveling cloak, his journal hidden under his shirt in a waterproof oilskin along with a quill and ink bottle and a few sticks of charcoal to work with, Wick stood ready to leave.

Wheezing with effort, Cap'n Farok joined Wick beside the longboat the crew had prepared to lower over the side. The sulfurous air hadn't agreed with the dwarven captain the whole day. Now he looked pale and wan.

"Ye keep yer head about ye while out there," Cap'n Farok said in a no-nonsense tone. "I don't like losin' crew, an' I won't stand for it outta stupidity."

"Aye, Cap'n." Unconsciously, Wick stood a little taller and puffed out his chest. There was something innately noble about the old captain, something that reminded Wick of Grandmagister Ludaan, who had accepted him

as a Novice and shown him the secrets of the Vault of
All Known Knowledge.

"Ye come back to us when ye've finished yer quest,
Librarian Lamplighter," Cap'n Farok said. "We'll see ye
through the monster's eye an' come to fetch ye when
ye've got Oskarr's battle-axe."

The monster's eye Cap'n Farok referred to occupied a
large bottle kept under the captain's bed. The ship's captain could use the eyeball (which still lived inside the jar)
to see any past or present crewman that yet survived, no
matter where they were.

Unfortunately, the sea monster could also keep watch
over the ship and—every now and again—track it. *One-
Eyed Peggie* had been attacked a number of times so far.

"I will, Cap'n Farok," Wick promised. "We've still got
your memoirs to write."

"In due time," the old captain said. "In due time." With
that, he ducked in for a quick, fierce hug that touched
Wick's heart. "Fair weather an' followin' seas to ye, Librarian."

"And you, Cap'n."

Wick stepped into the longboat, joined by Hallekk and
Craugh. The wizard's decision to risk stepping ashore
surprised Wick, but he didn't say anything. Three more
crewmen joined them, filling out the longboat crew.

Luckily, the ocean was calm. Wick took up one of the
oars and pulled with a trained stroke, falling easily into
the silent rhythm with Hallekk and the dwarves. They had
to make an adjustment because Craugh didn't pull an oar,
but the wizard kept watch.

Wick knew his hands were the roughest of any Librarian. They were even rougher than those of Librarians who
made most of the paper at the Vault of All Known
Knowledge. That process involved harsh chemicals.

Grandmagister Frollo faulted him for his worker's
hands on several occasions, but Wick took a curious pride

in them. There were several scars in with the calluses, from knife and rope and other sharp edges and fires, and looking at them was almost like studying a table of contents in a book. Each of those scars told a story.

Only a short time later, with the moonlight blunted by the thick smoke that shrouded the islands, the longboat ran up on the shore. Hallekk and the others got out, shipped the oars, and pulled the boat up so the retreating tide wouldn't carry it back out.

After a brief search of the coastline by torchlight, they found a cave where Wick could weather the night. With the area heated by the volcanic activity, it was warm enough that he didn't worry about being cold. He had precious few supplies.

Besides his hidden journal and writing utensils, he had only ragged clothes and a patched traveling cloak. All of it was clothing an escaping slave—if he were fortunate enough—could have stolen.

"Well then, little man," Hallekk said a little uneasily, "we've put ye up as best as we can with what we've got to give ye."

"I know," Wick said.

"I'll be askin' the Old Ones to keep an eye on ye."

"Just make sure the cap'n does the same," Wick said. "If he sees me running ahead of a goblinkin horde, or the dwarves are intending to chop me up, it's probably time to come get me."

Despite his anxiety, Hallekk grinned. "We'll come get ye straightaway. Ye got me word." He held out a big paw, and when Wick took it, he pulled the little Librarian in close and held onto him for a moment. "Ye just take care of yerself. I 'spect to hear all ye stories when ye come aboard again. Make sure yer knob stays attached properlike."

"I will."

Hallekk turned away, leaving Craugh standing there to say his good-byes.

"This is uncomfortable," the wizard said after a moment.

Wick silently agreed. Although he and Craugh had journeyed together in the past and had shared meals, stories, and hardships in their adventures, they weren't close friends.

"You're not making it any easier to leave," Craugh growled.

"If you ask me, the easy part is getting back in that longboat to return to the ship. Not staying here," Wick said.

Craugh grinned at him then. "I guess you're right. Well, we've seen harder times than these. You haven't gotten yourself killed before, so just keep doing that." Without another word, Craugh turned and walked away.

An empty feeling opened up in Wick's middle and spread quickly outward.

"Oh." Craugh turned around. "There is one other thing."

"Another warning?" Wick asked.

"No. I see no reason not to believe you've been given a sufficient number of those." Craugh reached inside his travel cloak. "You'll need a guide of sorts while you're here."

"I thought no one was staying."

"No one is. This guide will blend into the surroundings. Taking out his hand, Craugh held a foot-long skink by the tail. He opened his fingers and dropped the lizard with a *plop* to the ground.

The skink immediately slithered away and raced over to a clutch of rocks. It sat there looking at them with big, unblinking eyes.

"You're leaving me a lizard to act as a guide?" Wick asked in disbelief. *Maybe I could use it as bait for fishing.*

"Yes. I think you'll find him useful. His name is Ro-hoh. There's more to him than meets the eye."

Good, Wick thought, *because what meets the eye isn't even worth throwing into a kettle and using as soup stock.* "Sure," he said.

Quietly, with a few last-minute well wishes, the ship's crew—including Craugh—was back in the longboat and pulling for the ship. *One-Eyed Peggie* sat at anchor, riding the ocean's gentle swells. A few lanterns used as running lights marked her for Wick to see.

He stood there on the shore, listening to the slap of the waves, and watched as the pirate ship unfurled part of her sails and got underway again. Getting seen by an incoming ship or by dwarves looking for new ore wasn't a good idea. It would be easy to guess that perhaps Wick wasn't an escaped slave.

After a while, *One-Eyed Peggie* disappeared over the horizon.

"Hey," the skink said.

Wick glanced at the lizard in surprise. "You talk."

"Sure I talk." The skink whipped his tail around as if taking pride in his accomplishment, or maybe it was to show disdain.

"It figures. Don't tell me, you're here to tell me what Craugh would do whenever there's a problem."

"Actually," the skink said, rising on his two hind legs to address Wick from the rocks, "I'm not any happier about this than you are."

"Getting stranded on this lump of rock in the middle of the Rusting Sea?"

The skink looked around. Moonslight gleamed over the small scales. "This is actually a pretty good place. Warm and cozy." He took a deep sniff. "And it has a certain . . . aroma about it that seems fascinating." He glanced back at Wick and sniffed. "Craugh lied to me."

"Craugh lies to everybody. It's one of those dependable things in life."

"He told me you were a bonafide hero."

"I'm a Librarian," Wick said because he was tired and he wasn't thinking straight what with all the worry and fear clamoring inside his head.

"Oh," Rohoh said disdainfully. "A *book* person."

"You know about book people?"

"Mold, mildew, and dust. Those are terrible smells. Yes, I know books." He inhaled again. "Not like this."

"How do you know about books?"

"I've traveled with Craugh to different places. I've been to the Vault of All Known Knowledge. There was a man there. Grandmagister Ludaan. I played chess with him."

Wick *was* surprised. "You knew Grandmagister Ludaan?"

"Yes. A fascinating man. For a human with no wizardly abilities." The skink rubbed his light green stomach. "He was always generous with his food."

Suspicion darkened Wick's thoughts. "Were you something else before you met Craugh?"

The skink blinked. "Yes, I was. I was much safer. And I was happy."

"You weren't a human? Or an elf? Or a dwarf? Or a dweller? Or something else?"

"Please." Rohoh crossed his skinny arms over his narrow chest. "Why would I want to be *anything* else than what I am now? Being a skink is perfect for me."

"Then why are you here?"

"I owed Craugh a favor. He told me I'd be working with a hero who had dunderheaded tendencies."

" 'Dunderheaded tendencies'?"

"Yes. But I wouldn't take it personal. Craugh doesn't have a high opinion of anybody." The skink used his thin, pointed tail to pick his teeth. "Except for Grandmagister Ludaan, of course. I think Craugh likes his food, too."

Sighing, Wick marched back to the small cave they'd chosen for him to spend the night in.

"That reminds me, I'm hungry," the lizard said. It

scurried after him, its lightning quick skills easily making up for Wick's longer stride.

"So?" Taking off his traveling cloak, Wick folded it into a rough pillow at the back of the cave and laid down. "Go catch a bug."

"Have you ever tried to clean bug legs out from between your teeth?"

"You don't have teeth." Wick struggled in his bed on the hard rock and succeeded in finding an almost comfortable position.

"I was trying to put it in perspective for you. And if you swallow them whole, you end up swallowing them again and again. All night long. It's not worth the bother, I tell you."

Wick turned away from the skink and ignored him. *What have I gotten myself into?* Something scurried across the cave ceiling above him. When he looked up, the lizard hung upside down by its hind feet, regarding him with unblinking eyes.

"Don't you have anything to eat?" Rohoh asked.

"No," Wick said. "Craugh and the others took it away from me. I'm supposed to be an escaped slave."

"You don't have *anything*?"

"No."

"Can I search your pockets for crumbs?"

"No."

"You might have missed something."

"If you crawl inside my clothing," Wick promised, "I'm going to feed you to the first goblinkin I find."

Just then, light flared into the tunnel, chasing away the darkness. The skink hung frozen for a moment, his mouth wide in surprise. Then he bolted for the back recesses of the cave.

"Now an' why would I want to eat a skinny ol' lizard what's probably tough as leather when I could fetch me a nice plump halfer fer me stewpot?" a rough voice demanded. "Lookee here. I told ye I thought I smelt me a halfer."

Putting a hand up to block the torchlight, Wick spotted three horrible shapes standing in the cave mouth. Goblinkin! He was doomed even before his task got underway!

5

On the Menu

Springing to his feet, Wick tried to run for his life. The skink had managed to escape. But the cave ceiling was low. Wick didn't see the overhang that caught him across the forehead and knocked him from his feet. Nearly senseless, he landed flat on his back and couldn't move.

I'm paralyzed! he thought. Panic coursed through him.

The light from the goblinkin's torch came on into the cave, trailing the rude laughter from the approaching goblinkin.

"Stupid halfer," one of the goblinkin snarled. "Goin' a-runnin' through a dark cave like that when ye can't see. Ain't got no sense."

"Well," another said, "we ain't gonna eat him 'cause he's smart. We're gonna eat him 'cause he tastes good. Leastways, he'll taste good once we get him all stewed up."

"Maybe ye don't care for 'em none," a third commented, "but I like halfer brains. They's soft. I can swallow 'em down without even chewin'."

Wick discovered that he wasn't totally paralyzed because his stomach turned queasy at that revelation. He'd never made a study of what goblinkin ate. The information he had came as a result of misfortune. And he surely didn't want to learn about the culinary delights of goblinkin firsthand.

Bats fluttered on the ceiling, hanging upside down like dried figs. Several of them turned loose their holds and dropped, then spread their tiny wings and flew toward the cave mouth.

"Look out!" one of the goblinkin shouted.

The torchlight danced crazily as the goblinkin dodged the bats. Then the bats were gone from the cave.

Wick suddenly discovered that he wasn't paralyzed anymore. He tried to get to his feet. Only then a clawed goblinkin foot came crashing down on his chest and knocked the breath from him as it pinned him against the cave floor.

"Good thing ye didn't let him run," one of the goblinkin said. "Halfers is almighty quick. I hate fast food."

"Where do ye a-think ye're a-goin'?" The goblinkin leaned down, thrusting his ugly face into Wick's.

"N-n-nowhere," Wick stuttered, wishing he wasn't so afraid. But even after years of trekking around the mainland chasing after books and legends and seeing goblinkin many of those times, he still wasn't used to them.

Goblinkin were particularly ugly. Baby goblinkin were even more so, which was why they started out in the world unloved and pretty much on their own. Besides that, there was always another goblinkin that came along in case the first was eaten by something larger than him, killed while on a battlefield or falling from a mountain, or beneath the tusks of a wild Borhovian skurulta (which, for some odd reason no one knew, fancied goblinkin flesh), or was butchered and eaten by siblings who had grown tired of him.

The goblinkin's face was a triangle shape, with the narrowest point being the chin. Using the allotted space for features, nature had spread the piggy eyes apart so there was plenty of room for the bulbous nose to take root over the narrow mouth jammed with crooked, yellow fangs.

The hair was tied back in a ponytail festooned with rocks and gems and bones that told the story of the goblinkin's tribe and accomplishments.

A sparse sprinkling of bushy black hair on the chin formed something of a beard. The ears were huge sails as big as the bats that had fled the cave, and both were punctured several times over with earrings fashioned from victims' bones. In proper daylight, the skin was splotchy gray-green that maintained an unhealthy pallor.

"That's right," the goblinkin taunted, "you ain't a-goin' nowhere."

"Uh, Sebble," the smallest goblinkin said hesitantly.

"What, Droos?" Sebble snarled.

"The halfer." Droos nodded at Wick. "He's gotta go somewhere."

"No, he ain't," Sebble said, "'cause I said he ain't a-goin' nowhere. An' I'm the chief of this here patrol."

"Okay," the younger goblinkin said, looking around. "We can eat him here, I suppose. But he's gonna be cold an' tough if'n we don't cook him up proper."

"Oh." Sebble appeared to give that some thought. He scratched his head with a black talon. "We need to cook him, don't we?"

"We could eat him raw," the third goblinkin suggested. "Just open him up like a melon an' he can be his own bowl. After we scoop him clean, we can eat the rind. We've done it afore." He kicked Wick with a big toe. "That way we don't have to share him. Ain't enough meat on his bones to share with the others anyway."

"You don't want to eat him raw," a voice called from the back of the cave. Wick recognized the skink's voice but apparently the goblinkin didn't.

"Right," Sebble said. "We don't want to eat him raw, Kuuch."

"Why not?" Kuuch asked.

"Well," Sebble said, evidently thinking it over again.

Some chief, Wick thought.

"Because if you eat him raw, you'll get a bad belly and . . . and . . . a case of the spoilt meat trots," Rohoh called from the back of the cave.

Sebble slapped Kuuch with an open hand. "We doesn't want to eat the halfer raw, ye idjit. It'd give us the spoilt meat trots, is what it'd do."

"Take him back to the camp and put him in a stewpot," Rohoh suggested.

If I ever see that turncoat again, Wick thought, *it's going to be too soon!*

"We have a stewpot back at the camp," Droos said.

"Yeah." Sebble nodded. "We'll cook him up there. Let's go. We gotta find some potatoes."

"An' some carrots," Droos said. "I like carrots. But we don't wanna cook 'em too long. I like 'em crunchy."

"That's 'cause ye still got all yer teeth," Kuuch snarled, slapping the back of the younger goblinkin's head. "I like me carrots mushy. Otherwise I have to pick 'em out."

"Ain't my fault ye lost yer teeth," Droos sniveled, backing away from the others. "Told ye eatin' that many carrion rats at one time wasn't good for ye. Give ye gas an' rotted out yer teeth. Ye shoulda mixed 'em better with them slimeweed greens."

"I hate slimeweed greens," Kuuch moped.

"You'll want some salt and pepper, too," Rohoh called from the back of the cave.

"An' salt," Sebble said.

"An' pepper," Kuuch added.

Sebble glared at the other goblinkin. "I was gonna say that."

"And onions," Rohoh said.

Sebble turned to Droos. "Are ye rememberin' all this?"

Droos shrank back. "Maaaaybeee."

Sebble slapped the younger goblinkin again, making

Droos yelp. "Remember it, ye worthless gullet. Potatoes an' carrots an'—"

"Salt an' pepper," Kuuch said.

"I was gettin' to that," Sebble whined. "I wasn't gonna forget salt an' pepper."

"I think maybe we used up all the pepper," Droos said.

"We got pepper," Kuuch said. "Banna still has some he's hid up an' I know where he hid it."

"There was somethin' else," Sebble said. He'd been counting ingredients on his fingers and had nearly a full hand.

"*Onions*," Rohoh said.

"Oh yeah," Sebble said. "Onions. There's them wild onions what grows on the hill."

"I don't want them wild onions," Kuuch whined. "They gives me gas."

"Ever'thin' ye eats gives ye gas," Droos said. "I tell ye, ye shouldn't got a sweet tooth fer them carrion rats."

"Well, I like them wild onions," Sebble said. "But ye're a-sleepin' downwind of us after we eat."

Wick lay still under the goblinkin's foot. He couldn't believe he was fated to become indigestion after years of serving as a Novice and a Third Level Librarian. He'd practically only just gotten promoted to Second Level Librarian. Maybe First Level Librarian wasn't going to happen any time soon, but it was a possibility he was looking forward to. Everything happened eventually.

But not if he ended up as a repast for goblinkin.

"Firepears would be nice," Rohoh said.

Sebble nodded. "They would at that. I like firepears." He looked for another finger on his first hand and discovered that he was all out. He turned up a finger on his other hand like it was something he'd never seen before.

"C'mon," Sebble said. "We ain't got all night if we're gonna have the halfer stewed by mornin'."

Wick knew pleading for his life wasn't going to do any good. But he still felt inclined.

Together, the three goblinkin turned and walked away, arguing among themselves how best to prepare a dweller stew. Wick lay on the ground unnoticed. They were so involved in planning their meal they'd forgotten the main ingredient. Cautiously, head aching from the impact, Wick got to his feet.

"Wait," Droos said from outside the cave. "We left the halfer."

Seeing the torch hurrying back toward him, Wick turned to run again. Perhaps he could lose himself in the back of the cave. All he needed was—

"Look out!" Rohoh yelled.

The familiar impact slammed across Wick's forehead again. He was lying on his back, seeing stars, when Sebble returned for him.

Grinning, the goblinkin fisted Wick's clothes and lifted him from the ground. "Ye're really stupid, halfer. I hope I don't catch it from eatin' ye."

A short while later, Wick trudged up the mountain in the darkness. The rope around his neck chafed something fierce. Tied behind his back, his hands had gone numb. He fell again and again, bruising his face and cutting his lips and chin.

Every now and then, when he didn't fall fast enough to suit Sebble, who held the rope around Wick's neck, the goblinkin yanked the line and caused him to fall. Sebble and Kuuch hooted with laughter at the sport.

"Mayhap we could walk closer to him with the torch so he could see," Droos suggested. For a goblinkin, he seemed to have a more tender heart.

"Nah," Sebble replied. "All that fallin' down he's a-doin' is just tenderizin' him some."

"Well, if'n ye keep a-playin' with our food like that," Droos said, "ye're liable to lose him over the side in one of them firepits."

So much for the tender heart theory, Wick thought. Then, *Firepits!* He peered over the side of the trail and noticed that, indeed, he felt an occasional wafting of heat from that direction. Evidently the island still had vent tubes that ran to the heart of the smoldering volcano on the ocean floor.

Up and up and up, Wick went, following a narrow path that had been worn into the stone. Since there wasn't any game on the island that he knew of, Wick felt certain goblinkin or dwarves had made the trail.

Without warning, something ran up Wick's leg. Tiny claws bit into his flesh. Memory of Hallekk's description of the goldengreed weed ran through his mind and he couldn't help thinking that he'd stumbled against one of the plants in the dark and was now infested with flesh-eating insects. He halted in the middle of the trail and howled helplessly, jumping up and down. The claws just bit in more fiercely.

Concerned by their prisoner's antics, the goblinkin halted. Sebble raised his torch and looked at Wick. "What are ye about, halfer?"

"Something's on me!" Wick cried, jumping and flopping his elbows—which was all he could manage with his hands bound behind him. "I think I was bitten by a goldengreed weed!"

Anxiously, the goblinkin stepped back. That didn't help because Sebble kept a firm grip on the rope and yanked Wick off balance. He hopped and skipped a short distance back down the trail. Instantly, the goblinkin retreated farther and started yelling threats, but that tactic didn't do any good because Sebble kept hold of the rope and kept pulling

Wick after them. Down and down they skipped, till finally the little Librarian lost his balance and fell with a thud.

Frantic, Wick rolled and accidentally tumbled into one of the craters. Suddenly the only thing keeping him from plunging into one of the volcanic vents was the hateful rope around his neck. Thankfully the goblinkin had tied it well and it was a strong rope.

But he was strangling.

"Quick!" one of the goblinkin cried. "Pull him up afore we lose our dinner!"

"Maybe we should let him go," another suggested. "I don't want to eat any of those weevil eggs."

"Or we could just let him dangle a bit until he's properly steamed. Likely as not, the meat would fall right offa the bone in a little bit."

Wick felt like his eyes were about to pop from his head. He couldn't breathe and hot air from the vent came close to scalding his legs. It didn't take much for him to imagine the red-hot lava waiting only a short—or long—distance below.

Whatever was on Wick ran up his back, hooking claws into his shirt, then clung in his hair by his right ear. "Shh-hhh!" Rohoh hissed. "It's me. I came to help."

Help? Wick thought. *How is a skink going to help me? Especially since it's the same skink that gave the goblinkin the stew recipe?*

Rohoh crawled along Wick's shoulder and hid behind his hair. "Just keep quiet," the skink whispered. "I'll get you out of the mess you got yourself into soon enough."

Mess I got myself *into!* Wick tried to speak but couldn't. He kicked against the side of the crater wall, trying in vain to find some kind of purchase. At the same time, he was afraid his struggles would yank the rope from the hands of the goblinkin.

"If he's got weevils in him," Kuuch said as if he'd given the matter grave consideration, "we could just lop off that part. Would mean we'd have less to share, but I'd still like to have me dinner. I worked up an appetite just bringin' it this far."

"Gggggghhhhh!" Wick managed. Even he didn't know what he was trying to say, but he felt certain something *had* to be said.

"I wasn't bitten," Rohoh called up. "It was a mosquito."

"All that noise over a mosquito?" Sebble pushed his ugly face over the crater's edge and peered down with the torch in hand. "Ye've got mighty sensitive skin, halfer."

"Yes," Rohoh said. "It just means I'll be more tender."

"Tender is good."

Strength drained from Wick. He thought this was the end after all. In Hanged Elf's Point, he'd escaped the slave market (he'd had help, of course, but that was beside the point) and here in the Cinder Clouds Islands, he couldn't even make it into a goblinkin stewpot.

"Pull me up," Rohoh cried again.

"All right," Sebble told his companions, "heave ho."

Wick thought his head was going to separate from his shoulders when they started pulling him up, but it didn't. By the time he reached the top of the crater and solid ground again, his tongue was protruding from his mouth.

The goblinkin loosened the rope around his neck and peered down at him.

"Is he dead?" Kuuch asked. "If he's dead, maybe we could just eat him here. Doesn't make much sense to cook him if he's dead. Now I can work me up an appetite watchin' him flop around in the stewpot when the water gets hot."

"He was talkin'," Sebble argued. He kicked Wick in the head. "Are ye alive, halfer?"

"Yes," Wick croaked, even though he couldn't believe it. "I'm . . . alive."

"Good. Now get up an' walk. We got a stewpot waitin' on ye."

6

The Goblinkin Chef

Weak and hurting, Wick finally stumbled to the goblinkin lair in a cave formed from a large vent hole at the top of the island. Ten other goblinkin sat around a large fire made of timbers that looked like they'd once belonged to a ship.

"What's that ye got, Sebble?" one of the other goblinkin asked. The foul creature stood up and hitched up the belt around his bulging waistline that held up his ragged breeches.

"Dinner," Sebble said. "Thought I smelt me a halfer, an' I did."

"Bring him over here."

Barely able to stand, Wick walked over to the fire and stood while the goblinkin poked and prodded him with calloused fingers.

"Ye got a scrawny little thing," one of the goblinkin said. "Couldn't ye a-taken a better one?"

"This 'un was the only one there was." Sebble pulled Wick back, then stepped in front of him. The goblinkin's hand tightened around his club. "He's ours, Hesst. We foun' him an' we catched him."

"You a-gonna roast him?" another goblinkin asked.

"Thought we'd make stew," Kuuch answered.

"Well then," a particularly loutish goblinkin said with a grin, "if ye're a-gonna be makin' stew, ye'll be wantin' to use me stewpot." He tapped a foot lazily against the heavy iron cauldron sitting crookedly against the wall.

"We do," Sebble said.

"I can let ye use the stewpot," the goblinkin offered, "but it's gonna cost ye."

"What's it gonna cost?"

"A few bowls o' stew, 'course."

Angrily, Sebble pinched one of Wick's arms. "Ye can see for yerself there ain't much here, Ookool. We'll be lucky to have enough for ourselves."

"If'n ye roast him, ye're gonna lose a lot of the fat to the fire," Ookool pointed out. "The fat's some of the most flavorful. That's why makin' a stew out of him is such a good idea."

Wick couldn't believe he was standing there listening to the goblinkin figuring out how best to serve him. And where was Cap'n Farok and the crew of *One-Eyed Peggie*? Shouldn't they be putting in an appearance about now?

"I'd really like a nice stew," Droos said. "I kinda had me heart set on it."

Sebble sighed as if put upon. "All right. We'll make stew. Ookool, we'll use yer stewpot an' ye can have a bowlful or two. We'll be needin' some vegetables, too. Some potatoes an' carrots . . ."

"Salt an' pepper," Droos added.

"An' onions an' firepears," Kuuch put in.

Sebble tied Wick to the kettle and went searching for ingredients. The goblinkin set about their savage scavenger hunt. There were a number of ale kegs, proof they'd taken cargo from ships.

As they sorted out the vegetables, Wick spotted the broken bones piled against one of the cave walls. Evidently the goblinkin had been getting by on fish, turtles, dwellers, and dwarves.

"Get a grip," the skink said from his hiding place beneath Wick's hair. "I've got a plan."

"If they put me in that stewpot," Wick promised, "I'm taking you with me."

Rohoh snorted derisively at that.

"What's the plan?" Wick asked.

"They're not going to cook you with the rope around your neck and wrists," Rohoh said. "When they take it off—*run*!"

Wick shook his head. The goblinkin were more successful in their hunt for side dishes than he'd thought. The vegetables were piling up in front of the stewpot, which Ookool was filling with fresh water from the barrel they had.

"That's it?" Wick asked in disgust. "*That's* your big plan? *Run for it?*"

"If you get a better idea," the skink said, sounding miffed, "maybe you should let me know."

Watching the goblinkin bring up the vegetables, Wick suddenly remembered a story he'd read in Hralbomm's Wing. Actually, the tale had gotten handed down through several different cultures that had written it up.

Thinking quickly, Wick latched hold of a desperate idea. He tried to be calm and rational, but it was hard to when presented with becoming the main course for goblinkin gluttony.

"Wait!" Wick yelled.

The goblinkin all frowned at him.

"I hate food that talks," Ookool grumped.

Several of the other goblinkin agreed.

"Have you ever eaten dweller surprise?" As soon as the words were out of his mouth, Wick wished he'd remembered the name of another dish. He needed something more exotic if he was going to get their interest. But smoked dweller, dweller al fresco, and—especially—shredded dweller or blackened dweller sounded worse.

The goblinkin looked at each other.

"Have ye ever had dweller surprise?" one asked.

"No, not me. But I've *surprised* a few now an' again."

"I can fix dweller surprise!" Wick yelled.

"Ye can?" a goblinkin asked. He turned and nudged the fellow next to him. "Hey, the dweller says he can fix dweller surprise."

A large goblinkin with a prodigious belly shoved through the others till he stood in front of Wick. Judging from the finger and toe on his necklace, he was the chief of the goblinkin tribe. "Ye can make dweller surprise?"

Wick swallowed hard. His legs trembled. "I can. I've fixed it before."

"Have you?" Rohoh whispered in his ear. "Well, now that's just disgusting. Craugh really left me in the dark on this one. I bet you're a real favorite at all the goblinkin parties."

Wick shook his head, trying in vain to dislodge the skink.

"Well," the chief said, scratching the tuft of hair that grew on his bony chin.

"C'mon, chief," Droos said, rubbing his belly in anticipation. "Let him fix the dweller surprise. Ye can' have the first servin'."

The chief slapped Droos and made him yelp. "I get the first servin' anyway," the chief snorted.

But the other goblinkin joined in, all clamoring for dweller surprise.

"Okay then." The chief grudgingly gave in. "Ye can fix the dweller surprise, but if'n ye mess it up—" Here he drew a scarred forefinger across his own throat.

"Wouldn't you already be dead after you make the dweller surprise?" Rohoh asked.

Not if I can help it, Wick thought.

A few minutes later, after some of the feeling had returned to his hands, Wick stood on an empty ale keg in front of the kettle. The keg didn't sit terribly well on the uneven cave floor and he risked falling into the kettle every time he moved. Beneath the scorched iron bottom, flames licked out. Heat played over him. The goblinkin had even found a chef's hat in the piles of clothing they used as bedding. Chief Zoobi had plunked it on Wick's head. Overall, Wick was not happy about his current situation.

"Careful, you little cannibal," the skink hissed.

"I'm not a cannibal," Wick whispered back angrily.

"Why? You *fix* dweller surprise but you don't *eat* it?"

"Don't talk to me."

Chief Zoobi glared at Wick. "Were ye a-talkin' to *me*, halfer?"

"Noooooo," Wick replied, smiling charitably. "I was talking to myself."

"Wouldn't make a habit of it if'n I was ye."

On the verge of going into a goblinkin kettle for dweller surprise, I wouldn't think any habits would be forthcoming. But Wick kept that observation to himself. Instead, he cleared his throat. "I need the potatoes now."

While he'd been waiting for his hands to return to life, the goblinkin had been busy preparing vegetables at his direction. They handed over buckets of potatoes, some of them black with bruising. Wick didn't hesitate; he poured them into the bubbling kettle, then he stirred the pot with a ship's oar that was barely big enough for the job. The kettle was easily big enough for him to swim in.

"And some ale," Wick said.

"Ale?" Zoobi asked.

"Ale." Wick nodded. "It will help season the meat."

After a little grumbling, one of the ale kegs was broken open. Wick poured a bucket into the kettle. Then, as he'd hoped, the goblinkin fell to and quickly helped themselves to the rest of the ale. He stirred the kettle while they finished off the keg.

"Carrots," he called.

The goblinkin brought the carrots by the bucketful.

"More ale," Wick said.

"More ale?" the chief asked.

"If you want the true dweller surprise instead of a pale imitation," Wick said.

Another keg was opened. Another bucket was passed up to Wick, who poured it into the kettle and began stirring again.

While the goblinkin waited on their stew, they helped themselves to the open keg.

Wick started a song while he stirred, keeping an eye on the goblinkin.

Dweller surprise!
Dweller surprise!
Oh what a feast
For our hungry eyes!
Dweller surprise!
Dweller surprise!
It's warm and good,
I'll tell you no lies!

All of the goblinkin just looked at him.

"Onions," Wick called out. "And another bucket of ale."

They passed along the buckets of onions, then opened another keg of ale. He repeated the process with the salt and the pepper, asking for a bucket of ale after each. The kettle slopped over the sides from time to time. Steam boiled up as the liquid hit the flaming boards under the kettle. He stirred for a long time, hoping the ale the goblinkin had drunk would start to affect them, all the while singing his song over and over.

"Your singing really stinks," Rohoh muttered.

"They don't think so," Wick whispered back.

Several of the goblinkin started singing the "Dweller Surprise Song" in off-key voices. It sounded like several cats getting strangled at once. But they were singing.

"Firepears," Wick yelled, knowing it was the last ingredient before they plopped him in.

"Firepears!" the goblinkin yelled happily. This time when they formed a line to pass the firepears along, they weaved and swayed unsteadily. Several firepears spilled out of the buckets.

Wick led the song again, and this time the goblinkin readily joined in. After he poured the last of the firepears in, he called for more ale.

The ingredient caused a minor celebration. The goblinkin sang even louder. Wick gave them another song to sing.

Ale for me!
Ale for you!
Wouldn't you like to drink
Ale from a shoe?

Learning the song almost at once, the goblinkin joined in and their raucous voices filled the lair.

"You've gotten them drunk," Rohoh said.

"Yes," Wick agreed.

"Well that's stupid. Goblinkin are mean drunks."

"They're singing right now."

"If that's what you call it. This is still stupid."

"Want me to tell them that the last secret ingredient is skink?"

"No."

"Then be quiet and let me get us out of here." Wick stood atop the keg and turned to face the goblinkin. "Hey."

They looked up at him.

"Is it soup yet?" one of the goblinkin asked.

"Put the dweller in," another suggested.

"No," Wick said, holding his hands up. "It's got to simmer for a while. I need more wood for the fire and another bucket of ale."

The goblinkin lurched to fulfill his requests. Several of them shook his hand and thanked him for his time. A number of them told him the concoction bubbling merrily in the kettle was the finest thing they'd ever smelled. Then the latest keg of ale made the rounds.

Wick stirred some more, listening to the drunken versions of the songs he'd made up, and grew more hopeful about his plan. Then he turned to the goblinkin and put his hands together, clapping to a definite beat.

"It's time to dance!" Wick yelled out.

Crying out in excitement, the goblinkin raced around the lair. Three of them grabbed leather-covered drums and started laying down a fast-paced beat.

"Do ye know how to dance, halfer?" Chief Zoobi asked, grinning wildly.

"Yes," Wick replied.

"Then show us a dance step while we wait on the dweller surprise to cook."

Astounded, too surprised for a moment to even think straight, Wick listened to the rapid beat. Then he began a Swalian Grassroots Elven Clan dance that he'd choreographed in a recent book.

"What do you think you're doing?" Rohoh asked.

Wick waved his arms around. "Saving my life," he whispered to the skink.

"You've got an odd way of doing it."

Ignoring the comment, Wick tried to stay erect on his trembling knees. He'd mixed in all the ingredients. All that was left to finish off the dweller surprise was tossing in the dweller.

The goblinkin had trouble following the convoluted dance steps and gave up, complaining loudly. Upon reflection, Wick admitted that perhaps he'd selected the wrong dance. The Swalian Grassroots elves were given to complicated movements.

"You're losing them," Rohoh said. "They're going to want stew soon." The skink abandoned his position behind Wick's head and ran down his body to stand on the keg. He stood on his back legs and looked up at Wick. "Get off the keg. You don't have any rhythm."

Reluctantly, Wick abandoned his post. He jumped down and nearly lost the chef's hat. He pushed it back to the top of his head. So far, that hat was the only thing that marked him as something other than a stew ingredient.

"All right now!" the skink bellowed in a voice that somehow filled the goblinkin lair. "It's time to party!"

The goblinkin just stared at Rohoh.

He, Wick thought, *is supposed to help me? When I get back to* One-Eyed Peggie, *Craugh and I are going to have a* serious *talk.*

"Is that a lizard?" one of the goblinkin asked. He struggled to keep his eyes open. The effects of the ale showed throughout the goblinkin ranks.

"Aye," another goblinkin said, "that's a lizard all right."

"Ye ever ate a lizard?"

"I have. Crunchy little thing, it was."

"But was it good?"

"It was good enough."

"Might be good in the stew is what I'm a-thinkin'."

"Get that lizard in the stewpot," Chief Zoobi ordered.

Three of the goblinkin staggered forward. For a moment, Wick felt sorry for the skink. Then he remembered all the hateful things it had said to him. Still, he was loath to see it thrown into the bubbling pot.

Wick glanced at the entrance to the lair and wondered if he could grab Rohoh and make a run for it. After all, the rude little creature might come in handy later. *The skink can run faster than me*, he realized.

Then he slid his right foot in the direction of the lair's entrance. None of the goblinkin even noticed. Emboldened, he slid his right foot out and took another step.

"Wait!" Rohoh cried out, lifting his tiny hands and arms.

The goblinkin halted, looking at each other in consternation.

"It's a-talkin'," one of the goblinkin said. "Anybody ever seen a *talkin'* skink?"

"Ye're not there to talk to it, Uluk. Just toss it in the kettle."

"I'm a magic skink," Rohoh shouted.

That stopped the goblinkin. Since he was talking and that wasn't a normal thing for skinks to do, it was obvious that he was different.

"Magic, ye say?" Chief Zoobi forced his way to the front of the goblinkin.

"Yes," Rohoh said.

"What can ye do?" The goblinkin chief squinted at him.

"Well," Rohoh said, taking a moment to think, "I can talk . . . and I can dance."

"Let's see how he tastes," another goblinkin yelled out. "I get dibs on the head."

Rohoh stepped to the back of the teetering keg, waving his arms to keep his balance. Desperate, he yelled, "Also, I know the way to a fabulous treasure."

Wick groaned. *How often has* that *been used in the romances in Hralbomm's Wing? Talking fish. Talking snakes. At least if he was a talking bear he'd be big enough to defend himself.*

But the goblinkin hadn't read the romances in Hralbomm's Wing.

"A treasure, ye say?" Chief Zoobi asked.

Rohoh held his tiny arms as far apart as he could. "A *huge* treasure. Toss me in the pot and you lose your chance at the treasure."

"Well now," the goblinkin chief said, "I could do with some treasure. This bears a-thinkin' on."

"Great," the skink said, clapping his hands. "While you're thinking, let's dance." He turned to the drummers. "Give me a beat. Something with some feeling. Remember, you're going to get a treasure!"

Enthusiastic now in addition to being well in their cups, the drummers pounded their instruments. The skink started dancing, waving his arms and tossing his head to the beat.

Wick was so mesmerized by the sight that he forgot he was supposed to be escaping. Then he noticed that the skink's hand and head gestures grew more pronounced. So did that of the goblinkin.

Aggrieved, the lizard stopped dancing long enough to stomp his foot and point toward the lair's entrance. "Go!" he shouted.

Immediately, the goblinkin followed his lead, stomping their feet and pointing at the lair's entrance. They also shouted together, more or less, "Go!"

Understanding then, Wick turned and fled.

"Hey!" someone yelled. "The dweller's gettin' away!"

Okay, maybe it would have been better if I'd figured this out for myself! But it was too late now. Wick ran as fast as he could. As he turned the corner to head outside, he ran straight into a bear.

7

Dwarven City of Industry

actually, Wick didn't run into a bear. He just thought it was a bear. But that was before he bounced back from the huge bulk, landed on his backside, and was able to get a better look at what he had collided with.

A dwarf in full armor peered fiercely down at Wick. Thick and burly, with fair hair and beard, he stared at Wick through solemn gray eyes. He wore his hair back in a long braid that draped over a massive shoulder and was tied up with silver chains.

The dwarf had his battle-axe lifted over his helmed head and was prepared to strike. Moonslight glinted from the sharp, double-bitted blade.

Wick covered his head with his hands, yanking the chef's hat down over his eyes. "Don't!" he yelped, certain that he was about to become—mostly—asymmetrical halves.

The axe didn't descend.

Unable to bear the suspense, Wick peered under the edge of the chef's cap and between his trembling fingers. *I'm not cut in half!* He touched his middle because he couldn't believe his eyes.

"A halfer," the dwarf growled.

Wick saw that the dwarf wasn't alone. Of course, it would have been foolish for him to attack a goblinkin stronghold all alone. Gazing beyond the first dwarven warrior, Wick saw that at least a dozen others followed the first up the narrow trail leading to the goblinkin lair.

"What's the halfer doin' here, Bulokk?" another dwarf asked.

"Looks like he was cookin' for the goblinkin," Bulokk replied.

"No," Wick protested. "There's been a mistake. I was just—"

The arrival of the staggering goblinkin interrupted his explanation. "Dwarves!" one of them yelled. "Dwarves is upon us!"

"Axes!" Bulokk roared. He took his battle-axe in hand and set himself. Two dwarves flared out to either side of him, a full step back to give him plenty of room to swing.

The goblinkin responded as swiftly as they could, but the ale they'd consumed made them slower than normal. They fumbled with their weapons. Roaring a deafening war cry that echoed from the hilltop, Bulokk swung his axe. Goblinkin went down like felled wheat under a harvester's scythe. Covered in a wave of green goblinkin ichors, Wick rolled over and tried desperately not to get trampled. Getting to his feet, he found himself pressed along with the action, trapped between the advancing lines of dwarves and the goblinkin.

"Anvils!" Bulokk yelled.

Immediately, the dwarves shifted until they faced the goblinkin two by two. Bringing their shields up, they pushed the goblinkin back into the cave.

"Axes!" Bulokk roared once they were inside the cave that served as the goblinkin's lair. Lit by the flames under the boiling kettle in the center of the cave and by torches that were shoved into the ground, the battle continued.

Goblinkin and pieces of goblinkin rained down on Wick. He dodged, using his dweller's quickness, barely staying ahead of the axes, clubs, and cudgels. Once he'd even managed to get clear of the action and grab onto the wall. He panted, breathing hard, hoping to let the battle pass him by so that he could make his escape.

Then the fierce-faced dwarf with the braid spotted him. "So there ye are, cook."

" 'Cook'?" Wick put a hand to his chest and shook his head. "I'm no cook. I'm a—" He managed to stop himself before he said *Librarian*. Then the poofy top of the chef's hat, which had somehow—for *once*—managed to stay on his head, collapsed slowly down over his face. He pushed it aside. "They made me wear the hat."

The denial seemed a weak defense at best. Especially with the sound of steel meeting steel all around them. Shadows danced on the wall as the battle was waged. There was no doubt about the outcome. One of the dwarves grabbed a goblinkin and threw him into the boiling pot.

"Ye're a-comin' with me, halfer," the dwarf promised grimly. "I'm sure Master Blacksmith Taloston can think of a suitable punishment for him who'd cook up his mates an' serve 'em to the likes of these here goblinkin."

"But I didn't serve the goblinkin anything!" Wick said. "I swear! You've got to—"

"Shut yer cakehole, halfer, afore I shuts it fer ye!"

Wick shut. The chef's hat collapsed down in front of his face again. Surely *One-Eyed Peggie* was on her way back by now.

Only a few goblinkin survived the dwarves' surprise attack. The rest were quickly routed and went screaming down the hillside to disappear into the trees. Their longer legs served them in good stead in that regard.

When it was over, Bulokk spent time taking care of the wounded. Three of his warriors had to be carried out on

litters. Despite his small stature, Wick was assigned one
of the corners of a litter.

"We should just cut his throat here," one of the dwarves
grumbled to their leader.

"No," Bulokk replied, giving Wick a hard stare. "We'll
leave his fate to Master Blacksmith Taloston. Mayhap
he'll think of something evil enough for the likes of a
dweller what would cook up his own kind for goblinkin
stew."

"It wasn't stew," Wick said before he thought about
what he was saying. "It was dweller surprise." He clapped
a hand over his mouth.

In the Vault of All Known Knowledge, he'd gotten
used to speaking his mind when someone got his or her
facts wrong. It usually saved that Librarian a lot of time
and effort. Although Wick's contributions weren't generally acknowledged or appreciated, he couldn't help
making them. He was in the business of correcting facts,
after all.

Bulokk scowled at him. "Ye're beginnin' to tires me,
cook."

Wick shook his head. He opened his mouth to deny
the charges.

Throwing a finger into Wick's face, the dwarf said, "Ye
want to stay alive long enough to find out what Master
Blacksmith Taloston has in store for ye, ye'll grab ahold
of that litter an' get to movin'."

Since it took both hands to lift the corner of the litter,
Wick didn't have a free hand to keep over his mouth to
remind him to keep silent. He bit his lips instead.

Then they were on their way.

The trip down the hillside, encumbered as they were by
the wounded, took a long time. Going without sleep after

being frazzled and worried for days aboard *One-Eyed Peggie*, then being an unwilling guest of goblinkin who wanted only to eat him, hadn't agreed with Wick's nerves. He barely had the strength to make the trip. He didn't even argue when Rohoh caught up to the procession and climbed up his leg, undetected by the dwarves.

At the bottom of the long, crooked trail down the hillside was another long hike to the caves where the dwarves lived. After being around the dwarves in Greydawn Moors, who lived mostly outside, it was always a small shock to find dwarven villages inside the earth.

Only a few fortifications existed aboveground. The caves were vent holes for the volcano at the bottom. As they approached their destination, Wick felt the heated air and sulfur stink coming from them.

The dwarven entrance was little more than a hundred paces from the coastline, which told Wick at once that they lived below sea level. That seemed awfully risky to him. Parts of the Vault of All Known Knowledge extended down into the bedrock of the Knucklebones Mountains. In places, bridges to the lower levels even crossed the underground river that flowed through the area. However, the Vault of All Known Knowledge seemed so . . . invulnerable Wick never worried about drowning inside it.

Beyond the dwarven fortifications, the Rusting Sea rolled out and upward, meeting the sky. The sun was just beginning to rise in the east, coming out from behind the hillside they'd left. The light caught the shimmering orange coloration of the sea.

At the end of a short pier, a ship sat at anchor. Wick studied the vessel, hoping it might be *One-Eyed Peggie*. Even if Craugh wasn't there to admit that he'd shoved Wick into a job far too difficult and dangerous for him and was there only to berate Wick for laying waste to whatever carefully constructed plan he'd wrought, the little Librarian figured he would at least be among friends.

Not dwarves who chose to believe he was a cook for goblinkin.

But it wasn't *One-Eyed Peggie* who lay at anchor in the natural harbor. It was a human ship that was there merely to trade. A line of carts moved onto the pier, loading up and taking away cargo. Boom nets swung over the ship's side to make the transfer easier.

Idly, Wick wondered what the dwarves manufactured to trade. Locked on the island as they were, it was easy to see that the Cinder Clouds dwarves would need several things. Then he noted the shabby quality of the clothing under the dwarves' fine armor. *Maybe they're used to living hand-to-mouth.*

Once the carts were emptied then full again, the drivers drove them back among the fortification. A great, hinged stone gate swung open and allowed entrance.

"Move along, halfer," Bulokk's rough voice said. "Ye've done just about enough gawkin'."

Taking a fresh hold on the litter he helped carry, Wick trudged forward once more. He was looking forward to sitting down, but he was afraid it might be the last thing he would ever do.

"Who goes there?" The challenge rang out strong and bold from the stone fort.

Wick stood at the large stone slab that served as the gate. He was tired and ached all over, and his eyes were fatigued and grainy.

" 'Who goes there?' " Rohoh repeated. "Like he doesn't have eyes in his head to see."

"Quiet," Wick told the skink. "You're going to get us both killed."

"Bulokk," the dwarf called back up. "Open up. Ye've got injured warriors a-waitin', an' all of 'em tired."

The dwarf manning the gate tower grinned down from above. "Did ye do for 'em then, Bulokk?"

"Aye," Bulokk called back up. "We did. Got rid of one nest, but there's more of 'em out there."

"There always will be," the other acknowledged. "Until we find a way to take these isles back to ourselves. At least them beasties won't be tryin' to get our fishin' crews for a while." He turned and shouted over his shoulder. "Open the gate!"

The cry was repeated. Then, a short time later, the mechanical clank of a windlass ratcheted to life. Chain links clinked as they wrapped the drum. Slowly, grating smoothly, the huge slab of rock raised along the cunningly wrought tongue-and-groove channels fashioned for it. When it rose to its full height some five feet above (plenty of room for a dwarf to walk through), other gatekeepers locked it into place with stone chocks.

"All clear," the dwarf above called down. "Come ahead."

Stumbling into motion again, Wick walked through the gate.

"That's a big rock," Rohoh said. "If it fell, we'd be smashed flat."

Not, Wick thought, *a pleasant thought*.

"Probably be relatively painless, though," the skink went on.

Wick chose to ignore his unwanted passenger. Some of the fatigue dropped away as Wick's interest flared anew. He'd been in dwarven fortifications before, by himself and with Craugh, and he was constantly amazed at the architecture. Each underground village or city took advantage of the lay of the land, which resulted in a unique experience each time.

Inside the fortification, three hills filled the center. All of them, Wick knew, led to different and separate sections of the dwarven village. One would lead to the forge area.

Another would go to the living quarters. And the third was reserved for the storage area and wells that tapped into groundwater directly or used a filtration process involving a limestone-lined cistern.

The carts unloaded in front of one of them. Bulokk's warriors headed for another. Wick followed along. They handed off the wounded warriors to dwarven women, who picked up their men and carried them down into the passage.

Then Bulokk grabbed Wick by the shoulder and aimed him at the third aboveground entrance.

Upon entering the tunnel, hot air circulated around Wick, letting him know that this passageway probably led to the forge. Bulokk and some of the warriors took up torches to light the way. Several twists and turns later, all of them part of a corkscrew descent into the earth, they arrived in the main forge chamber.

Intense heat baked Wick to the core. He couldn't imagine remaining in the large cave for long. Only dwarves, with their natural resistance to heat, could hope to endure a lengthy stay. The stink of sulfur was almost unendurable. Metallic thuds and clanks of dwarven hammers striking superheated metal resounded throughout the cavern.

At the other end of the chamber, an open lava pit glowed yellow-orange against the wall and ceiling above it. Judging from the wall that separated the lava pit from the chamber, the design was intentional, providing the dwarven blacksmiths some respite from the roasting heat.

A score of anvils stood on sturdy tables made of stone. All of them shared a form, but Wick knew from his studies that each of them had been poured from molten ore and beaten into the proper shape and hardness by the blacksmith. When a dwarven blacksmith worked on an anvil, he had to know it as well as the back of his own hand. Every flaw and imperfection showed on his work, and a blacksmith had to know how to use those to his advantage.

The dwarves plunged long-handled tongs bearing the metal they were working with to a point just above the sluggish lava. In a short time, the metal would glow red-hot and they withdrew it. Back on the anvil, they held the piece with other tongs and picked up their hammers to beat the piece into the desired shape.

Most of them, Wick saw, worked on pedestrian items like bands for wheels or barrels. Others made frying pans and pots. Others worked on chains and collars. Farm implements, plows, and harness tack were also in evidence. A few of the younger dwarves, noticeable because of their lack of beards, made nails.

Wick couldn't believe that the Cinder Clouds dwarves, who had once made some of the best armor ever to be found, had been reduced to making items for sale from a peddler's cart. Looking at the work they were doing, he felt incredibly sad for them. In the Vault of All Known Knowledge, he'd read a few books that had praised Master Blacksmith Oskarr and the dwarves of his forge for their work.

Bulokk shoved Wick forward so hard that he nearly fell. Stumbling, he came to a stop in front of a dwarf whose hammer fell with a rhythmic clangor. They stood waiting till the dwarf finished with the piece for the time. When he stepped back, his massively thewed body glistening with sweat and glowing from heat and exertion, he nodded to another dwarf.

The other dwarf picked up the piece with a set of the long-handled tongs. In that instant, Wick saw that the piece was a nearly finished shield. At least, it was the backbone of a shield.

"Master Blacksmith Taloston," Bulokk called.

"Aye," the dwarf said, watching as the shield was carefully hung back over the lava pit. "Is that ye, Bulokk?"

"It is," Bulokk replied.

"Did ye put an end to that nest of goblinkin the scouts spied?"

"We did. But we come up on a surprise."

Still holding onto the huge hammer, Master Blacksmith Taloston turned to face Wick. The dwarf's face was broad and scarred by battle and fire. Sparks burned in his brown hair and beard. His arms showed scars from the ironwork.

"Don't like surprises," the master blacksmith said. His glance took a quick measure of Wick. "A halfer?"

"Aye," Bulokk said.

"What'd ye bring him back here for?"

"Didn't know what to do with him."

The master blacksmith grabbed a ladle from a water bucket and took a long drink. Then he poured another ladleful over his head. "Shoulda let him go. There's other halfers in these islands. Mayhap he can stay free an' catch a ship like some of them others have. Otherwise he can be a slave in the goblin mines again. Either way, it ain't our problem."

"He's a goblinkin cook," Bulokk accused. He held the crumpled chef's hat out as evidence. "When we come up on that goblinkin lair, this 'un was fixin' them goblinkin a meal an' leadin' the dancin'."

"Dancin'?" The master blacksmith's bushy eyebrows closed together.

"Aye."

"I wasn't leading the dancing," Wick said. "The skink was leading the dancing."

"Skink?"

Moving quickly, Wick plucked the skink from his hiding place on his shoulder. "This skink." He held Rohoh up by his tail, dangling him for all to see.

The lizard tried to get free, but he didn't open his mouth to complain.

"Ye have a dancin' skink?"

"Yes."

Before Wick could go on, Taloston looked at Bulokk. "Is this halfer infested with them things?"

Two dwarven warriors quickly searched Wick. They didn't find any additional lizards.

"No," one of them answered. "That appears to be the only one."

"Good," Taloston said. "I can't abide them lizards. Ate me fill of 'em, I have. Dwarves wasn't meant to feed on such creatures. Them goblinkin can have 'em all."

Rohoh stopped squirming to escape. For a moment Wick thought the skink was going to protest the comment. That would have been fine because it would have brought further proof to his claims.

"So he was cookin' fer the goblinkin, eh?" Taloston rubbed a hand through his smoldering beard.

"Aye."

The master blacksmith nodded, said, "Take him up top, cut his throat, an' throw him into the bay," and turned back to his work.

8

Banished

What!" The exclamation burst from Wick before he knew he was prepared to launch it. The sound of his incredulous voice pealed over the forge, bringing an end to all work. He almost dropped Rohoh to the cavern floor. "You're going to just order them to cut my throat and throw me into the bay?"

By that time, Bulokk had his hand on Wick's shoulder and was dragging him back from the master blacksmith.

"I'll be merciful," Bulokk said quietly.

"I don't want merciful," Wick bellowed.

"No?"

Realizing what he'd said, Wick held up his hands, one of which was still holding onto the skink. "What I mean is, I don't want to die."

"Should have thought of that before you started whipping up dweller surprise," Rohoh said only loud enough for Wick to hear.

"Ye shouldn't have been cookin' for the goblinkin," Taloston said.

"I'm not a cook." Wick felt entirely helpless.

Shoving his face into Wick's, making the little Librarian cringe, Taloston asked, "An' do ye know any recipes for cookin' dwarves?"

At last! Wick thought happily. *A question I can answer!*
"I do! I do!" He put his free hand to his head and started
imagining the pages of Prendergorf's *A Short Course of
Dwarven Dishes: Being a Horrifying Account of Famous
Dwarves Eaten by Goblinkin*. "There's dwarf tort with
spiced apples. Creamed dwarf. Jellied dwarf. Dwarf-ka-
bobs. Dwarf cake, though that's generally served for holi-
days and is made out of dried dwarf bits that have gotten
particularly leathery with age and—" He was suddenly
aware of every dwarven eye in the forge on him.

"An' how many dwarves have ye cooked up?" Taloston
asked.

"None," Wick answered immediately. "I swear. The Old
Ones strike me dead if I'm lying."

At that moment the lava pit bubbled violently, throwing up a huge gout of lava and causing a massive *boom!*
that echoed through the forge. Thinking that the volcano
below was about to erupt and throw burning lava everywhere, Wick dropped to his knees and covered his head
with his arms. Cowering, he waited for the end.

The skink, which he'd dropped, ran up his arm and
curled once more behind his head. "Get up," Rohoh said.
"You're embarrassing me. If you're going to die, at least
go out with some dignity."

Cautiously, Wick opened one eye. He looked around.
Dwarves stared at him with derision and dislike. But that
was okay. While he was on the mainland, that was how
most beings looked at him.

"The lava pit didn't erupt?" he asked.

"No," Taloston said. "Get this cook outta me sight."

Strong hands gripped Wick. He tried to fight against
them but it was no use.

"They were going to cook me and eat me!" Wick
wailed.

"Oh, that's just softening them right up," Rohoh said.
Taloston turned and looked out at the lump of metal

hanging over the lava pit. It was starting to glow cherry-red.

"I didn't escape from the goblinkin mines!" Wick shouted as he was dragged away. "A wizard sent me here in search of Master Blacksmith Oskarr's magic battleaxe!"

Bulokk stopped dragging immediately, calling to his men to halt. The dwarven warrior looked at Wick. "Are ye tellin' the truth, halfer? About comin' here fer Oskarr's magic axe?"

Terrified of answering, Wick just stared at the dwarf, wondering which response would let him live and which would get him instantly killed. Because he felt certain that was what it was coming down to.

"Yes," Wick squeaked, gazing into Bulokk's eyes. "It's true." He waited for the end.

After a moment more spent staring at him, Bulokk swung to face Taloston. "Did ye hear what the halfer claimed? That he came here fer Master Oskarr's axe?"

Slowly, Taloston faced Bulokk. "Aye," the master black-smith said. "I heard him." He shook his head. "Doesn't mean it's true. Master Oskarr's axe has been lost fer a thousand years. Mayhap it was destroyed."

Wick thought Bulokk was going to argue, but the dwarf maintained his silence.

"Don't go gettin' yer hopes up, Bulokk," Taloston said.

"The axe . . . means a lot to me family," Bulokk said.

Sighing, Taloston picked up his hammer and walked over to Wick. "There's tales ever'where about Master Os-karr's enchanted battle-axe an' how it was lost when Lord Kharrion caused the volcanoes to erupt an' bury them islands in the sea while spewin' up new ones. Is that what ye're hopin', halfer? That some half-told story about Master Oskarr is gonna save yer neck?"

"You're in for it now," Rohoh whispered in his ear.

"It's true," Wick insisted. "I was sent here for the axe."

"Why?" Taloston demanded.

"The wizard, he thinks he can use it to find out what really happened at the Battle of Fell's Keep. He doesn't think that Master Oskarr betrayed the other warriors holding Painted Canyon while the south evacuated ahead of the goblinkin hordes." Wick met Taloston's accusing stare.

"What do ye know of all that?"

Slowly at first, but becoming immersed in the story just as he had back at Paunsel's Tavern in Greydawn Moors, Wick told the dwarves the tale of the Battle of Fell's Keep.

Later, as Wick wrapped up with what he knew of the battles fought in the Cinder Clouds Islands—embellishing the telling with all the skills he'd learned as well as the sense of the dramatic he'd picked up from the romances he'd read in Hralbomm's Wing—the dwarves sat around him like dweller children during story time.

The clangor of the hammers falling on metal had silenced. Only the bubbling of the lava pit continued. Water buckets were passed around, and one had been made readily available to the little Librarian.

Finally, though, he was through and had once more sunk the Cinder Clouds Islands beneath the Rusting Sea. Looking out at the sad reaction of the dwarves, Wick felt a little sad for them himself—even though they'd been ready to cut his throat and heave him in the bay only a few hours ago. He knew at least that much time had passed because he was starving.

"Do ye know where Master Oskarr's axe is?" Bulokk asked.

"No," Wick answered truthfully.

Taloston scowled at him. "Then how were ye gonna find it?"

"I've seen—" Wick stopped himself from saying *map* because no one outside the Vault of All Known Knowledge had ever seen one. "I've *heard* a number of tales about how the islands were before Lord Kharrion sank them. I think, after I travel around on a few of them, that I'll be able to figure out where Master Oskarr's forge was."

"Likely it's at the bottom of the Rusting Sea," Taloston growled.

"There's tunnels," Bulokk pointed out. "All the minin' the goblinkin been doin', they've uncovered some of the vent tunnels that blew out of the volcanoes. Some of them dwellers we freed an' put on ships—"

Oh ho! Wick thought. *They've helped other dwellers who have escaped the clutches of the goblinkin! But not me!*

"—have said the goblinkin have dug up remnants of dwarven cities," Bulokk finished.

"'Tis a forlorn hope ye're insistin' on," Taloston said.

"I would know that Master Oskarr was not the traitor the humans an' the elves believe him to be," Bulokk stated.

"What the humans an' the elves think of us or of Master Oskarr don't matter," Taloston said.

"It matters to me," Bulokk disagreed.

"An' me," another dwarf said.

"An' me," another echoed.

"It's the past," Taloston said. "Ain't no way of changin' the past."

"'The past lays the bedrock for the future,'" Wick quoted. "'If you want to change your future, find a way to change your perspective of the past in your present.'"

"What are you talking about?" Rohoh asked.

"What's yer meanin', halfer?" Taloston growled.

Bulokk looked at Wick with interest. "What he's a-sayin' is that if'n we find Master Oskarr's lost battle-axe, there's a chance we can know what really happened at the Battle of Fell's Keep. An' if'n we know, it'll change how we see ourselves today."

Taloston looked at Bulokk and shook his head. "Ye get a lot more from what that halfer's a-blatherin' about than I do."

"Mayhap," Bulokk said, "it's 'cause I'm willin' to listen."

Waving the comment away, Taloston stood. "We're a-wastin' time here now." He looked around at the other dwarves. "On yer feet. We got things to make. There'll be another ship along soon."

Bulokk pushed himself up, too. "What about the halfer's story?"

"It's a story, Bulokk," Taloston said. "Just like them tales the elders tell around the community firepits in the common rooms at night. It's just entertainment fer the young, that's all. Don't go a-gettin' all caught up in his story. It's hard beatin' disappointment out of a tender heart. Without a-losin' the heart it's attached to."

Silently, Bulokk studied his leader.

"What wizard in his right mind would send a halfer to do somethin' so important?" Taloston asked.

Bulokk kept his own counsel, setting his jaw stubbornly.

Something's going on, Wick thought. But he didn't know what it was. He didn't dare utter a word.

"Don't work that ore," Taloston said in a softer voice. "It's too hard for ye, an' when ye get it hot enough, ye're just gonna shatter it."

After a moment, Bulokk broke eye contact with the master blacksmith and nodded.

"Now take him on out of here," Taloston said. "Mayhap ye don't want to kill him, in case ye believe him, but make certain that halfer's off this island. Put him aboard one of the trade ships what's out in the harbor an' send him on his way, if ye like. But get him outta here. He's banished from our home."

"All right," Bulokk replied. He shoved Wick from behind and got him moving.

Long minutes later, Wick was once more above ground. The outside air was cooler, almost chill after he'd gotten acclimated to the forge chamber. Shivering a little, he pulled his light cloak more tightly around him. Rohoh scampered up under his hair to lie along his collar. Wick reached for the skink twice, but the creature avoided his efforts with ease, hiding inside his coat.

Bulokk and a dozen dwarves escorted Wick to the huge gate. Dusk had settled over the Rusting Sea, leaving black clouds hanging in a chartreuse sky. Land lay in that direction, Wick knew, because the sunset would have been practically colorless over the water. In order for the sky to have color, it had to pick up dust in the wind over land, not sea.

After they passed through the gate, during which time Wick once more had the uneasy feeling while walking under the immense stone, the wind held more of a chill, but he willingly admitted that the fear inside him may have caused that. On the other side, Bulokk steered him to follow the well-worn cart ruts that led down to the harbor.

Wick looked up at the moons and wondered if Craugh could see him. And, if the wizard could see him, if Craugh was unhappy with the way things had turned out.

Of course, there was always the possibility that Craugh had sent Wick on ahead simply to use as bait and was finding Oskarr's fabled axe himself even now. That seemed to be a favorite tactic.

"Halfer," Bulokk said.

"Yes." Wick was trying to work up the courage to ask for something to eat. He was certain he wouldn't get anything aboard a trading vessel if he weren't paying passage. And realizing that led to even further worries. Where would the trade ship put him ashore? He didn't have any gold as he usually did. It was possible they'd simply dump him over the side and have done with him.

"Do ye really think ye can find Master Oskarr's forge an' mayhap his axe?" Bulokk walked beside him but wouldn't look at him.

Wick measured his words carefully, well aware that they held the possibility to change his course. He tried to figure out if it would be safer to go on the cargo ship and hope to find another vessel that traveled to Greydawn Moors and try to take passage on it.

Still, the question was almost a challenge to his skills as a Librarian.

"Yes," Wick said. "I think I can."

"Why?"

"Because the Cinder Clouds Islands were made a certain way, in a half-moon shape that's distinctive." Wick looked out at the sea and saw the furled sails along the ship's 'yards riffling in the breeze. "I memorized some of the landmarks. There were lighthouses, cliffs, and reefs that I can use to figure out where I—where we—are in relation to where Master Oskarr's forge was. If we can find them." He gave the dwarf a sidelong glance. "Your familiarity with the islands would help us in that search."

They walked a while longer in silence.

"Do ye think it's still there?" Bulokk asked.

"Do I think what's still there?"

"The axe. Master Oskarr's axe."

Wick considered his answer, letting the strained silence gather weight and speculation. "I do. Magic weapons have a tendency to outlast all attempts to destroy them."

"An' through it ye could know what happened at the Battle of Fell's Keep, could discover what took place all them years ago?"

"The wizard who sent me here has such powers," Wick said. "If anyone could do it, he could."

Bulokk looked at him. "Do ye believe that in yer bones? 'Cause that's the bedrock of a man."

"I do," Wick said. Even though he wasn't absolutely sure of Craugh's powers, over the years he had seen the amazing things the wizard could do.

"All right then. Wait here." Bulokk turned back to his fellows.

Wick stood alone at the side of the cart trail and wished he were back home in the Vault of All Known Knowledge. Or at least safe back on *One-Eyed Peggie* where he could finish reading the romance about Taurak Bleiyz.

He stared at the lanterns along the rails of the human ship anchored out in the harbor. With the sun setting behind the vessel, the men all but lost in the shadows aboard her, the sight was beautiful. His hands itched to take out his journal and writing utensils and capture the memory in inks. More than that, he wanted to write up his latest adventures, all the things that he had seen and the people he'd met.

"Stop your wool-gathering," Rohoh admonished. "We need to find that forge."

"I don't even know if that's possible," Wick argued in a low voice. He looked out over the broken masses of islands scattered over the Rusting Sea.

"Craugh sent you here."

"As I recall, he sent you here as well. Why?"

"To help you."

"How?"

The skink was quiet for a moment. "I don't know. Craugh just said I was to keep you out of trouble."

"Well," Wick said, "that hasn't worked so far."

At that moment, the dwarven huddle broke up after a fierce, final debate. Bulokk returned to Wick.

"We're a-goin' with ye," the dwarven warrior declared.

Wick blinked at him. "Why?"

"Why? Why to find Master Oskarr's lost axe an' clear his good name is why!"

"Oh," Wick said.

"Yer quest, halfer, whether 'tis yer own or ye're a-workin' fer or with someone else what cares about Master Oskarr's relationship, 'tis a noble one."

"That's why you want to accompany me? To get glory?"

"No," Bulokk said more somberly. "I'm part of Master Oskarr's kith an' kin, halfer. 'Tis me own family we're a-talkin' about here, too." He sighed. "Master Taloston is a good 'un. He's a-runnin' this forge the best he knows how to, but we've gone a far piece down in the world."

The sadness in the dwarven warrior's words touched Wick's heart.

"Was a time," Bulokk said softly, "when armor made by the Cinder Clouds Forge with Master Oskarr's mark on it meant somethin'. It meant a warrior—be he a human, dwarf, or elf—could stand up in a battle an' know he was protected. But since them accusations after the Battle of Fell's Keep, no one wants to buy anything from us. Except a pittance of what we used to make." He pulled at his beard. "By the Old Ones! We're a-makin' nails an' horseshoes an' plows when we should be a-makin' armor an' weapons meant to be carried into battle by kings an' heroes!"

Several of the other dwarves came closer to Wick and Bulokk, as if finally making the last decision to throw in their lot with him. They murmured similar feelings.

"Ye're the first one what's ever come to these islands a-sayin' ye could find Master Oskarr's axe," Bulokk said. "So if'n ye'll have us, we'd be right proud to journey with ye."

"If I'll have you?" Wick stood dumbfounded.

Rohoh moved so that he could whisper in the little Librarian's ear. "This is the part where you say, 'Yes, thank you.' And then you swear undying fealty to one another."

Bulokk looked uncomfortable. "We know we said some unkind things about ye—and *to* ye—be we're a-hopin' ye'll find room in that tiny little heart of yers to overlook that. At least fer a while. Ye see, it's a-mighty dangerous out there where ye'll be lookin'. Goblinkin roam unfettered over several of these islands. If ye're a-gonna be a-searchin' fer that axe, ye might want some help."

Gathering himself, Wick said, "Of course. Of course I'd like help."

The dwarven warrior shoved out his big hand. Unconsciously, Wick took it, finding his own hand engulfed in Bulokk's.

"But won't Master Taloston be upset?" Wick asked.

Bulokk turned him and started him toward the harbor again. "Aye, that he will, because he don't like no one a-questionin' his authority none. But it ain't his ancestor we're a-talkin' about. It's mine. An' come what may of our little hunt, I'm through a-makin' nails an' horseshoes. I'm wishful of a-doin' true dwarven armorer's work." He laid a heavy hand across Wick's shoulders, almost crushing the skink.

They walked down to the harbor but turned away from the ship. Several dwarves and humans called out to Bulokk, for he was known to a number of them.

They chose one of the single-masted longboats tied up at shore. From the lay of the boat, Wick guessed that it was used for ferrying goods among the islands, possibly to supply other dwarven outposts that weren't as large. Bulokk quickly assigned three of the dwarves to gather food and water to supply them on their excursion. After a short while, they returned with a cart loaded with several water skins and bags of food.

Wick crawled into the longboat with Bulokk and most of the other twelve dwarves. Four of them remained on shore to push the boat out into the retreating tide. The waves crashed against the longboat's side and the cold spray dappled Wick.

"Good job," Rohoh whispered in the little Librarian's ear. "Now just keep a civil tongue in your head, and maybe they won't cut it out."

9

Collision!

Once they had the craft shoved out into the ungentle caress of the sea, the four dwarves heaved themselves into the boat, aided by the others who grabbed their armor and pulled. They crowded together in the small boat, and Wick's stomach heaved, certain they would all sink under the combined weight. For a moment he sat petrified among the dwarven warriors, constricted between their massive shoulders.

After a while, a few of the dwarves assembled the single mast and raised the sail, which promptly filled with wind and drove them forward. The wind wasn't directly behind them, so they canted over to port. Bulokk sat in the stern and managed the tiller with a sure hand.

Then, with the tangy scent of pepper cheese in Wick's nostrils reminding him how hungry he was, his stomach growled. He immediately felt embarrassed.

That broke the tension on the boat and several of the dwarves laughed. Hunger was something they all understood and shared.

"Are ye hungry then, halfer?" one of the dwarves asked.

"Yes," Wick answered timidly, not knowing if his admitted weakness was merely going to be made sport of.

"Didn't get yer fill of goblin stew, I suppose?"

Wick didn't know what to say.

"Dweller surprise, I think it were, Hodnes," another dwarf said, chuckling. "I believe them ugly goblinkin was properly surprised, too!"

They all had a good laugh at that for a moment, and the sound combated the darkness of the night that pressed in all around them. Wick even laughed a little.

Then Hodnes opened one of the bags of food and carved up a cheese wheel, passing it out while another dwarf handed out biscuits.

"What's the landmarks ye was needin' to find?" Bulokk asked after they were well into the impromptu meal and the dwarven fort was fading in their wake.

"There was a lighthouse," Wick said. "It was built in the shape of a hammer." He crossed his arms to demonstrate. "During those days it was called Zubeck's Hammer, named after the dwarven god of the stars. It was supposed to be over a hundred feet tall. Red and green lanterns hung in either end to let ships' captains know whether they were on the sea side or the lee side of the island."

"I've never seen anything like that," Bulokk replied.

"Mayhap I have," a dwarf said.

"Where did ye see something like that, Drinnick?"

"'Twas north of here." Drinnick glanced up at the sky, seemed to study the stars a minute, then pointed more or less in the direction they were traveling. "It ain't above water no more, but if'n ye know where to look, ye can find it."

"What's another landmark?" Bulokk asked.

"A domed amphitheater," Wick answered. "It was called Trader's Hall. Back before the Cataclysm, there were several such structures. Guildsmen and craftsmen met there twice a year, in the summer and in the winter, to show their wares and do business. The Trader's Hall in the Cinder Clouds Islands was unique. Besides being shaped like a dome, the builders had hammered blue foil all over it, making it very distinctive. According to what I've re— been *told*, the dome could be seen from miles away."

Apparently, none of the dwarven warriors had ever seen the amphitheater in their travels and battles with the goblinkin.

"Anything else?" Hodnes asked.

Quickly, Wick described Hullbreaker Reefs (two of them thought they knew where that might be), the Dragon's Aerie (so named because it once was home to a dragon), Delid's Circle (a semicircle of underwater mountains whose peaks appeared above the surface of the sea), and Jerrigan's Landing (a natural port that was too small to be used for commercial industry, but was renowned for a shelf of vertical granite that set it off from the rest of the island).

The dwarven warriors compared notes to what they had seen over their years of traveling through the Rusting Sea, describing in detail the things they'd observed and heard about. Wick continued eating till he was full, then grew sleepy. The skink's slight rustle as he burrowed through his clothes in search of the fresh crumbs didn't inspire the little Librarian to chase the creature down. He wanted his pipe and he wanted a bed instead of being jammed between the dwarves, but he went to sleep anyway.

Only a little while later—Wick was certain about that because he knew from the way he felt he hadn't slept long—dwarven cursing woke him.

"'Ware there!" someone said. "It's a-comin' straight fer us!"

Wick tried to dive for the bottom of the boat—not that there was any real room there, but it seemed safer there than sitting up if they were under attack. Being caught out in the open was one of the worst things to happen to anyone under attack. However, he was jammed too tightly among the dwarves to move.

"Show 'em the lantern," Bulokk ordered.

One of the dwarves brought out a small pot of coals they'd kept out of sight. So far, Bulokk had wanted to remain unseen. When the dwarf removed the lid, the glow formed a translucent orange ball in the moonlit darkness.

Wick was curious about what had changed the dwarven leader's mind about remaining hidden. Fatigued and a little frightened, he turned and gazed in the direction the dwarves seemed to be focused on. There, parting the great steam clouds that lay over the area from the volcanic activity, a ship designed solely for speed bore down on them. If it hit the small boat with its narrow prow, the ship would only leave splinters in its wake.

"Ship!" Wick squalled, managing to lever up an arm and point at the approaching craft. *"Ship!"*

"Ship!" Rohoh squealed in his tiny voice in Wick's ear. The dwarves didn't appear to have heard the skink's cry of warning, but the shrill scream in Wick's ear almost deafened him.

"Aye, we seen it already," Bulokk said, holding the tiller hard so the boat cut back toward the land. But the smaller craft was coming around too slowly to avoid the oncoming ship.

Staring through the darkness, Wick realized the ship was sailing without running lights, like a smuggler might. *Like we're doing*, he thought.

Her sails were black-gray, almost invisible against the sky and noticeable only because they were blank fields and held no lights. She was fully strung, even flying jib sails, not moving with any trepidation, obviously familiar with the waters.

The lantern wick caught flame from kindling lit by the

coals. Handing the coal pot off, the dwarf replaced the hurricane glass on the lantern and turned the wick up. Bright, cheery light filled the lantern.

"'Ware!" the dwarf called as he stood and waved the lantern. "'Ware! There's a boat out here!"

Figures shifted on the black boat, all of them lean shadows. Moonslight glinted on steel. Then, between a momentary gap of sails that allowed the moonslight through, Wick spied an archer bending his bow.

"Look out!" Wick called. "Archers!" even as he was wondering who would just fire at them without hailing.

Before his voice drifted away, an arrow crashed through the dwarf's lantern, shattering the glass. Another arrow took the dwarf through the chest. Oil splattered the boat, then the wick fell through and the oil lit the dwarf holding the lantern and the boat on fire. Flames wrapped threatening tendrils around both.

The burning dwarf cried out in alarm and beat at the flames with his hands. He flung the remnants of the lantern into the sea.

Fear clawed through Wick and his instinct screamed at him to burrow as deeply into the press of dwarves as he could. Instead, he fought to get free, to try to reach the burning dwarf, but he couldn't.

"Adranis!" Bulokk barked. "Get him into the sea!"

Instantly, one of the dwarves pushed up, caught the burning dwarf in his arms, and threw them both from the boat into the sea.

Another arrow found a second dwarf. Two more arrows were embedded in the gunwales. Eight or nine shafts (things were confusing at this point) pierced the boat's sail. And a half dozen more arrows spiked the water around the boat as it pitched.

"Got me in me leg!" the wounded dwarf yelped. His big hands closed around his thigh. Flames from the spilled oil licked at his boots.

Wick gazed in disbelief as he drew his own feet up. *Where did they come from? Why did they attack?*

"To port!" Bulokk roared. "Turn the boat over! Save her if'n we can!"

The dwarves reacted to their leader's orders at once, standing on the port side and grabbing the gunwales. Three of them even took hold of the mast and boom and pulled those over to port as well.

Overbalanced, the boat turned on its side as the ship came abreast. Wick held onto the seat, not wishful of dropping into the deep, dark water. The ship collided with the boat, hammering it unmercifully. Then it was done. The boat capsized completely and he submerged. The dark water pulled at him but he held onto the bench.

Long, loud crashing filled the water around Wick. Holding onto the seat, Wick felt the longboat shudder and shake as the black ship ran up against it all along its side. More *thumps!* signaled the arrival of more arrows. One of them cut a furrow along the back of one of the little Librarian's hands. He grew instantly more worried because blood in the water would draw marine predators.

Once the boat stopped bucking and pitching in his grip, he took a fresh hold and pulled himself up into the dark of the upside-down boat. He felt at least three more arrows that had poked through the boat's hull.

Then he thought about the dwarves, wondering how many of them had learned to swim.

Taking a deep breath, Wick ducked under the side of the overturned boat, swam free of it, and popped up above the surface of the water. Shaking the wet hair from his eyes, he gazed around, glad of the full moon.

"What were you trying to do?" Rohoh squalled. "Drown me?"

"You're welcome to take your leave at any time," Wick invited. He wasn't sure where the skink had gotten to, but he was certain wherever it was couldn't be dry.

Adranis surfaced near Wick. The dwarven warrior was striving to keep his head above the water and was failing miserably due to the weight of his armor.

Wick pulled his knife from his water-filled boot and seized hold of Adranis's support straps. In the pale moonslight, the little Librarian saw the dwarven warrior's face.

Stay back from him, Wick told himself. *If he lays hold of you, he'll drown you as well as himself.*

As Wick started to saw at the support straps with the knife, Adranis figured out what he was doing.

A fierce, "No!" escaped from Adranis's mouth, emptying his lungs of air. Bubbles from his unheard bellow rushed through the water. But the deed was done quickly because Wick had learned to keep his knife sharp if he was going to keep it at all. The dwarf's armor peeled away from his body and slid away into the sea.

Angry, Adranis closed his hand over Wick's arm, pulling the little Librarian underwater. Sinking, Wick fought to free himself but couldn't manage the feat by strength alone. Lungs burning, he gripped the knife in his free hand and tried not to let fear claim him entirely. Drowning was a horrible death.

But Adranis couldn't remain underwater any longer either. Releasing Wick, the dwarf kicked upward. Wick swam up as well, aiming for the other end of the overturned longboat.

Partially submerged in the sea, the longboat still maintained a little buoyancy. Wick grabbed hold of the stern and clung there, sucking in deep breaths. *No matter how many times I venture to the mainland, I'll never get used to the idea of death dogging my footsteps!*

Gazing around the longboat, listening to Adranis's curses, Wick saw that the mystery ship had continued on its way. Relief washed over Wick. The vessel could have stuck around to either finish killing them or take survivors as slaves.

"Ye stupid halfer!" Adranis growled. The dwarf thumped the longboat's hull with his fist. "That was me family armor ye just sent to the bottom!"

"You would have looked really good wearing it there," Rohoh snarled.

Before Wick could assure the dwarf that he hadn't said that, Adranis erupted in a torrent of foul curses that left the little Librarian in fear for his life. If he could have found the skink, he would have thrown him into the sea.

"Ain't no replacin' that armor!" Adranis worked his way around the lifeboat, obviously meaning Wick bodily injury. "I'll thump yer melon for ye, I will!"

For a moment, Wick continued around the boat in order to avoid the angry dwarf. Then he gripped the longboat's edge and flipped himself up onto the hull, which was riding a few inches out of the water. His weight (slight for a dweller!) didn't affect the overturned boat's buoyancy.

Adranis, unable to pull himself up out of the water, had to content himself with cursing Wick soundly.

A few feet away, Bulokk surfaced, spluttering and gasping for air. He, too, had sacrificed his armor. Still other dwarves came up as well.

When Bulokk asked for a quick count, they discovered that three of the dwarves had been lost. The warrior who'd held the lantern and gotten shot and set on fire had been sunk in the depths without recovering. Arrows had accounted for one more, dead with an arrow through his neck before the boat flipped. The third had evidently gone down too fast. Repeated diving turned up no results.

Setting his sights on continued survival, Bulokk gave the orders to those who could swim (and only about half of them could) to push the longboat to shore while the others held on.

Wick dove from the boat and joined the swimming effort. His mind raced, trying to remember everything he could about the black ship. Then he focused on swimming because, with the tide going out, getting to the beach was almost impossible.

Nearly an hour later, winded and worn, the dwarven party and Wick made a landing. The beach was inhospitable, craggy and rocky, but at least they wouldn't drown there. They pulled the boat up on shore. Bulokk and two other dwarves tore out the arrows and examined the extent of the damage.

Wick sat by himself, as far away from Adranis as he could manage. Even in the moonslight he could see the dislike the dwarves held for him.

They think this is my fault, he thought. *If I hadn't arrived and gotten Bulokk interested in finding Master Oskarr's lost axe, they wouldn't be here now*. He wanted to argue with them and point out the fact that he had nothing to do with the attack.

"The damage can be repaired," Bulokk told the group after he returned from the longboat. He put the lantern he carried on the rocky shoal. They'd found it floating to shore and miraculously intact. The light played out over the semicircle of glum faces. "With the tools we have at hand."

Wick knew the dwarves had packed for the eventuality they would have to work on the boat. Or, perhaps, another boat if they couldn't repair this one.

"The food an' fresh water remained on board, too," Bulokk said. It had been strapped under the benches in waterproof containers. "So we have a choice about what we do."

The impulse to tell the dwarves about *One-Eyed Peggie* thrummed inside Wick. When *One-Eyed Peggie* arrived, they would all be safe. But in the end he chose to tell them nothing about the Blood-Soaked Sea pirate ship. *In case Craugh keeps them away too long.*

"We can turn back," Bulokk said, "an' hope that our absence hasn't been noted."

"But if'n we has been noticed missin' an' someone has told Taloston that the halfer wasn't on that ship, he won't be happy with us," Adranis said.

"I know." Bulokk scowled, striding across the rocky shoal where they'd landed.

"If Taloston grows vexed with us, we'll be out on goblinkin patrol permanentlike. Ain't gonna live any too long if'n that's the case."

"I ain't afeared of Taloston's displeasure," Bulokk said, "but I set out to find Master Oskarr's axe." He glanced around at his men. "That still ain't been done, an' I mean to see it finished."

Slowly, then with increasing alacrity, the dwarven warriors echoed his sentiments.

"Then, in the mornin'," Bulokk said, "what we'll do is patch up the longboat as best as we can an' continue with what we're about."

Sullenly, the dwarves agreed. Their leader chose to ignore their lack of enthusiasm.

"Until then," Bulokk said, "get what sleep ye can. Ain't none of it gonna be easy."

"Wait," Wick said, not knowing he'd spoken out loud until all the dwarves were looking at him.

"What?" Adranis growled.

For a moment Wick thought about telling them to never mind. But he knew he'd never sleep that night if his curiosity didn't get assuaged. "Did anyone know that ship?" he asked. "The black ship that nearly ran us down?"

"'Tweren't but one out there," Adranis said unkindly.

"Does it make a difference if'n someone's seen it afore?" Bulokk countered.

Wick hesitated. "I don't know. But generally, according to Dreizelf Mochanarter, the more that is known about a problem, the better able the solver is to deal with it."

"So," Drinnick said, clawing fingers through his thick beard, "mayhap the knowin' will prove important?"

"Yes."

"I never seen the ship meself," Drinnick said, "but I heard she plied her trade in these waters."

"What trade?"

"She has an alliance with the goblinkin."

"What kind of alliance?"

"The ship's captain is interested in things that the goblinkin find in their mines."

"What things?" Bulokk stepped closer, taking over the questioning. "The ore?"

In that moment, Wick realized that the goblinkin were actually in competition with the Cinder Clouds dwarves, all of them ripping iron ore from the guts of the earth. He hadn't even considered that before, just assumed that the goblinkin were there in hope of finding gold or silver mines. But with the islands vomited up by the sea-based volcanoes, chances of finding those kinds of mines would be unlikely. The goblinkin were there supplying other forges, ones the goblinkin ran themselves with dwarven slaves or had trade agreements with.

"Not just the ore," Drinnick said. "I heard these humans—"

"They're human?" Wick asked, picturing the image of the lean archers along the ship's railing again in his mind. Those lean shapes could have been human or elven. They'd been too narrow and tall to be dwarves or dwellers.

Of course, the possibility existed that they were other kinds of creatures. Humans, dwarves, elves, dwellers, and goblinkin comprised most of the population of the world, but certainly not all of it.

"Aye," Drinnick said. "They're human."

"How do ye know?" Bulokk said.

"I spied on 'em a time or three whilst I was on patrol."

"Then surely others among you have seen it," Wick said.

No one answered.

Drinnick scratched at his beard. "I sometimes go a mite closer than these here warriors."

Bulokk took a deep breath, obviously not pleased about this revelation. "I told ye to stay away from the goblinkin."

Narrowing his eyes, Drinnick nodded. "I will. Just as soon as I get me four more Nathull Tribe heads. I told ye I'd claim ten of their heads for them a-killin' Broor the way they done. I swore me out an oath of vengeance. I means to live up to it."

Bulokk cursed and told Drinnick that he was being a fool, but Wick knew from the calm way Drinnick listened to his leader that the assessment was falling on deaf ears. A dwarven oath of vengeance was a fearful thing.

"Where did they do their trading?" Wick asked.

"West of us." Drinnick pointed in the general direction they'd been headed. "Not far from here."

Bulokk glanced at Wick. "Do ye think this is important?"

Wick pondered the question, and all the questions his fertile mind had already raised. "How often do you hear about humans traveling to trade with goblinkin?"

Shaking his shaggy head, Bulokk said, "Never. Leastways, *never* afore this. It's always them goblinkin what's a-tryin' to trade with humans. Ain't no dwarf or elf gonna work with 'em. But humans, now, they got short memories."

"Then it couldn't hurt to keep our eyes peeled for this ship while we're searching," Wick said.

With years of long practice behind them, the dwarves

chose up guard shifts and made themselves as comfortable as could be on the hard rock. Wick took his own bed beside a tall stand of rock, telling himself that sleeping up next to a rock wall wasn't the same as sleeping out in the open. He didn't really fool himself, but he was so fatigued that he quickly went to sleep.

10

"D'Ye See Anythin', Halfer?"

Someone planted a toe in the middle of Wick's back, kicking the little Librarian hard enough to get his attention but not hard enough to injure him. Still, the unaccustomed violence—at least, it was unaccustomed in the Vault of All Known Knowledge—filled Wick with fear and he threw his free arm over his head to protect it. His other arm had gone numb from pillowing his face from the hard rock and now flopped rather uselessly.

"Wake up, halfer," a dwarf muttered. "Got no time fer beauty sleep. An' it ain't gonna help ye none anyway."

Dwarves, Wick grimaced, relaxing a little. Groggily, he pushed himself into a sitting position, not wanting to get kicked again because he suspected it would only get harder after the first effort. Dwarves weren't ones to lollygag around. They were always ready to do something.

To the east, the sun was barely peeking above the horizon. Gulls cried low in the sky overhead, evidently hoping for some left-behind morsel. Gesa the Fair looked like an empty silver ring in the western sky.

Bulokk gathered the dwarves quickly, breaking them into two groups. One was responsible for repairing the longboat and the other was supposed to fish for breakfast. Adranis and Wick were assigned to gather coal.

In short order, three of the dwarves waded out into the water with fishing lines and Bulokk led the five remaining ones to the longboat, which they immediately dragged completely onto shore and flipped over so they could start working on the holes made by the arrows the night before.

Adranis crossed over to Wick and kicked his feet. "C'mon then, halfer. That coal ain't gonna find itself."

Reluctantly, Wick got up and went.

Finding coal wasn't a simple affair, Wick discovered. Although all the upheavals caused by volcanoes in the past had revealed much of the bedrock and mineral underpinnings of the land comprising the islands and the sea floor, coal wasn't readily found. Cooling lava formed most of the islands, but here and there throughout most of them, chunks of the ocean floor had been shoved up as well.

Wick trudged in Adranis's wake along through the hills and valleys of the island. He'd seen coal before, of course. A few communities outside Greydawn Moors used coal as a primary source of fuel. Most of them preferred to use wood logs, but if they couldn't get that, they burned coal.

Only a little while later, Adranis called a halt and dropped down into a shallow crevasse.

Alert to the danger around them, Wick found himself interested nonetheless. More than anything, though, his fingers itched to be at his journal. There was so much he needed to record. For a while last night, he'd been able to sneak his journal out and make a few quick notes, just to make certain he didn't forget anything when he had a proper chance to catch up with his thoughts and experiences.

Adranis ran his hand across the jagged faces of the crevasse. An uneven black stripe showed on both sides. When the dwarf picked at it, pieces of black rock tumbled down.

He looked up at Wick. "What are ye a-doin?"

"Watching you," Wick answered.

"Hmmph. Ain't ye ever seen coal mined afore?"

"I have. It's still interesting." Wick felt a little embarrassed about his curiosity, but not so much that he quit watching.

Adranis scowled. "Ain't near as interesting as minin' gems or iron ore. An' minin' ain't what I'm for anyways. I'd rather be at me anvil, a-workin' on armor." He reached into the pack he carried and drew out a pickaxe. He kept his battle-axe close to hand. Drawing back, he swung the pick. The point dug into the black vein and broke chunks free. "Get on down here an' make yerself useful."

Wick slid over the side and scooted down.

Working like an automaton, Adranis dug into the crevasse side. Coal chunks flew and dropped at his feet. "Pick up them pieces an' fill that bag."

Kneeling, Wick did so. "Did you know that you're digging into history?"

"What do ye mean?"

"Do you know where coal comes from?"

Adranis scowled at Wick as though he were a buffoon. "From the earth, of course. Can't ye see me a-excavatin' it?"

"Yes, but do you know how the coal got in the earth?"

"I never give it any thought." Adranis returned to his pick work.

Wick sorted through the coal chunks, picking up the smaller ones rather than the larger. The large pieces would have filled up the bag with too much wasted space, and a fire burned better with the smaller pieces close together.

"Finding coal here means that this land was above the sea once," Wick said.

"It is now."

"I know, but judging from all the metamorphic rock lying around, I think this section was once part of the ocean floor that got ripped up and pushed to the surface again."

"So?"

"Thousands of years ago, though some say it was millions, forests grew here," Wick said. "Trees grew to maturation and fell, covered over by more trees and organic growth. Eventually they rotted and were buried by more and more trees that kept growing on top of the old ones. Then, when enough time, heat, and pressure was applied to the organic rot, it became coal."

Adranis paused and looked at Wick. "So coal was once trees?"

"Yes," Wick replied. "Trees and plants. Everything that grew in the forest."

"An' this is true?"

Wick nodded.

"I have to admit, halfer, that's mighty interestin'. But it don't make no difference to me. Ain't gonna change the way I do things." Adranis shook his head. "Don't know how come ye fill yer head with such useless knowledge. At least it ain't as bad as knowin' how to cook dwarves."

No, Wick agreed. *At least that bit of knowledge about coal is only wasteful, not offensive.*

Adranis put away his pick, then grabbed his battle-axe and laid the weapon across his broad shoulders. "I'm gonna warn ye about somethin' else, too, halfer."

A cold chill chased down Wick's spine. He dropped the coal chunk he'd been fumbling with and glanced up at the dwarf's hard expression.

"Bulokk seems taken with ye," Adranis commented. "Even when we found ye with them goblinkin, was his hand what spared ye when ever' other warrior there would have spilled yer tripes for ye on general principle on account of bein' with them goblinkin."

Wick hoped that wasn't true because such an announcement was in nowise restful, but he suspected the statement was exactly what was on the dwarven warriors' minds.

"Bulokk's one to get to the truth of somethin'," Adranis said. "Me an' the others, we've mostly had hard lives an' are set to keep on livin' 'em."

"But Bulokk wants more," Wick said.

Narrowing his eyes, Adranis glared at Wick. "Ye seen that in him, did ye?" he demanded. "Plannin' on takin' advantage of it, are ye?"

"No. That's what he said last night before we left the fort. The part about being tired of smithing the things you've been making out here."

"It's work with a hammer an' anvil," Adranis said. "Good work for a dwarf. I ain't ashamed of it. An' it's what the Old Ones has give us to do. Fer now." He took a deep breath. "What I'm a-doin' here, halfer, is a-givin' ye fair warnin'. I don't even owe ye that. But I'm a-doin' it to save Bulokk if'n I can."

"Save him from what?"

"From gettin' his hopes up just to have ye bring 'em a-crashin' down, is what!" The dwarf's voice thundered in the stillness around them.

"How would I do that?"

"By a-leadin' him on a wild goose chase around these islands. Mayhap it ain't too late for us to go back to the fort. Taloston might be somewhat peeved, but he ain't gonna banish us. Not if'n we go back soon enough."

Wick thought about the threat but didn't know what to say. Suddenly, everything he remembered about the area and about Master Blacksmith Oskarr seemed jumbled in his mind. Even if it hadn't been, the land where all those things had taken place was jumbled. By Lord Kharrion's evil magic, by volcanic eruptions, and by time.

It's not fair to hold me accountable for so much, Wick thought desperately. He met Adranis's hard gaze with difficulty. "I can't promise that we'll find Master Oskarr's axe. Or that we'll even find his forge. For all I know, it may still be underwater. You can't just—"

Snarling, Adranis lifted his battle-axe as if preparing to swing it.

Throwing up his arms to defend himself, Wick closed his eyes and ducked his head, certain he was about to be killed. *This is all Craugh's fault! He should be the one getting beheaded! Not me!*

He waited. Then he took another breath. And waited some more. Finally, he opened one eye and saw Adranis glaring at him.

"Ye do yer best then," Adranis said. "An' don't ye take too long to get it done."

Don't take too long? Don't *take too long.* Wick couldn't believe it. Since he'd arrived on the island, everybody had been willing to kill him. Then, when he was simply try-ing to accomplish the impossible task Cap'n Farok and Craugh had left him to do, dwarven warriors wanted to take over. But not be responsible for the task. *Oh no, never take on the responsibility. Just figure out whom to blame.*

And kill. That was a very important part to remember.

Adranis climbed to the top of the crevasse and glared down. "Are ye a-gonna fill that there bag or do ye expect them chunks to up an' jump in theirselves?"

"I'll fill it," Wick grumped.

"Then get 'er done."

Wick felt a slither over his right shoulder. "If I was you," the skink whispered to him, "I'd fill that coal bag. Adranis looks like he'd push you over the side of a cliff and tell Bulokk you slipped and fell."

Silently, Wick agreed. "You know," he said, "you might let the dwarves know you can talk."

"Why?"

"Because we could convince them I have magical pow-ers. Maybe they wouldn't treat me so harshly then."

"Why do you have to have magical powers?" Rohoh asked. "Why couldn't I have magical powers?"

"Because," Wick said, thinking furiously.

"Because why?"

"I need to be the important one. It'll empower me."

The skink slithered out onto Wick's shoulder and sunned himself while the little Librarian worked. "You're already empowered."

"How?"

"They can't find Master Oskarr's forge without you."

That, Wick knew, was true. *However, I don't know if I can find Master Oskarr's forge.*

The skink slithered back into his coat and became still. Wick concentrated on gathering the loosened coal.

When the bag was full, Wick passed it up to the dwarf, then clambered up. At the top, Adranis handed Wick the bag again, claiming that he had to have his hands free to defend them in case of attack. Wick sighed and shouldered the bag, following the dwarven warrior back to the campsite.

"I says we let the halfer cook," one of the dwarves suggested. "After all, he was cookin' fer the goblinkin when we found him."

Wick sat and looked out to sea, deciding not even to deign notice of the slight the men threw at him. The dwarves quickly put the suggestion to a vote. The little Librarian wasn't at all surprised to find himself suddenly in charge of the makeshift kitchen.

As he built a proper fire there on the beach, he set up—with Adranis's assistance—a clever framework of metal rods that became a spit. The dwarves fishing the waters off the bank had experienced good luck and brought in several edible fish, and other dwarves had dug up clams in the mud.

In short order, with the addition of the cooking supplies, Wick had fish smoking over the fire on the spit and a large pot of clam chowder simmering on the coals. He also made pan bread in a large iron skillet that Drinnick proudly admitted he'd made. Wick made the bread partly because he had a hankering for it and partly because he wanted to prove to the dwarves that he could cook. If he could cook, there was at least some worth he could continue to bring to them once his days as guide were over.

If we don't get killed looking for the axe, he told himself.

The dwarves' disparaging comments quickly gave way to interest as the concerns of their empty stomachs outweighed the work of heckling Wick. The pan bread was new to them, and was something Wick had picked up in his travels. He'd even added the recipe to the book of favorite recipes he was in the process of writing.

The dwarves kept themselves busy with the repairs to the longboat and with guard duty. They rotated in and out at regular intervals. Lunch was ready before the boat was, but only just.

Once Wick announced everything fit to eat, the dwarves chose up and posted guards, then hunkered in and started eating.

While he was serving, Wick went ahead and cored a few apples, stuffed them with cinnamon, butter, and sugar and drenched them in firepear juice to heat up the flavor even more. During that, Rohoh kept slipping down his arms and snatching choice bits. Even though the dwarves protested that they couldn't eat another bite, Wick saw that the apples disappeared easily enough.

Afterward, Bulokk pronounced the longboat seaworthy again, then gathered his men and said a few words about the companions they'd lost. The sun was setting in the west, and the sky was bleeding orange shot through with purple veins.

Seeing the dwarves with their caps and scarves doffed and in hand touched Wick's tender heart as they listened to Bulokk's words. Wick had seen similar scenes aboard *One-Eyed Peggie* while on his excursions aboard the ship. Humans had a tendency to float among families, taking what they needed wherever they were at the time. Arrogance kept elves together, and avarice and fear generally kept dwellers together.

But love and a long sense of history bound dwarves. Their world was the earth, given to them by the power of the Old Ones during the Beginning Times when things were created.

"All right then," Bulokk said, clapping his hat back on his head. He gestured to the setting sun. "As ye can see plainly as the nose on yer faces, we ain't goin' nowhere tonight. We'll rest up once more, get us a fresh start in the mornin'."

The dwarves grumbled, not truly happy spending life out under the stars when they were used to being able to burrow up whenever they liked.

Wick wasn't happy about it either. Especially when he realized that he was going to have to cook another big meal. This time, though, Bulokk posted guards and assigned two dwarves to help the little Librarian.

"The meal ye fixed were helpful," Bulokk said in an aside to Wick. "Kept them men from feelin' hollow, it did. So I'm gonna see to it ye get help."

"Thank you," Wick said. "I won't let you down."

Bulokk looked at him and smiled a little. "I don't think ye will, halfer. Just get me to where I can find Master Oskarr's lost axe, I'll be thankful to ye the rest of me days."

Weakly, not at all certain he could deliver on the promise he was being asked to give, Wick nodded. Then, when his crew showed up, he put his plans into action to organize the evening meal.

Later, with fish chunks floating in a seaweed soup made a little more exotic with the firepear pulp he'd saved from juicing earlier, Wick wiped sweat from his brow with a forearm and wondered where Craugh and *One-Eyed Peggie*'s crew were. The bottom of the cook pot glowed cherry-red and the soup bubbled.

Several of the dwarves looked on with fond expectation. Bulokk had organized a guard rotation and taken one of the posts himself.

"Them stories ye were a-tellin' back at the burrow," Drinnick said. "The ones about Master Oskarr, them was true stories, wasn't they?"

"They was, er . . . were," Wick agreed.

Drinnick scratched the back of his neck with a big forefinger. "Would ye, uh, mind tellin' us a few more of 'em? We ain't ever heard the like. An' the way ye tell 'em, why folks would pay to hear ye a-tellin' 'em."

So as he cooked and fried (and tried frightfully hard not to think that his life might be on the line), Wick told the dwarves stories about the Cinder Clouds Islands dwarves. He included tales of Master Blacksmith Oskarr as well as that worthy's ancestors.

During the telling of Varshuk's Blockade, when a human pirate named himself king of the area and tried to enforce his laws, none of the dwarves said a word. Wick employed all the tricks he'd learned in Hralbomm's Wing to tell the tale properly. He continued the tale while he filled the dwarves' metal plates and tankards, then feigned distraction to the point that they washed the dishes in the sea so that he would be free to speak. It was a bit of chicanery he'd learned while making his way across the mainland hunting down lost books.

Later, when the coals had burned low and were deep orange, Bulokk put an end to the tale-telling. Several of the dwarves thanked Wick for the meal and for the stories. That night, the little Librarian slept without wondering if he was going to wake up with his throat slit.

But he kept wondering where *One-Eyed Peggie* and Craugh were, and why they had abandoned him.

"*Easy.* Go easy there, ye great-eared lummox," Bulokk growled from the longboat's stern. "We got this boat fixed up good as we could, but she ain't gonna take a fierce poundin'."

Despite the dwarves' best efforts, the longboat scraped the jutting teeth of the rocks they passed through. The hoarse sound carried over the water.

Wick swallowed hard, telling himself that the water probably wasn't that deep there if the rock was jutting above the sea surface. But he knew that might not be true. Slender spires of rock drove up from the sea bottom a hundred feet and more sometimes. The forces contained within the earth and unleashed through the open sores of the volcanoes festered with tremendous power.

All around them, the gray fog closed in swirling waves. The manifestation happened every time cool air came down from the north and hit the blast furnace that was the Cinder Clouds Islands.

Wick sat in the longboat's prow and peered out. The dwarves had since admitted that Wick had some of the best eyes among them. The fog glided over Wick's skin like damp silk and he resisted the impulse to claw it out of his face.

Although it was mid-morning, darkness covered the Rusting Sea and the sun couldn't be seen. Gull cries echoed across the water so much that Wick couldn't determine the true direction of the birds.

Stiff and sore from sleeping on the hard ground a second night in a row, Wick disliked acting as lookout now. There was too much moving around involved.

"D'ye see anythin', halfer?" Drinnick asked.

Wick sighed. He wanted to be angry, but he was afraid to be. Even though he'd told them stories last night, and cooked meals for them, he didn't trust the dwarves to be so thankful that they wouldn't throw him overboard while reacting to their own frustrations. Wick had already seen two saurian creatures gliding through the murky water.

However, *D'ye see anythin', halfer?* from the dwarves was becoming as irritatingly monotonous as *Are you sure that brushstroke was made by the Dalothak Canopy elves, Second Level Librarian?* from the Novice and Third Level Librarians. (And, truthfully, even a few Second Level and First Level Librarians still asked that! Wick thought that was shameful.)

The demand was repeated on the heels of Wick's sigh. "D'ye see anythin', halfer?"

"These dwarves," Rohoh whispered irritably, "are awfully short-sighted." Then the skink laughed at his attempt at humor.

Turning, controlling his ire only through excessive fear, Wick said (as politely as he could while trying to sound capable), "No. If I had seen something, I would have said that I had—"

Of course, at that point the longboat ran aground.

11

Landmarks

Loud grinding filled Wick's ears. From the deep-throated sound and the way the longboat continued to glide evenly over the surface of the hidden object, Wick believed they'd hit stone. Then his thoughts immediately flew to the holes that had been so recently repaired in the longboat's hull.

"Good job," Rohoh commented. "Maybe you should have been watching instead of getting all sensitive."

"Reverse!" Bulokk commanded, keeping his voice down because it carried across the water and he didn't want to alert anyone that might be in the area that they were there, too. *"Reverse!"*

Immediately, the dwarves churned their oars in the other direction, pulling back away from whatever they had hit. Their efforts yanked the longboat backward.

Caught unprepared, Wick nearly went ears over teakettle into the water. He flailed for a moment, certain he was going to land in the sea and be a mere gobbet for some passing monster. Then Adranis flicked out a lazy hand and caught him, keeping him in the boat.

"Ye think ye mighta seen *that*, halfer," Adranis griped.

Chagrined, Wick sat in the prow and concentrated on staying aboard and staying alive.

Adranis peered forward. "Don't see nothin'."

"We hit somethin'," Bulokk said.

"Aye. I know that. But I'll be jiggered if'n I can find it."

Curious, though he felt certain he should just try to stay out of everyone's way, Wick turned and looked into the water. A small fish broke the surface only a few feet away. Reaching into the small bag at his feet, Wick palmed a handful of pan breadcrumbs and scattered them over the water's surface.

"What do ye think ye're a-doin'?" Drinnick growled. "Tryin' to bring us face-to-face with one of them beasties?"

"Face-to-face with ye, Drinnick?" another dwarf asked. "I'm a-thinkin' there ain't a monster in these waters what's brave enough fer that."

A few of the other dwarves chuckled at that.

"Quiet!" Bulokk ordered.

They all fell quiet.

As Wick watched, several small fish broke the surface and fed on the crumbs he'd spread. "There's something down there," he announced.

"Why?" Bulokk asked.

"That's a school of small fish. You won't find them out in the open because the bigger fishes eat them." Motivated by that same powerful pull of curiosity that had gotten him into so much trouble over the years, Wick grabbed the sides of the longboat and peered down into the water. He still couldn't see anything.

"Are we ashore, then?" Bulokk asked.

"Don't see no shoreline," Adranis replied.

"It's an underwater structure." Wick was certain he was right. He thought about how the longboat had glided across the submerged surface. "A big one."

"What makes ye say that?" Drinnick challenged.

"Because we moved across it evenly. If it were the shallows, it would have tapered up and probably stopped us in our tracks. And it has to have hollows or be porous in some way to hide the small fish." Wick searched the bottom of the boat and found the weighted line they used to test the depths.

"D'ye think it's Zubeck's Hammer?" Bulokk asked.

"That's what we were here searching for." Wick wasn't really thinking about the dwarves or their reaction to him. He was excited about possibly finding the dwarven lighthouse.

Standing in the prow of the longboat, Wick cast the line. But the rope was more tricky to manage than he'd thought. When he released it after spinning it around, the weight sailed backward.

Dwarves cursed and covered their heads.

"Give me that!" Adranis snarled. "Afore ye brain somebody!"

Meekly, Wick handed the line over and knelt in the prow again.

After a few casts, Adranis found the underwater surface about twenty feet forward and to port. The weight landed solidly on it.

"Slow," Bulokk said. "Slow an' easy as we go."

The dwarves barely moved the oars and eased the longboat through the water. A moment later, they bumped up against it again.

"All right," Bulokk said. "Drop anchor an' let's see what we found."

The water, though shallow, still came up to just under Wick's chin. Although he didn't want to, he had a tendency to bob on the tide and Bulokk had finally assigned Adranis the task of keeping the little Librarian anchored. It wasn't a task Adranis was particularly fond of, and he occasionally waited until Wick was over the edge and had started to swim. Then the dwarf would yank Wick back like a wandering toddler. The skink clung to the back of the little Librarian's head, hidden by his hair.

Thankfully, the Rusting Sea was warm. On the negative side, though, there appeared to be plenty of depth for a sea monster to come by and try for a quick catch. Wick's attention was divided between the mystery of what they'd found and survival. In the end, though, the discovery devoured his attention.

Walking across the underwater surface, Wick found that it was thirty feet long and eight feet wide. Although Wick and two of the other dwarves had dived and followed the line of the submerged structure, they hadn't been able to go more than forty or fifty feet down.

Given the measurements, Wick was certain they'd found Zubeck's Hammer. The lighthouse was in surprisingly good shape. Nothing had appeared broken, though there were some pitted places on the surface.

Unfortunately, the ocean held too much sediment for Wick to see the lighthouse. The only way he'd ever see Zubeck's Hammer would be for some freak of chance to thrust the structure to the surface once more. Since the Hammer was reputed to be one hundred forty feet tall, he didn't see how that would happen.

And besides, he thought glumly, pacing across its submerged surface once more with his bare feet, *it was a miracle that the lighthouse wasn't destroyed when it sank.*

"Is this it then?" Bulokk asked.

"It has to be," Wick said.

"Then where should we head next?"

Wick sighed and ended up with a mouthful of salty, metallic-tasting seawater for his trouble. He also snorted some up his nose and it burned strong enough to bring tears to his eyes.

"Do you understand how important this is?" Wick asked. "We're standing on a piece of history."

Bulokk frowned. "There's lots of history. Everywhere you go, there's old things."

"But don't you realize how much those old things can tell us?"

"About what?"

"The past," Wick moaned. He gestured at the light-house, a feat that was incredibly hard to do because he had to wait between waves of the incoming tide and even then the water was up well past his armpits. "Can you even imagine what it would be like if we could get inside this place?"

"We'd drown," Adranis said. "This place is under-water." He shook his head. "Ye know, to be as smart as ye are, ye got some awfully dumb ways."

"He's speaking the truth there," Rohoh muttered in Wick's ear.

"Not while it's underwater," Wick argued. "If we could somehow raise it up and go inside."

"Everything inside is ruined," Bulokk said. "The only thing that survives the sea is gold. Even silver rots away."

"Some enchanted things survive, too," Wick said.

Bulokk frowned. "I don't hold much with magic. Can't see a need fer it."

"But you want Master Oskarr's battle-axe."

"Master Oskarr's axe ain't magicked up none," Bulokk replied. "It's just . . . Master Oskarr's axe. Something that touches all them before times."

Wick was thinking of all the books that might have survived. Some books were magical in nature and couldn't be easily destroyed by the vagaries of weather. But other books, especially ones that were kept around water or the constant threat of fire, tended to be kept in protective bindings. Just as his own journal was wrapped securely in oilskin beneath his clothing.

There have to be books in there, he thought desperately. *The Rusting Sea can't have claimed them all.*

"Which way?" Bulokk demanded.

Wick had difficulty wresting his thoughts from books and maps and journals that might still be lurking in Zubeck's Hammer. The lighthouse would have been a natural gathering place for seafarers, tale spinners, and those seeking their fortunes in legends and maps of old.

"Which way is the sun?" Wick asked.

Bulokk pointed.

Squinting up at the light that had grown somewhat brighter, Wick silently admitted that the sun probably did lie in that direction. He thought about it for a moment, then turned back to Bulokk. "Is it morning or afternoon?" He'd lost all track of time. It had been morning the last he'd looked.

"Afternoon," Bulokk answered.

"Then that way is west?" Wick pointed toward the sunniest part of the haze.

"Aye."

"We need to go still farther east, but in a northerly direction."

"Then let's be about it." Bulokk turned and walked toward the anchored longboat.

Wick couldn't make himself move. He was loath to leave the lighthouse and whatever treasures it might have inside.

"Perhaps we can get inside," he said, thinking about Luttell's *Guide to Undersea Vessels in Fact and Fiction: Their Design, Construction, and Uses.* Nearly all of those used magic in one form or another, though. Still, there had been a few workable designs, and dwarves were certainly most capable when it came to manufacturing things that—

"We're a-leavin'," Adranis declared. He yanked Wick and the little Librarian's feet left the lighthouse as he skimmed through the waves like a fat-bellied merchant's cog. Closing his eyes against the spray, Wick clapped a

hand over his mouth and nose to protect himself from in-
haling the ocean.

Hours later, Wick glumly sat in the prow of the longboat.
In short order, proceeding on the information he remembered, they'd found Hullbreaker Reefs and managed to
stay well clear of them, then Delid's Circle. Both of those
landmarks had been above the ocean's surface.

Now, if everything was right, Wick felt they had to be
closing in on—

"There!" Drinnick said, standing and pointing, which
caused the longboat to tip precariously and take on a little
water.

The rest of the dwarves set about cursing Drinnick's
thoughtless action, but he protested and said he'd never
claimed to be a sailor. The imprecations and defense
didn't last long. The sight out in the middle of the ocean
drew all of their attention.

For there, only a couple feet above the whitecaps
rolling in from the sea toward the Cinder Clouds Islands,
the very top of a blue dome could be seen. Wick's heart
leaped. He knew from Brojor's *Physical Laws of the Natural World* that a dome often maintained air pressure in
quite the same manner an empty tankard could be pushed
to the bottom of a sink filled with water. In fact, that
thought had been buzzing through Wick's mind because
he was thinking that one of the devices he could use to
get inside Zubeck's Hammer was similar in nature.

But the Trader's Hall had windows. Only the top half
of the dome might have maintained an air pocket. Surely
nothing had been up there.

But it might have floated, Wick thought optimistically.
*Pots. Trunks. Kegs. Anything that might have an airtight
seal.*

"No one knows this is here?" Wick asked, having trouble believing that.

"These ain't the primary trade routes," Bulokk said. "We're well away from them right now. Few comes through here, an' them not often." He looked at the blue dome. "Besides, what ye a-gonna do with somethin' like that a-stickin' up outta the water except make sure ye don't hit it?"

Wick had to concede that the dwarf had a point. As they got closer, though, the little Librarian's heart broke. Over the years, someone had broken through the dome, punching a big hole in the top. From his vantage point, he clearly saw the sea sloshing around inside.

He barely heard Bulokk asking him which way they were supposed to go. Despondent by the terrible realization that probably nothing inside Trader's Hall yet remained, Wick took a moment to get his bearings, then pointed north.

The dwarves immediately set out on the new tack, pulling all the harder as if they were racing the sunset to the west.

Twilight draped the Rusting Sea as they came within sight of the island chain. The water turned muddy black with it, and the white curlers held a glow like glimmerworms.

Wick had grown tired with the passing of the day. He wasn't used to having to spend whole days without something to distract his thoughts. He hated spending hours by himself with nothing but thinking to dwell on. Left to their own devices, his thoughts often chose to spin around and around like water gurgling through plumbing. Only he was unable to divest himself of those thoughts because he was afraid that he'd never rethink them. That was different when he had quill and paper at hand, because then he could jot down whatever was on his mind and trust that nothing would be forgotten.

It was terrible having a headful of thoughts with no proper place to put them. His mind and fingers cried out for the luxury of putting quill to paper, of transferring all that thinking to a more forgiving and permanent medium, then sorting through it to make it make sense.

"Is that it, halfer?" Bulokk asked in a quiet, reverential voice.

Wick studied the coastline, looking for landmarks that he could recognize from the maps he'd seen of the Cinder Clouds Islands. Although most Librarians were able to remember prodigious amounts of information, he was more able than most of his fellow Librarians.

"Sail to the east," Wick said. "We need to travel up the eastern coast for a bit."

Bulokk gave the orders. "But is this the island where Master Oskarr's forge was?"

Wick shrugged. "I don't know. It could be. We need to be in closer."

The skink slithered on his shoulder. "This is it," Rohoh whispered. "And this is where this thing starts to really get dangerous."

"Hug the coastline," Bulokk ordered his warriors. "Keep a weather eye peeled."

Later, when the full dark of the night had descended upon the Rusting Sea and the island as well, Wick spied campfires nestled in a cove that looked like the scar from an old axe blow. Steep cliffs forty and fifty feet tall soared above the ruins of a city. Alabaster rock showed signs of expert quarry work. Since no one had truly built like that among the Cinder Clouds Islands in a thousand years, Wick assumed the village was at least that old.

Thin wisps of fog floated through the chill breeze that continued from the north. The campfires filled the ruins with orange light. There was no mistaking the creatures that maintained watch over the area.

"Goblinkin," Adranis whispered with real loathing. "Quite a mess of 'em, too."

Wick silently agreed. The goblinkin encampment was spread throughout the ruins. It was easy to see that they had been there for some time. A stone pier made up of broken rocks thrust a short distance out into the Rusting Sea. Two ships, both of them ragged and worn, jostled against each other on the tide.

Most interesting, though, was the ship lying at anchor next to the pier. Lanterns lit her deck and dark figures that might have been human moved around onboard. Her sails were furled and her rigging rang against the masts and 'yards in the breeze.

If that's not the black ship that tried to run us down, Wick thought, *then it's her sister.* He didn't think it was a coincidence.

"Slavers," Drinnick growled. "They got halfers there."

Shifting his attention from the buildings he could see, Wick spotted the slave pen tucked at the back of the canyon. Wire nets made up the enclosure. Skulls—most of them from dwellers but some from humans, dwarves, and elves—hung on the wire nets and picked up a warm cast-off glow from the campfires. Nearly a hundred slaves lay practically on top of each other on the stone floor. Goblinkin guards lounged around the slave pen.

"Are they a-sellin' 'em then?" another dwarf asked.

Wick surveyed the rest of the city. Then he spotted a narrow trail that had been cut into the cliff wall. The trail zigzagged up the wall. A torch burned at the entrance to a cave mouth.

"They're digging," Wick said.

"Fer what?" Adranis asked.

"I don't know." Farther up the cliff, Wick made out the block-and-tackle assembly that he assumed was used to lower excavated rock to the ore cars on the ground. A worn path led from the ore cars to the stone pier.

"Are they a-diggin' fer gems?" Bulokk asked. "Or fer gold?"

"Maybe it's iron ore," Wick said. "You mentioned that the goblinkin were mining iron ore and shipping it to the mainland."

"This ain't an iron mine," Bulokk said.

"No," Adranis agreed.

"How do you know?" Wick asked.

"Can't smell any iron," Bulokk said. He touched his nose.

Adranis and the other dwarves agreed.

"Was iron here once," Adranis said, sniffing again. "But it's been gone a long time."

"Mayhap even a thousand years or more," Bulokk conceded. "Master Oskarr an' his forge smiths had to import iron ore even durin' his day." He paused. "Either way, we have to find out what they're doin' there. An' this is the spot where ye said Master Oskarr's forge was."

Wick had been afraid the dwarves were going to come to that conclusion. Even though he was afraid, part of him was hypnotized by the possibilities the goblinkin presence presented. The goblinkin wouldn't be there if no reason existed.

Neither would the mysterious black ship.

"Time to get moving, halfer," Rohoh said. "This is what you've come all this way to find."

"How do you know that?" Wick whispered back, knowing the sound of the sea would carry his words away before they reached dwarven ears.

"Because," Rohoh said, "this is what Craugh sent me

here to help you find. Now you just have to stay alive long enough to find it."

And what about after *I find it*? Wick wondered. *What then?* But he was afraid to ask.

12

A Daring Plan Is Made

I think the halfer should stay here," Adranis said. "He'll just be underfoot."

"So do I," Wick piped up. "I think the halfer should stay here, too."

All of the dwarves shot the little Librarian a glance of annoyance.

"Or not," Wick whispered.

"You can't stay here," the skink told him. "Your place is down there. Either you can go with them, or you'll have to go alone."

Wick didn't want to go alone. "Of course," he added swiftly, "if you think I can help . . ."

Bulokk had given the order to set up camp on the other side of the island. A half mile of crooked rock and ridges separated their camp from the ruins of the city where the goblinkin had set up base. A hidden reef lay only a few feet below the ocean surface where they'd tied up. The longboat had negotiated the area with difficulty, so they knew the black ship couldn't close in on them without risking its hull.

The main focus of the mission, though, was not to get caught observing in the first place.

"He's goin' with us," Bulokk declared, "an' that's that."

"Why?" Adranis asked.

So I can be the slow one if we get caught, Wick was certain. *The sacrificial lamb. By the time the goblinkin get through tearing me to pieces, you'll all have made your escape.*

"Do ye know anyone else who might know his way around them ruins?" Bulokk demanded. "We get down in them ruins a-runnin' fer our lives, might be a good idea to have a guide."

"Ummmm," Adranis said. "Hadn't thought about that."

Oh, Wick thought, and realized that he hadn't considered that either. Upon reflection, Bulokk's reasoning was without fault. Wick was of mixed emotions, though. He didn't like the idea of potentially ending up in slaver's chains (or dead!), but he knew that Bulokk and his men wouldn't recognize a book if they saw one.

If *any* of the books Master Oskarr used, or—and the hope left Wick giddy with anticipation—wrote himself still existed, that knowledge would be worth every risk he took.

As long as I don't die, Wick told himself.

Wick's back and feet hurt by the time they reached the ruins. The dwarves acted like the rocky climbs and journey over the rugged terrain was something they did every day. Given that they lived on an island a lot like this one, though, Wick had to admit that they probably did.

They came to a stop on the side of the canyon across from the block-and-tackle. No goblinkin guarded the boom arm or the mine entrance. Since the coast was clear, they went to the other side and soon grouped under the block-and-tackle assembly.

Bulokk quickly divided the dwarves into two groups. One was assigned to stay by the boom arm to manage a retreat. The other was descending down into the goblinkin camp to assess the possibility of freeing the slaves.

Wick didn't even have to be told which group he was going with. Heart in his throat, he crept along behind Bulokk and the other dwarves as they sneaked down into the goblinkin camp.

The stone steps tracking up the cliff were so narrow Bulokk almost had to go down while turned sideways. Of course, carrying his battle-axe in both hands made the effort even more difficult. But he managed. The steps were uneven and sometimes poorly placed. Dwarves hadn't made those steps and Wick had the feeling that dweller or human slaves had.

But why? Despite the terror that never stopped vibrating through him, Wick couldn't let go of the question. If Bulokk and the others said there was no iron ore coming out of the mine, he believed them. *So why would the goblinkin be interested in a mine that didn't promise gold or gems or some other wealth? And what relationship did the ship have with the goblinkin?*

Finally, after what seemed like an eternity to Wick, he reached the ground level and stood in hiding with Bulokk. But that just meant that although he was no longer in fear of falling over the edge of the narrow steps, it was now a long way back up to safety. He would have felt better if there had been a few elven warders with longbows posted among the dwarves.

Craugh, he thought miserably. Surely the crew of the pirate ship could see where he was and how much trouble he was potentially in.

"It's here."

Wick clapped a hand over his mouth automatically. Glancing back over his broad shoulder, Bulokk glared at him.

It wasn't me, Wick thought desperately. Of course, at first he'd thought it had been him who had spoken. Then he'd realized that the voice was tiny, not a whisper or an inadvertent slip.

"Oskarr's axe is here," the tiny voice said.

The skink, Wick realized. Keeping one hand over his mouth to show Bulokk that he wasn't talking, Wick frantically searched for Rohoh with the other. Then he figured he probably looked like he was patting himself on the back.

"Should have slit his throat when we found him a-cookin' fer them goblinkin," Hodnes growled.

"It ain't too late to do it now," Drinnick whispered.

"If you two keep talking, maybe you'll wake the goblinkin and they'll come after us," Rohoh said. The skink crawled out from hiding and stood on Wick's shoulder waving an angry, curled-up claw at the dwarves.

"Ye got a talkin' lizard?" Drinnick asked.

Now he decides to talk. Anxious, Wick peered around the goblinkin camp amid the ruins. So far none of the goblinkin appeared to have heard them.

"It dances, too," Hodnes reminded. "We saw it dancing when we found the halfer a-cookin' fer the goblinkin." He smiled. "A dancin' lizard what knows how to talk. Now that could fetch a pretty price."

Rohoh crossed his forelegs and stood up on his hind legs. "You two are idiots."

"'Course," Drinnick said, "he could have him a better disposition."

"Don't you think the important thing is figuring out why he chose *now* to speak?" Wick asked.

"Quiet!" Bulokk commanded.

All of them quieted.

"Lizard!" Bulokk pointed at the skink.

"Yes," Rohoh said.

"Why do ye talk?"

"Because I have something to say, you ninny."

"Enough to get all our throats slit?" Bulokk demanded.

"Look," the skink said, "I was sent here by a powerful wizard to make sure this numbskull—"

Numbskull! Wick thought indignantly.

"—managed to find Oskarr's battle-axe," Rohoh went on.

"Why?"

"Because the wizard wants to find out the truth of what happened at the Battle of Fell's Keep in the Painted Canyon."

"Why does he want to know that?" Bulokk demanded.

"It's time everyone knew what happened in those days," Rohoh stated.

Glowering, Bulokk leaned in close. "Does he think Master Oskarr betrayed them warriors?"

"I don't know. He doesn't talk to me about things like that."

Nor me, Wick thought glumly.

Bulokk ran his fingers through his beard thoughtfully. He clearly wasn't happy about the turn of events. "So why did this wizard—"

"Craugh," Rohoh said.

That does it, Wick thought, and prepared to run for his life. Craugh had a large reputation, but those who'd heard of him either liked him or hated him. The wizard tended to divide people into those two camps immediately. Generally the ones who didn't care for him had a relative who had been turned into a toad.

"Aye," Bulokk said. "I've heard of Craugh."

Wick's legs quivered. He thought if Bulokk chose to vent his anger on the skink he might gain a step on the certain pursuit. Of course, he'd be running straight into the arms of the goblinkin and the mysterious humans.

Of course, there existed the possibility that Bulokk would choose to take off Wick's head and cut the skink in twain in one fell swoop.

"Craugh's been around for a long time," Bulokk said. "There's some even say he was around for the Cataclysm and fought against Lord Kharrion."

Wick knew it was true. He'd read journals and books of the Cataclysm, and Craugh had been featured prominently in them.

"Why is Craugh interested in this?" Bulokk asked.

"He wants to know the truth," Rohoh said.

"Why?"

Wick couldn't keep quiet any longer. He stepped forward on trembling knees. "Bulokk."

The dwarf turned his harsh gaze on the little Librarian.

"I really think this is neither the time nor the place to discuss this at length," Wick said. "We've already been longer at it than we should have. What matters is that we're all here to recover Master Oskarr's axe."

Bulokk wanted to argue. That showed in every hard line of his body. Finally, he sighed. "Ye're right. But we're not even sure if the axe survived—"

"It did," Rohoh insisted. "In fact, we're not far from it."

"How do ye know that?"

"Because finding things is one of my skills," the skink answered. "That's why Craugh put me with this inept dweller."

Inept? Wick didn't know whether to be hurt or angry. He supposed he was both.

"Ye *find* things?" Bulokk asked. "How?"

"By magic," Rohoh said.

"Ye're a wizard?"

"No. I just have a talent for things like this. It's more like a—" The skink hesitated. "—a *knack*."

"Like a dwarf what can put his hand on a chunk of iron ore an' know he's gonna find something special in it," Adranis said. "A sword. An axe. A ring with a little extra good luck in it."

Rohoh nodded. "Exactly like that."

Immediate curiosity filled Wick. Although he'd heard of *knacks*, he'd never before seen anyone who possessed them. Magic was something that came two different ways: either as a discipline through years of tutelage, or as a more primitive means of tapping into the elemental forces that drove the power. Having a knack for finding magical things only made sense.

If you accepted the existence of knacks, Wick thought.

Bulokk didn't appear convinced.

"What this un's talkin' about," Adranis told the dwarven leader, "I've seen it fer meself. It's a true thing. Just seldom seen, is all." He turned and peered down at the skink standing on Wick's shoulder. "Ye're a-sayin' ye can sense Master Oskarr's axe?"

"I can."

"How did ye get the scent of it?"

Wick wanted to know the answer to that question as well.

"Craugh gave it to me," Rohoh answered. "He knew Master Oskarr and had touched the axe. It was enough to give me the scent."

"Even after a thousand years an' more?" Bulokk definitely had a hard time believing that. "Where's the axe?" Bulokk asked.

The skink pointed. "Somewhere inside the mountain. It's buried in there. But it's near."

Bulokk took a deep breath. "All right, then." His gaze raked the goblinkin and the mysterious ship. "First things first. We need to see what we're up against."

Wick decided he didn't like the sound of that. He liked it even less when Bulokk told him what he intended they do.

"An' ye," Bulokk threatened the skink, "no yappin'. Ye talk again before I tell ye it's okay to do so, an' we'll be a-takin' our chances on findin' Master Oskarr's axe ourselves."

The goblinkin guards stood their posts but didn't put any effort into it. There was more activity aboard the mysterious ship.

Of course, that was where Bulokk insisted they go. Even worse, he ordered Wick to follow him.

Cautiously, they crept down to the small harbor, easily avoiding the goblinkin guards, most of whom slept or stood in bored groups grumbling about their lot in life. The worst thing (if the constant fear of getting caught was discounted!) was the noxious smells coming from the great cauldrons that continued to simmer over fires in the center of the goblinkin camp.

Wick tried very hard not to think about what was cooked in those vast metal pots. That was hard to do when he saw the pile of bones—most of them from humans, dwellers, and dwarves with a few elven bones thrown in for good measure—that lay scattered at the water's edge on one side of the stone pier.

Lanterns glowed in the stern of the ship, stronger than the moonlight that peered again and again between clouds. Hidden in the shadows gathered at the base of the cliffs where they met the Rusting Sea, Wick hunkered down beside Bulokk and listened.

Up close, Wick saw the ship was crisp and clean, showing definite signs of immaculate care. The captain and his crew obviously cared about her the way a dwarven warrior cared about his axe. In the darkness, Wick couldn't make out her name, or even if she carried one. She rode light and easy on the tide, obviously carrying no cargo.

She carried something into the port, then, Wick thought, unable to keep from puzzling it out. *But what?* He gazed around the camp and knew at once. *She's a slaver.*

But that didn't sit right either. A ship that clean, that well cared for, Wick knew from experience that she shouldn't be a slaver. Ships used in that profession tended to be slovenly and piggish, cared for enough to keep afloat and keep turning a profit, but there was no pride in those ships. No matter what a captain and crew did, they could never wash the stink off such a vessel.

So who made you a slaver? Wick wondered. *And why did you agree?* All of the crew appeared to be human. *How did you come to deal with goblinkin if you're as successful as you look?*

After a few more minutes, Bulokk waved them back. Wick went willingly.

Once more at the foot of the stone steps, Bulokk conferred with Adranis. "We've got a two-fold problem," the dwarven leader said. "I want to find the axe, an' I'm not leavin' here without at least attemptin' to rescue them prisoners."

"An' I wouldn't let ye shirk on either of them duties," Adranis declared.

"The way I see it," Bulokk went on, "we've got to manage both of them things at the same time."

"Means splittin' our forces," Hodnes said.

"Not till we get the prisoners to the top of the cliff."

"We get them free," Adranis asked, "how are we gonna get them off the island?"

"Once we get them free an' up the cliff, we'll alert the goblinkin—"

"Assumin' they ain't already been alerted," Adranis said sourly.

Bulokk nodded. "Even so. As long as we get 'em clear, it should only take a few men to hold the cliffs against the goblinkin. All we need to do is hold the goblinkin fer a while, long enough for the prisoners to circle around the island. Then whoever holds the cliff top simply has to outrun the goblinkin to the longboat."

"Simply, he says," Drinnick grumped.

"At the longboat, them defenders will cast off. If'n we get lucky, an' the Old Ones are known to favor the bold, them goblinkin will think their prisoners got away in other boats an' aren't circlin' around the island to take their ships."

"That's a daring plan," Wick said, because it was. "But even if the goblinkin fall for the trick, I don't think the crew of the black ship will leave their vessel unprotected. They'll be aboard her."

"That's a risk we'll have to take," Bulokk stated. "I don't see anything else we can do." He paused. "We ain't got all night, so let's be about it."

13

Walls of History

Crouched in the shadows, Wick watched in helpless terror as Bulokk and his handpicked warriors crept across the shadow-covered space. They moved in concert, as if they'd committed actions like this all their lives. Swiftly, each of them targeted a goblinkin guard and brought him down, finishing them all off quickly with their knives.

At that moment, the risk elevated to the point of no return. All it took was one goblinkin guard checking on another to throw them all into danger.

"Relax," Rohoh said, standing on Wick's shoulder. "Bulokk and his warriors know what they're about. They're good at this sort of thing."

"You've never seen them at work before," Wick whispered back.

"I saw them in front of the goblinkin you were preparing the banquet for."

"You were the entertainment."

"Under protest, though. And if you'd been able to save yourself, I wouldn't have had to bother."

Wick didn't say anything, caught up in the drama taking place in front of his eyes. In seconds, Bulokk had the attention of the prisoners, then had the locks picked.

Adranis took the first one under his care and guided him through the shadows to the stone steps.

Several of the prisoners struggled to remain quiet as they made their way across the back of the campsite. They took advantage of the massive stone blocks that remained of the city, making Wick wish again that he could see the ruin in the light of day (which would have adversely affected the escape plan, though).

Only a few moments later, they began a staggered line back and forth up the stone steps cut into the cliff. Humans, dwarves, and dwellers aided one another in their bid to escape the goblinkin.

For the first time, Wick thought about how much the rescue attempt was like the Battle of Fell's Keep during the Cataclysm. He only hoped that this present effort didn't end so badly as that one had.

At Bulokk's direction, Wick joined in with the procession toward the end so they could split off once they reached the mine entrance. He went up and his legs ached with the effort. He couldn't remember sleeping last night, and now fatigue was hammering him. He truly wished he were back home, safely in bed at the Vault of All Known Knowledge, the only plunder on his mind one of the books from Hralbomm's Wing that Grandmagister Frollo frowned upon.

The escape proceeded at a snail's pace.

Long minutes later, the goblinkin noticed the escape attempt. It didn't happen the way Wick thought it would, which was pretty much through chance as a goblinkin went to relieve himself, or happened to glance up while a stray beam of moonslight penetrated the cloud cover and highlighted the fleeing prisoners.

Instead, what happened was that one of the escapees became too weak and lost his footing about thirty feet up the cliff face. Panicked, the man grabbed the man next to him and plucked him clean from the steps as well. Both of them screamed as they plummeted to the rocks.

Neither of them moved after they hit. Unconscious or dead, they weren't going to make their escape tonight. Wick felt badly for them. But only for a moment. Then panic exploded within him.

"What was that?" one of the goblinkin guards yelled.

"Something at the back," another called.

Hugging the cliff face because he'd suddenly grown aware of how far he had to fall, Wick glanced below, using his bare feet to search out the next step.

At first, three or four goblinkin started toward the back of the canyon. They took torches from supplies near the campfires.

"Hurry!" Adranis admonished from above.

But even though they were afraid of the goblinkin, the fleeing prisoners were suddenly afraid of the climb, too. Doubtless some had fallen while on their way to the mine from time to time.

The goblinkin guards called out. No answers came. Sensing that something was wrong, several other goblinkin roused from their beds and picked up torches as well. In practically no time at all, a horde of goblinkin had taken up the hunt.

"The prisoners have escaped!" a goblinkin yelled. "The slave pen is empty!"

"Over there!" someone shouted. "They're climbin' the wall to the mine!"

Immediately, the goblinkin started for the steps and the fight began in earnest. Thankfully none of them appeared to have bows. But Wick remembered that the human crew aboard the mystery ship did. And they knew very well how to use them. They didn't leave the vessel, though, presumably choosing to stay aboard and protect it.

Bulokk and two of his warriors protected the flank,

using short-hafted axes and shields to alternately attack
and defend. Their efforts slowed the goblinkin attack, but
also distanced them from their comrades.

"Quickly!" Wick cried out. "Quickly as you can!
More help is waiting at the top! Quickly!" As he moved,
he helped the elderly human behind him, grabbing him
once before he lost his balance and tumbled over the
side.

Loose stone, Wick discovered, also made footing more
problematic. But it also gave him an idea.

Adranis reached the mine entrance first.

Wick thought about passing the mine entrance by and
continuing up the steps. It would have been safer to do so,
but he wouldn't have gotten the opportunity to see if Rohoh was right about the axe. He stepped off the steps only
with extreme reluctance.

A torch flared to life, causing Wick to jump a little.

"Well, halfer," Adranis said, "I see ye made it."

"I did," Wick agreed. But he didn't know how the dwarven warrior felt about that, or if he felt any way at all.

Hodnes and another dwarf stood inside the mineshaft
with Adranis. The shaft was narrow and long, swallowed
up in darkness beyond the reach of the torchlight. Scars
from the iron wheels of mine carts scored the stone floor.
Four carts lined the wall.

Wick ran to the carts and peered inside. "Here," he
pointed to the first two. "Pour this one into that one."

"What?" Adranis demanded.

Grabbing hold of the cart, Wick barely managed to
shift one of the wheels from the floor. "If you want to
help Bulokk and the others, listen to me. *Empty this cart
into the other one*." Despite the fact that he'd been yelling
loud enough that he heard his voice echo down the mineshaft, Wick didn't really think the dwarves would listen.
In fact, he didn't know to whom he thought he was to give
orders.

Surprisingly, Adranis and the others put the torches aside and helped him lift the cart. Outside the door, the last of the escaping prisoners filed by. The gap opened up between them and Bulokk's delaying action.

"To the entrance!" Wick yelled. "Hurry!" He pushed the cart and—unbelievably—got it moving. The wheels creaked.

With the dwarves' help, Wick got the cart outside to the steps but he made sure to leave room for Bulokk and the others to get by. They were below, in anvil formation, taking the blows of the goblinkin on their raised shields. A dwarven prisoner filled out the quad formation.

"Here!" Wick yelled. But he was so scared he felt like he was going to throw up. Despite Hallekk and Cobner's efforts to train him, he wasn't a warrior. He was a Librarian. Thankfully, as such, his mind was his greatest weapon. He leaned down and chocked the cart's wheels. "Come on now!"

"Axes!" Bulokk roared.

The dwarves shifted into attack mode and chopped at the goblinkin, temporarily driving them back. A few of them fell, but others fell in pieces. Bulokk and his warriors were merciless.

"Back!" Bulokk ordered.

The dwarves moved together, thundering up the steps. Bulokk was bleeding from three or four wounds, but none of them appeared serious. At the bottom of the landing, the goblinkin regrouped and charged up after the dwarves.

Wick shoved on the cart, rocking it against the chocks. "Turn it over!"

Adranis and the others helped Wick lift the cart. A cascade of small rocks tumbled free and skidded down the steps. The initial plunge knocked a few of the goblinkin down, but the loose rocks tripped others. They screamed as they fell.

"Great idea," Rohoh said, hanging onto Wick's shoulder tightly.

"Thanks," Wick said. He stood watching till the goblinkin got everything sorted and started back up the steps more slowly.

"You're not as useless as you look."

Wick frowned, but he didn't let Rohoh's unkind words rip the glow of victory from him.

"Maybe you should get into the mine," the skink suggested.

A goblinkin threw a club that smacked into the wall only a few feet from Wick's head.

"You're probably right," Wick said. He ducked back inside the mine entrance.

A quick glance up the steps revealed that the last of the fleeing prisoners was now disappearing over the crest of the ridge.

Inside the mineshaft, Bulokk picked up one of the lit torches and wiped blood from his face. He had his shield slung over his back along with his battle-axe, and carried a short-hafted double-bitted axe in his other hand.

"That was quick thinkin', halfer," Bulokk said.

Wick nodded. "It won't buy us much time."

Bulokk grinned. "Then we'd best make the most of it, shouldn't we?" He nodded toward the other dwarf. "This here's Rassun. He knows this mine an' has an idea about what the goblinkin is after an' who owns that ship down to the pier." He nodded toward the mineshaft. "We can talk on the way."

Wick struggled to keep up with the dwarves as they ran pell-mell through the mineshaft. The flames clinging to the torches fluttered and snapped as they ran. Within a short distance, the mineshaft split into three different shafts.

"Which way?" Bulokk asked.

Rohoh stood on Wick's shoulder. The lizard's tongue flicked into the air a few times. "To the right."

"Ye have a talkin' lizard?" Rassun asked. He was fairly emaciated from his long imprisonment and the harsh life afforded at the mine. Scars crisscrossed his face and hands, offering testimony to past battles and hardships. Gray streaked his long, ill-kept brown hair.

"Aye," Bulokk replied. "An' one that knows what we're seekin'."

Only a short distance ahead, the mineshaft split again, but this time the choices were up and down.

"Down," Rohoh said before anyone could ask.

Bulokk plunged ahead, holding his torch high. Shadows swirled and twirled around on the narrow walls of the shaft.

In several places, building blocks and archways—the bones of the old dwarven city that had existed aboveground before the island sank or was covered in lava—showed through. Before he knew it, Wick stopped at one of them and studied the inscriptions he found there.

There weren't many words, of course, because the author had been dwarven. Most of the dwarven languages that had existed before the Cataclysm forced everyone to learn a common tongue were abbreviated. Except when it came to forging and armament. In those areas, the dwarven language waxed eloquent.

The inscription was in the Cinder Clouds Islands dwarven tongue. It was also short and to the point.

Welcome
This is Master Blacksmith Oskarr's Forge
Metalwork Done Here
Intruders Will Be Killed

"Halfer!" Bulokk called. "What are ye a-waitin' on? Fer them goblinkin to catch up?"

"No." Wick struggled to take his eyes from the stone block. He pointed. "This was a warning to everyone who entered Master Oskarr's Forge. This stone was once placed at the entrance to the master blacksmith's inner circle." Drawn by other stones with engravings, he stepped slowly toward them to begin a deeper examination.

"How do ye know that?" Bulokk asked.

"Why, it's plain as the nose on your face," Wick said, not thinking. He was so used to having to explain to Novice Librarians that he didn't realize what he was doing. "That's written in the original Cinder Clouds Islands dwarven language." He wiped at the blocks in front of him.

"Hey!" Rohoh whispered in Wick's ear. "Ixnay onay ethay eadingray."

It took Wick a second to process the broken verbal language the skink used. In all his years, Wick hadn't heard it more than a handful of times. *Nix on the reading*. Only then did he realize what he'd said.

"Writ, is it?" Bulokk asked. Suddenly he was there in front of Wick, a grim look on his face. "Ye can read, can ye, halfer?"

Wick cringed back, but the wall was behind him. He held his hand up with only a small gap between his thumb and forefinger. "Maybe a *little*."

"A little, is it?"

Wick waited, heart beating frantically.

"Okay," Rohoh said, "so the halfer can read. A little. You can teach a monkey to wear clothes. Doesn't mean it suits him."

"Goblinkin kills them what can read," Drinnick said. He added his glare to Bulokk's. "They hate readin' an' writin'."

"It's not like the goblinkin aren't already after us to kill us," Rohoh said.

Wick glanced at the skink and wished he would shut up.

"Is that how ye come to know all them stories ye told us?" Adranis asked.

"Yes," Wick said. "The wizard that sent me has a few books. He taught me to read." Guilt stung him as he lied. Grandmagister Ludaan had given him the gift of reading, as the Grandmagister had done for hundreds of other dwellers who were brought into service to the Vault of All Known Knowledge. But he didn't want to reveal anything about the Library.

Adranis turned to the other dwarves. "Think about all them stories he's done went an' told us over the last few days. Stories *we* didn't know, or only halfway misremembered." His voice thickened. "He give us a gift is what he done. Without him, we wouldn't know where to even start lookin' for Master Oskarr's battle-axe."

"Master Oskarr's battle-axe?" Rassun echoed. "That's what the goblinkin are here lookin' for."

Bulokk wheeled on the onetime slave. "What?"

"The goblinkin," Rassun said. "They've been a-lookin' fer Master Oskarr's axe, too. That's why they've had us a-rootin' around in these caves."

"Maybe we could be moving while we're talking," Rohoh suggested sarcastically. "Or does standing around waiting for the goblinkin to catch up to us work for you?"

Wick raised his torch and studied the engravings made into the stones again.

"Do they tell ye anythin'?" Adranis asked. His voice was softer than normal.

Unconsciously, Wick raked dust and earth from the lines of the etchings. "These engravings," he said, "tell me that we're near Master Oskarr's forge. It also tells me some of the history that the town faced while they were here. This was part of the town's history wall, a place where travelers could visit and see much of what had taken place here."

Adranis pointed toward a block showing a goblinkin

and ships out in the harbor. "Was this attack part of the Cataclysm?"

Wick rubbed the inscription across the top and translated the words with ease. "No. This was from hundreds of years before that. A goblinkin slaver raid that followed on the heels of a storm."

"An' did the goblinkin succeed?" Adranis asked.

Shaking his head, Wick grinned. Happiness filled him. "No. I recognize this story. This was Farrad's Stand."

"Farrad was Master Oskarr's da," Adranis said.

"He was," Wick agreed. "But he was also Master Blacksmith during his time. The goblinkin slavers came in greater numbers that year than ever before. There was some talk that the storm that ravaged the coastline was summoned by a wizard so the goblinkin would have an easier time of it."

The next block showed dwarven warriors standing on a bridge above two massive stone gates. Since Wick hadn't seen those gates when they'd sailed in, he assumed that they'd been lost during the Cataclysm.

"Master Farrad stood with his warriors above the gates to Hammer Cove." Wick indicated an oval of islands and reefs that included the dwarven forge. "Hammer Cove was held together by the Treaty of Vovaln, which was made when the Master Blacksmiths all acknowledged Master Sarant—one of Master Oskarr's ancestors—as the greatest among them. In exchange, Master Sarant taught those blacksmiths and their sons all the secrets of his forge. That was when the Cinder Clouds Islands armor became prominent among warriors."

"I didn't know that," Adranis said.

"There's a lot you don't know," Rohoh said. "Like where Master Oskarr's axe is. Come on!" He marched to the end of Wick's shoulder and halfway down his biceps like it was a bridge.

Wick shifted his attention back to the previous stone.

"Master Farrad and his warriors triumphed against the goblinkin slavers. In fact, the beating the goblinkin received was so vicious that no slavers ever again tried their luck in the Cinder Clouds Islands."

"Not until the Cataclysm," Adranis said in a low voice.

"The goblinkin didn't try to enslave dwarves then," Wick said. "They came only to finish the destruction of the forges."

"They've been enslavin' ever since. An' now they're here to steal Master Oskarr's axe."

"Running," Rohoh said. "Us. Going to go get that axe. Does that sound familiar?"

Ignoring the skink, Wick turned his attention to Rassun. "How long have the goblinkin been here looking for Master Oskarr's axe?"

"Three, mayhap four years," Rassun answered. "I been here the last five months. Been right hard work we been doin'."

"Why are they looking for the axe?"

"Them thieves hired 'em to."

"What thieves?" Bulokk asked.

"Them in the black ship."

"They're thieves?" Wick asked.

"Aye. What did ye take 'em fer?"

"Slavers."

Rassun spat and shook his shaggy head. "They're thieves. Part of some guild down to Wharf Rat's Warren."

Wick had only heard rumors of Wharf Rat's Warren. Located far into the Deep Frozen North, the port city provided a haven for the murderers and cutthroats that profited from robbery and death. Filled with pirates, thieves, and assassins, Wharf Rat's Warren was a lawless place of superstition, avarice, and double-cross.

"Why would a thieves' guild be interested in Master Oskarr's battle-axe?" Wick asked.

Rohoh marched back up Wick's arm. "Because they

want Craugh to keep from finding out the truth of what happened at the Battle of Fell's Keep!"

"What good would that do?" Wick asked.

"If Craugh can find out what truly happened during that battle," the skink replied, "he might be able to engineer a peace treaty along the mainland that can start to rebuild the Unity."

The Unity.

The words struck a chord deep within Wick. Was this what it was truly all about? This mission that Craugh had sent him on? If that was what the stakes had been, why hadn't Craugh told him?

Because you'd have gotten scared, Wick told himself. *Just the way you're doing now.*

He was a Librarian, not part of a diplomatic corps. He wasn't trained to deal in the fates of nations. Well, now that there weren't truly any nations left, he supposed he couldn't be afraid of that, but he couldn't be responsible for the fates of towns or even small villages. Give him a book and he could translate or copy it (provided it was written in one of the many languages he knew and read), or ask him to give reports about any number of subjects and he could do that.

"If'n the goblinkin find Master Oskarr's axe," Bulokk asked, "what are they gonna do with it?"

"I don't know," Rassun said. "But I'm guessin' they're gonna destroy it. Get rid of it once an' fer all."

Goblinkin yells echoed within the mineshaft, some of them near and some of them far. It was so confusing it was hard to tell where they were.

"They'll have split up to look for us," Rassun said. "It'll make for smaller search parties, but once they find us they'll come a-runnin'. Ain't no way back out of the mineshaft 'cept through the entrance. Ye can wager they'll put guards over that."

"Escape is all about the timin'," Adranis said. "We'll worry 'bout that *after* we get Master Oskarr's battle-axe."

"That ain't gonna be easy," Rassun said. "The goblinkin got creatures what helps 'em with the diggin'."

"What creatures?" Bulokk demanded.

14

Master Oskarr's Forge

"They call them Burrowers," Rassun said as they ran. "They look like giant worms. If worms had mouths big enough to swallow boulders the size of cows."

"How do they help the goblinkin with the diggin'?" Bulokk asked.

Rassun waved at the mineshaft. "Burrowers dug this mineshaft."

Wick glanced around at the mineshaft, which was at least eight feet in diameter. For the first time he saw how smooth the walls were. They hadn't been made by pickaxes. There were no tool marks. He thought back to the bestiaries and ecologies he'd read while at the Vault of All Known Knowledge.

Since he'd begun his journeys along the mainland, Wick had increasingly read more about flora and fauna and animals he'd found and would probably find there. Several of them he hoped he'd never meet, but there were others he looked forward to seeing.

But a Burrower? He'd never heard of a Burrower. At least not as the name of a species.

"When the goblinkin were first set to this task," Rassun said, "the thieves were unhappy with the amount of progress they were makin'. They brought over the first Burrower, then they brought over three more."

"What do they do?" Bulokk asked.

"They eat through the rock," Rassun said. "Faster than a pickaxe. 'Course, ye gotta clean up after 'em. They digest what minerals they want outta them rocks, then the rest passes on through."

"Ye mean ye're a-shoveling worm—"

"Aye," Rassun said. "But it ain't as grim as ye'd believe. They break the big rocks into little rocks. Most of 'em ain't no bigger than yer fist when they pass through."

"Does it stink?" Drinnick asked.

Wick couldn't believe they were running for their lives and the dwarven warrior thought to ask such a question.

"No," Rassun answered. "Ain't no foulness to it." Torchlight played across his emaciated face and showed the grimace carved there. "Leastways, ain't no foulness to it when them Burrowers just eats rocks. They eat a dwarf or an elf, it's a whole different tale I have to tell ye."

"Burrowers eat people?" Wick asked. Now that, he believed, was an important question to ask.

"Aye," Rassun said. "Burrowers eats flesh an' blood people like they was gingersnaps. One gulp an' a body's gone afore he even knows he's been et."

With all the wonders of the world, Wick wondered again why so many of the large ones seemed intent merely to eat everything else out there.

"What passes through a Burrower, the leavin's of a man or a beast," Rassun said, "why there ain't enough to fill a hat, there ain't. Bone chips. There's something in a person or an animal that don't quite agree with them. An' once they get the taste of blood, why Burrowers becomes a danger to the goblinkin for days. They have to keep 'em penned up till they forget they ever had the taste of flesh an' blood. 'Course, Burrowers, they ain't exactly long on memory."

"Left," Rohoh announced when they came upon another choice of three tunnels.

Bulokk took the lead, thrusting his torch into the opening and following it down. Wick's attention was divided as he saw still more stones that had once been part of Master Oskarr's town. The little Librarian's heart ached to pass up all the treasures from the past without even taking time to make rubbings of the stones.

"Where did they get the Burrowers?" Wick asked.

"Ain't exactly sure," Rassun answered. "There's a rumor that some wizard magicked 'em up fer the thieves' guild."

So they might not even be natural creatures, Wick thought. He immediately felt better about his lack of knowledge about the Burrowers. He had friends among the elven warders on Greydawn Moors and often talked with them about their creatures and others they'd seen or heard of in their own craft.

"How much farther?" Bulokk asked.

Clinging to Wick's shoulder and hair, Rohoh said, "Not much. We're almost there."

The band kept running through the darkness.

All the while, Wick wondered if the other escapees had made it over the ridge and if the dwarves Bulokk had posted there were canny enough to hold what they had. Even then, they'd have to have a lot of luck to take one of the goblinkin ships without getting killed.

Wick fretted over how things would eventually turn out. Then he realized he might not even live long enough to find out.

Long minutes later, the mineshaft Rohoh directed them to opened up into a large chamber. Given that they'd been running steadily downhill for nearly the whole time, Wick knew they were well below sea level. He didn't like thinking about that.

But his fears quickly evaporated as Bulokk held his torch high and revealed the surroundings. The torchlight didn't reach far enough to reveal the rest of the chamber, but if it was anything like what Wick saw before him it would have been an impressive sight.

Elegantly made buildings, homes as well as shops, stood out from the cave walls. The dwarven structures had been carved from quarried rock that was bluish-white and no match at all for the reddish-alabaster of the native stone.

"They used different stone to make the city," Bulokk said in awe.

"They did," Wick agreed. "I'd forgotten." Holding his torch high, he walked to the nearest building and ran his hand along the smooth sides of the stone. "Back when Hammer Cove's homestone was laid—"

"Homestone?" Rassun asked.

Wick looked at the dwarf in disbelief. How could a dwarf not know his roots? Then the little Librarian realized how much had truly been lost in the Cataclysm.

"A homestone," Adranis said in a voice filled with quiet reverence, "was the first stone laid of the first building built in a true dwarven city. A lot of thinking went into it, into the making of it, because it carried the hopes and dreams of the dwarves who built it. They carved images of history, legend, and aspirations on all six sides of the homestone and imbued it with all their love."

Adranis's voice carried throughout the empty space, indicating just how large it was.

"Then," Bulokk said, "the homestone was laid as cornerstone of the first building an' the city began."

"That's correct," Wick said. "As I was saying, back when Hammer Cove's homestone was laid, the builders decided to choose a rock not overly natural to the area. They wanted stone that could be found wherever there were dwarves. So they chose this." He tapped the rock and it made a hollow sound. "Limestone. Wherever there is a dwarven city, there is generally limestone. Even here in the Cinder Clouds Islands."

"But ye don't find much of it here in the islands," Adranis said.

Wick nodded. "Still, they quarried some of it. For the rest, though, they took in donations. Together, they built a city for all dwarves who wanted to learn to forge in the heart of a volcano."

"Volcano?" Rohoh piped up. "I suppose that's why I feel so hot."

For the first time, Wick noticed the heat as well. He'd been too overcome with worry and fear to be aware of it earlier.

"We're sitting on top of a volcano, aren't we?" the skink demanded.

"Aye," Bulokk said. He raked a massive arm across his sweating brow. "It is gettin' a mite heated in here."

"It's the forge," Rassun said. "It's still operational."

"Master Oskarr's forge?" Bulokk whispered.

"Aye." Rassun smiled grimly. "I been a miner all me life. Wasn't one to ever be overly interested in the makin' of things. I prefer findin' them in the earth. Give me a rich vein of gold or a gem mine, an' I'm happy as can be. But I ain't no blacksmith. Nor did I ever wish to be."

Following Rohoh's directions, the group of dwarves and Wick walked through the center of Hammer Cove. The buildings were three and four stories tall, straight and square. Many of them showed signs of stress fractures that ran through the stone, but nearly all of them were whole. But there were obvious places where others had once stood.

Since there were no pieces of buildings in the main walkways or in the buildings, Wick assumed that the goblinkin had ordered the area cleaned. He hated thinking about all the things that had been thrown away. Much about the past could always be told through everyday utensils in addition to books and records.

"I helped clear some of this area," Rassun said. "When I was first brought here. The goblinkin had most of it done by that time. It took a long time. When the goblinkin found out there were buildings here, an' they was likely to be them what held Master Oskarr's forge, they didn't want anything damaged. They kept the Burrowers out then, 'cause the Burrowers woulda et everything in sight."

"This was all cleared by hand?" Wick asked.

"Way I heard it," Rassun said, "this area was kept pretty much like this. Like a big bubble formed over most of it an' kept it mostly from harm durin' the Cataclysm, an' fer a while when it was under the sea."

"A bubble?" Bulokk repeated.

"Aye," Rassun said.

"It could have been caused by the heat of the forge," Wick mused. "If the volcano that fed the forge didn't erupt, that might explain it."

"I was also told Master Oskarr's forge was protected by magic," Bulokk said. "I heard that a wizard put a protective glamour over the forge."

"I don't know about that," Wick said. "Dwarves, as a general rule, don't hold with magic."

"But we're inspired by luck at times," Bulokk said. "I could see a dwarf wantin' a bit of good luck for his forge, especially with his family's fortunes an' well-being tied to it."

Only a short distance farther on, with Rohoh growing more excited with every step, Wick and the dwarves found themselves standing in front of an arched doorway that stood ten feet tall, an impressive height to a dwarf, though not so much to a human.

Engravings and writing stood out on the beautiful stonework. The engravings showed images of war and weapons, of brave warriors locked in battles where they'd just cut down enemies and ferocious beasts while dressed in beautiful armor and carrying splendid weapons.

The writing over the doorway simply bore the legend: *Welcome to Master Oskarr's Forge. If you're a friend, you have nothing to fear. If you're an enemy, may you die on one of our finely crafted weapons.* Baldly stated, but there it was.

Inspired by their good fortune, the dwarves took fresh grips on their weapons and strode through the forge entrance. It was smaller than Wick thought it would be. From the descriptions of the forge, he'd believed it would be huge, a vast series of anvils, one after the other. It was said that Master Oskarr had an anvil for every piece of armor that he made. Of course, Wick had mistrusted that piece of information because dwarves learned how to make everything they ever wanted to primarily on one anvil.

Without the ringing of dwarven hammers against metal, the forge seemed surreal, unfinished. Cracks ran the length of the floor, testifying to the elemental forces that had ripped through the city as lava covered it. Despite the goblinkin's orders to clean the area, gray ash still collected on most surfaces.

At the far side of the room, a pit of molten lava burned red-gold behind a cracked stone wall. The heat rolled over Wick and covered him in sweat at once. The lava stirred restlessly, like a baker's bread dough, constantly folding into itself as the top cooled and the hotter liquid rock below bubbled up to take its place.

Anvils lay tumbled from the specially carved stone

tables. Engravings decorated each of the tables, making each unique.

As if under some spell, the dwarves slowly made their way through the forge, touching each anvil and each stone table in awe. Mesmerized as well, Wick followed them. His quick hands darted over the engravings.

Unable to help himself, he took out his journal and began taking quick sketchings, but only of images that he didn't recognize or couldn't tie into one of the dwarven stories he'd been told. None of the dwarves even took an interest in him.

"We were sent here to get Master Oskarr's battle-axe," Rohoh said.

"I know," Wick said. "But—but—*this* is *history*." Journal in one hand and charcoal in the other, he gestured at the forge. "Can you even imagine the armor and weapons that came from this place? The blacksmiths that toiled here? Can you imagine what their lives were like? The hardships they had to endure?"

"Getting attacked by Lord Kharrion was probably pretty bad," the skink mused. "Probably even worse than if the goblinkin and those thieves catch the lot of us down here in this forge."

Wick craned his head around to face the skink. He focused on the lizard's face, then remembered again the danger they were in. There was, after all, only one way out of the forge.

"Where is Master Oskarr's axe?" Wick asked.

"There." Rohoh pointed toward the bubbling lava.

"Where?"

"In the forge."

Wick regarded the molten mass. "It can't be. If the axe were in there, it'd be melted to slag by now."

"It's not."

Although he didn't want to believe it, Wick put his

journal and charcoal away. Slowly, he made his way through the overturned anvils and studied the lava pit.

"Where are ye a-goin', halfer?" Adranis growled.

"To find the axe," Wick replied, his mind searching desperately for a way the skink's words could be true. Even dwarven-forged iron couldn't stand the heat of lava. Especially not a thousand years and more of it.

Wick's announcement drew everyone's attention. They abandoned whatever had distracted them and fell in with him. Close up to the rolling lava, the torches were no longer necessary because the bright glow filled the immediate surroundings.

"Where's the axe?" Bulokk demanded.

"He says it's in the forge," Wick answered.

The expressions on the dwarven faces around him told him at once that they didn't believe him.

Wick took an involuntary step back from them and pointed to the skink. "He's the one saying it. Not me."

Bulokk cursed. "Only a fool would believe that. Ain't no way even Master Oskarr's axe would escape bein' burnt to a crisp."

"It's there," Rohoh insisted. He slithered to the end of Wick's arm, then sprang to the low lip of the retaining wall holding the molten lava back. "I *smell* it. And I'm never wrong."

"Nobody's ever never wrong," Adranis said.

"Well," the lizard mused, scratching his chin in thought, "there was that one time in the Wizard Ekkal's treasure room that I was . . . incorrect. But how was I supposed to know that the Cup of Weligan had been turned into a person? I mean, that just hadn't been done before. In the end, though, I was right and just didn't know it."

Together, Wick and all the dwarves peered closely into the lava pit. Wick got so close the heat nearly blistered his face. Tears filled his eyes and dropped into the lava. They hissed into steam before they even reached the molten rock.

Suddenly, Drinnick yelped. He danced away from the lava pit, flailing with his free hand at the flames in his beard from where he'd gotten too close. The smell of burning hair filled the air. By the time he'd reduced the flames to smoking patches, his once beautiful beard was a charred mess.

Angry, he raised his axe and strode toward Rohoh. "Ye vexin' little varmint! Why I oughtta pound ye into jelly, I should! An' mayhap I will at that!"

"Wick!" the lizard squeaked, scampering along the wide lip of the retaining wall.

"You're on your own," Wick told the skink.

With incredible athletic ability, the lizard leaped and caught hold of the smooth wall. His claws managed to find precarious holds and he scampered up toward the roof and stopped out of Drinnick's reach. He stuck his tongue out, cursed, and waved a threatening clawed fist.

Wick ignored them and turned his mind to solving the puzzle. If Rohoh was right, and there was no reason other than logic that dictated the skink was wrong, then Master Oskarr's axe lay somewhere in the lava pit.

"What are ye a-lookin' fer?" Bulokk asked.

"Aren't there tongs somewhere?" Wick asked. "Isn't the metal heated and softened by plunging it into the lava?"

"Aye," Bulokk said. "That's one of the secrets of a lava pit. Fire-hardenin' the metal is a lot easier." He started looking around as well. "An' they did use tongs. An' a sieve in case somethin' were dropped." He raised his voice and gave orders to his men to find those tools.

They scattered with their torches. Even Drinnick abandoned his pursuit of the skink to help.

15

Unwanted Truth

𝒯he tools, tongs, and the sieve—all equipped with long metal poles encased with wooden handgrips at the end—were quickly found. Bulokk and some of the others began sorting through the lava pit, but they had to frequently stop because even with the wooden grips to cut down on the heat transfer, the metal got too hot.

Hodnes was even able, through the use of padded gloves and iron will, to leave one set of tongs in so long that the metal turned liquid and dripped off at the end. The other dwarves cursed and slapped Hodnes for ruining one of their tools.

"It's no use, halfer," Bulokk said after a while. "If that axe is in there, it ain't comin' out." He spat. "This is a fool's errand, is what it is. I just hope them prisoners got away of a piece."

And I hope we can do the same, Wick thought. "The axe has got to be there."

"It can't be here," Rassun said, coming over to them. "I tell ye, them goblinkin's been all over this area. After them Burrowers uncovered this part of the city, especially when they found the forge, they went over every inch of it. If Master Oskarr's axe had been here, they'd have found it."

Wick's mind examined all the angles, looking for a

lever. He lifted his torch and gazed at the anvils. "Where is Master Oskarr's anvil?"

"Over here." Bulokk led the way to one of the anvils.

Rather than the pristine thing he'd thought it would be, Wick saw a battered, much-used anvil sitting on the floor. The anvil arms were still straight, and every line looked as though it planed true. But stamped on the sides, the design still bravely cut, was Master Blacksmith Oskarr's forge mark. The design showed a hammer upright over an anvil, declaring the owner to be a full master of title and rank, with Oskarr's name and the Cinder Clouds Islands symbol below.

"Where's his table?" Wick asked when he found that the anvil was devoid of further illustration. Evidently Master Oskarr hadn't cared much for bragging.

A quick search ensued before Adranis found the table. "Here," he called.

The table lay on its side. A corner was chipped from it, but otherwise it was unharmed. Soot and ash covered much of its surface.

After tearing a sleeve from his shirt, Wick set to work cleaning all the images.

"Is there anythin' there about the Battle of Fell's Keep?" Bulokk demanded.

"No," Wick answered. And he couldn't help thinking how strange that was. Had Master Oskarr deliberately chosen not to reveal anything about that fight? Were the rumors true? The little Librarian sincerely hoped not.

Then, in small writing around the edge of the table, barely discernible in the torchlight, Wick found the newest entry, dated over a thousand years ago.

"What is it ye've found?" Bulokk knelt beside the little Librarian.

"This is the last entry on the table," Wick said. "It's written in an archaic dwarven tongue. The old language of the Ringing Iron Clan in the Iron Hammer Peaks."

"Master Oskarr's ma was from the Ringing Iron Clan," Bulokk said. "But I never heard of the Iron Hammer Peaks."

"They're called the Broken Forge Mountains now," Wick said idly. He translated the inscription with no little difficulty. The Ringing Iron Clan had always been small. "In addition to destroying Teldane's Bounty—which is now renamed the Shattered Coast—Lord Kharrion also made a deal with the dragon Shengharck to take over the Iron Hammer Peaks. The dragon lived there." He paused, remembering the dragon's treasure lair at the heart of the volcano where he and Cobner had fought for their lives. "Until very recently."

"The Ringing Iron Clan worked metal in volcanoes as well," Bulokk said.

"Yes." Wick nodded. "But they were never as successful as the Iron Hammer Peaks Clan. Many of the Ringing Iron Clan was apprenticed by the Iron Hammer Peaks Clan."

"That's how Master Oskarr's ma was born out here," Bulokk said. "But all I knew was that a few dwarven blacksmiths from near Teldane's Bounty ended up on the shores of the Cinder Clouds Islands. I don't remember anything being said about the Iron Hammer Peaks." He leaned in closer to Wick. "Can ye read it then, halfer?"

Satisfied with his translation, Wick started over at the beginning and read aloud in his best voice. " 'Let it be known that we are facing the end. Lord Kharrion has come calling for us, and we are all prepared to die this day. Let none say there were cowards among us, because we all stand prepared to shed our life's blood fighting the Goblin King. We are not merely blacksmiths, but we are warriors, too.' "

"Aye," Bulokk whispered, "they was. An' fierce ones, too."

" 'I fought Lord Kharrion's forces at the Battle of Fell's

Keep.' " Wick's heart raced as the translation came faster and easier. " 'There we were betrayed.' "

"They *was* betrayed!" Bulokk said. "There's proof enough fer ye that it wasn't Master Oskarr who betrayed the Unity!"

Wick didn't agree with that assessment, but he wisely kept his thoughts to himself. He wasn't fleet of foot enough to scamper to the top of the room as Rohoh had been. He continued with the translation.

" 'My axe,' " Wick read, " 'that I forged myself under the watchful eye of my da, Master Blacksmith Farrad, was cursed during that battle.' "

"*Cursed!*" Bulokk exploded. He grabbed Wick roughly by the shoulder and shook him, feet dangling above the ground. "What do ye mean the axe was cursed?"

Out of self-defense, Wick grabbed onto the dwarf's big hand. "I don't know. I'm just reading this part, too." He looked into Bulokk's eyes and saw the fear and hatred there, whipped into flames by the orange glow of the lava furnace. "Let me finish, Bulokk. This is what I do. For good or ill, this is what I can do."

"I don't want to hear Master Oskarr's good name sullied," Bulokk said harshly. His statement was a threat in Wick's ears.

"I know," Wick whispered. "I don't know what that inscription says, but I could lie to you." He paused. "If that's what you want." Hanging above the ground as he was, the little Librarian had to admit to himself that he'd have told the dwarven leader anything he wanted to hear at that moment.

Adranis stepped forward and put an arm around Bulokk. He looked at the younger dwarf and spoke calmly. "Is that what ye want, Bulokk? A lie? Even if it's a good one?"

Bulokk didn't take his eyes from Wick. "This was a mistake," the dwarf choked out. "We shouldn't ever have come here."

"Likely as not, there's a lot of freed slaves out there that don't feel all we done this night was for naught," Adranis said. "We done forged some good outta tonight. Freed them prisoners. Killed some goblinkin. No matter what else happens, we done that." He took a measured breath. "Now ye decide what ye want: the truth or the lie. An' try not to scare this little halfer so much that he ain't got him enough backbone to give ye the truth if it is bad."

Wick hung helplessly at the end of Bulokk's arm. *Where are Craugh and* One-Eyed Peggie*? It can't get any worse than this!*

Slowly, Bulokk uncurled his fingers and let Wick drop to the stone floor. The little Librarian's knees were shaking so bad that he fell on his rump.

"The truth then, halfer," Bulokk growled. "An' I'll know if'n ye try to lie to me."

"The truth," Adranis said, reaching down to help Wick to his feet. "Bulokk's made of stern stuff. He can take it."

Trembling, Wick turned back to the inscription. He traced his finger along it, finding his place. "'I didn't know about the curse till later,'" Wick read. "'We were too busy escaping, running for our lives after the sickness took so many of us and rendered so many others unable to fight. Then, back on the Cinder Clouds Islands and once more in this forge, I began to have nightmares of Lord Kharrion. He and others whom I can't name tried to talk to me. Every day their voices became more clear.'"

Bulokk growled.

Wick lifted his hands, covering his head and thinking that wouldn't truly help because then his head would be lopped off only with his hands holding onto it. He closed his eyes.

The blow didn't come.

"Continue," Adranis stated quietly, stepping up to place himself between Wick and Bulokk.

Wick didn't know if Adranis was there to reassure him,

which he did, a little, or to stop Bulokk in case he couldn't control himself—which kind of wiped out all the reassurance. He turned back to the inscription, driven as much by curiosity as survival.

" 'Afraid of the nightmares, I tried to destroy the axe,' " Wick went on. " 'You will never know how hard this was to contemplate, let alone try to accomplish. The axe, *my* axe, would not break or bend on my anvil no matter how hard I tried. The magic that had infected it had become too much a part of it.' "

Silence hung over the dwarves. Wick was certain that none of them could imagine trying to destroy something they had worked so hard to make. That was a true horror for them, and the curse only made the story more horrific.

" 'In despair, I sank the axe into the lava furnace and hoped that Lord Kharrion's forces wouldn't find it there. The axe,' " Wick read, " 'was one of the main reasons the goblinkin invaded the Cinder Clouds Islands.' "

"They came fer the axe," Hodnes said.

"An' they're still here today a-lookin' fer it," Drinnick said.

The fact amazed them all.

There is so much Craugh didn't tell me about this task, Wick thought. But he focused on the words and continued his translation. " 'Years ago, my da, Master Blacksmith Farrad, made home of this forge to an elemental being named Merjul. He is a fire elemental, one of those few oddities that exist even after the Darkling Times that came before Lord Kharrion, when it was said the Old Ones warred and destroyed several of the worlds they had created.' "

"An elemental?" one of the dwarves whispered. "There's no tellin' what one of them things will do. Likely as not, it'll melt ye down in yer tracks as look at ye."

Wick sincerely hoped not because he knew Bulokk wouldn't be able to let the matter rest. " 'Unless Merjul has died in Lord Kharrion's attack, he will still remain there. If you are of my blood, if you know the names of your ancestors, then you may call upon Merjul and he will bring you the axe from the fiery depths. Have a care, though, for the axe is cursed. My only wish is that you find a way to free it because it is the most beautiful weapon I've ever hammered out upon my anvil.' " He looked up at Bulokk. "It's signed, 'Master Blacksmith Oskarr.' "

Without a word, Bulokk crossed to the lava furnace. "Merjul!" he spoke in a loud voice.

Drawn by curiosity but well basted in fear, Wick followed. He stood beside Bulokk, hoping that the dwarven leader wasn't drawing down the wrath of an elemental. Not many lived through such a thing.

"Merjul!" Bulokk called again, impatient this time.

At first, the surface of the lava pit merely continued to roil. Then, out in the center, something *moved*. Lava elongated in a bubble, then suddenly popped and a fearsome, hulking creature stood atop the lava.

Elementals, Wick knew, could take myriad shapes. All of those shapes were fluid, based more on power than on any kind of skeletal frame. That was only one of the things that made them so hard to destroy.

Merjul stood at least nine feet tall, fiery skin smooth as worn stone and the color of ochre. The facial features were ill-defined, consisting only of two eyes and a mouth like a slash. Reflections of shimmering heat twisted against his skin. He faced Bulokk.

"Who are you?" the elemental asked in a deep, sonorous voice.

"I am Bulokk, descendant of Master Blacksmith Oskarr, come to claim his axe," Bulokk declared.

Wick took a tentative step back. Being intrigued, he'd often found, was something akin to having a death wish.

The elemental appeared unimpressed. "The axe was

left with me. That you know my name is one thing, but I was told a true descendant would know all Master Blacksmith Oskarr's lineage. He said that his descendant would know that."

"I do know the lineage," Bulokk declared.

"Then give it to me," the elemental challenged. "And know that if you fail, you will die."

"I am Bulokk, son of Farrad, son of Thumak, son of Azzmod, son of—"

"You're an imposter!" the elemental shouted. The fiery eyes narrowed and the slit of a mouth tightened in anger. "You don't know the lineage." Bending, he reached down into the lava and cupped a handful of molten rock. With the speed of a thought, the lava shot out in both directions and became a heavy war spear with a flared head. He poised to throw it, and there was no doubt that his target was Bulokk.

Bulokk raised his shield, which—in Wick's opinion—seemed like a pathetic thing to do. It was obvious that the elemental would strike the dwarf down.

The other dwarves scattered, except for Adranis, who chose to remain at Bulokk's side.

"Wait!" Wick yelled. Of course, he regretted speaking at once. It was evident that his mind responded much more quickly to solutions to puzzles than to self-preservation.

However, the elemental paused. "Who are you?" the creature demanded imperiously.

"Nobody, but I know why you believe Bulokk is an imposter. Which he isn't."

"He doesn't know the lineage," Merjul insisted.

"*You*," Wick said, "don't know the lineage."

"I was taught—"

"You were taught what the lineage was back in Master Oskarr's time," Wick interrupted, fearing that the elemental would choose to strike at any moment. "But a thousand years have passed since Master Oskarr met his fate in these islands."

Merjul seemed undecided for a moment. He kept the spear resting easily on his shoulder. "A thousand years," he mused. "Truthfully, I didn't count how long I've been here. Time holds no meaning to someone such as I. Even with the sun to mark its passage, I often don't pay attention. Oskarr's friendship, though it lasted years, seems like such a brief thing."

"This," Wick said, "is Master Oskarr's descendant. Blood of his blood. And if you gave your word to Master Oskarr, then you are honor-bound to Bulokk as well."

"Perhaps," Merjul agreed. He shifted his attention to Bulokk. "Tell me the lineage again."

Wick turned to Bulokk. "Again. Only this time begin with Master Oskarr."

Bulokk did. In spite of his fear, his voice rang out clear and strong as he worked back through the dwarven genealogy. At last he was finished, and everyone stood pensive, awaiting the elemental's judgment.

"You are as you claim," Merjul said. "You shall have your ancestor's battle-axe." The thin mouth curved into a frown. "I have to tell you, though, I will be glad to be rid of it. It's been a discomfort the whole time it's been here. The curse laid upon it is a powerful thing." He dropped the lava spear, which took back its original shape, and held forth his empty hand.

A tendril of lava plopped up, then grew like a vine. In its coils was a beautiful dwarven battle-axe. With careless strength, the elemental flung the weapon at Bulokk.

Wick ducked back, watching as Bulokk effortlessly caught the great axe. He fully expected to hear the dwarf yell out in anguish from the super-heated metal.

But Bulokk didn't. He acted as though the axe wasn't hot at all. Awe filled his face as he gazed upon the mirror brightness of the finish. Even after all those years in the lava pit, the wooden haft wasn't scorched. "By the Old Ones!" he gasped. "I have never seen such a blade!"

Merjul smiled. "Now I know for certain you are Master Oskarr's kith and kin. You share his love for the craft."

"With all me heart," Bulokk agreed.

Bowing, the fire elemental said, "Then I am glad I could keep my promise."

"Thank ye," Bulokk said, smiling. "I know me words ain't enough, but they're all I have. If'n ye ever need anything that I can ever help ye with, let me know."

If we live, Wick thought, remembering the goblinkin even now searching the mineshafts for them.

"Use the battle-axe in good health," Merjul said. "My friend would have wanted that." His face darkened. "But beware the curse. Master Oskarr wanted to trust no one except his own family with the weapon because of that curse."

"Why have you never left here?" Wick asked, unable to curb his curiosity.

"My promise to Master Oskarr held me here," Merjul answered. "Now that I have fulfilled that obligation, I am free to go."

"How?" Wick asked. "You can't travel except through the fire routes."

The elemental smiled. "I can travel. When I wish to. I can walk through the lava rivers that reach under the sea to the mainland, or I can become a candle flame and travel in a lantern. For now, though, I'll explore what's to be had here in the islands. Many things have changed since Lord Kharrion brought his destruction here."

"Wait!" Wick cried. "I have other questions!" *How often do you get to talk to an elemental face-to-face?* Without *dying*?

"This isn't exactly time for a parlor room conversation," Rohoh said. The skink ran across the ceiling and dropped back to Wick's shoulder, curling a claw in his hair at once.

"Another time, perhaps," the elemental said. Then he dropped into the lava and disappeared. The molten rock dimmed at his passing and Wick knew he was gone.

"Well then," Bulokk said, "I suppose it's time we should be findin' out if'n that escape attempt we planned for the prisoners is workin' out. Luck willing, they should be around the island by now." He slung his own battle-axe and shield, and took up his ancestor's, giving it an experimental swing. "By the Old Ones but this is a fine weapon." He smiled in pleased satisfaction, then took off at a trot.

Wick followed, falling into the middle of the group of dwarves, hoping that they all remained safe. That hope was quickly shattered, though. Only a few tunnels back, surely not even halfway back to the entrance, they were discovered by a goblinkin patrol.

"Halt!" a goblinkin ordered.

Turning, peering between the dwarves, Wick saw nearly twenty goblinkin in a pack just coming out of the mineshaft they needed to pass through in order to get out of the mine.

"There can't be more'n twenty of 'em," Adranis said. "I like the odds just fine."

Apparently so did the other six dwarves. They hefted their weapons. Then another goblinkin patrol closed on them from behind. Wick quickly verified that there were nearly twenty in that group as well.

"By the Old Ones," Adranis said, "most of the goblinkin must have been sent into the mine after us."

"This whole setup has been to secure the return of Master Oskarr's axe," Wick said. "It makes sense that they would safeguard that first."

"Well, it's to our rotten luck," Drinnick snarled. "Twenty goblinkin we could account for. Forty is pressin' the limit."

"In here," Bulokk said, dodging into the mineshaft to his right.

"No!" Rassun cried.

But it was too late. The dwarves, and Wick, had already plunged into the new mineshaft.

"This shaft holds the pens for the Burrowers!"

16

Burrowers!

Oy the Old Ones!" Adranis shouted, coming to a stop in front of Wick.

Unable to stop so quickly, Wick ran into the dwarf's backside and fell backward, tripping Hodnes.

"Stupid halfer tanglefoot!" Hodnes yelped. "Walkin' ain't that hard to—"

From the way the dwarf stopped in mid-deprecation, Wick assumed Hodnes had gotten his first sight of the Burrowers, too. It did take the breath away.

The torches lit up the large chamber surprisingly well. Or maybe it only seemed like that because the Burrowers could be seen well enough to inspire instant nightmares.

They were at least thirty feet long and nine feet in diameter, and they lay in a writhing mess at the bottom of a twenty-foot pit. A narrow ledge ran around the pit, but it went in an irregular oval, leaving only the one entrance to the chamber.

Their pale pink and cream skins looked tough as leather but gave them a deceptively harmless appearance. They had no eyes or ears or nostrils, only a huge gaping maw that opened the full diameter of their bodies so they looked on the verge of turning themselves inside out.

Rows of serrated teeth occupied the thick purple tongues that showed in the vast hollows of their mouths.

The tongues moved out again and again, like battering rams. Nets made of metal links covered the Burrowers' mouths/faces, though, and every time the tongues came in contact with the net, the tongues would withdraw at once. Chains attached to the nets were locked onto stakes driven deeply into the stone floor of the chamber.

"They can't chew through them metal nets," Rassun said. "An' the goblinkin put some kind of foul-tastin' brew on the net links to keep 'em from tryin'."

"How do they control them?" Wick asked.

"Got riders," Rassun said. "Humans with some kind of magical talisman what allows them to control the Burrowers. A little bit, anyways. If'n nobody watches after these beasties all the time, why they'll get loose an' wander off on their own. It's hard bringin' 'em back under control."

Wick didn't doubt that. What he had trouble believing was that anyone could exercise any control at any time. He pressed against the wall so hard that the stone dug into his back.

"Ain't any way forward," Bulokk said, face grimy and grim in the torchlight. He nodded back toward the entrance. "Gotta go back through them goblinkin."

Evidently the goblinkin knew that, too. They stood in the doorway, waiting and grinning in anticipation.

"There's only one way we're getting out of here alive," Rohoh yelled into Wick's ear.

Wick had forgotten the skink was riding there. "What?"

"We've got to set a Burrower free," Rohoh said. "Let it chase the goblinkin back."

Wick peered over the side of the pit. "I'm not going down there."

"Why would ye go down there?" Adranis asked, not taking his eyes from the goblinkin.

"The lizard says we should free one of the Burrowers to chase the goblinkin," Wick said.

Peering over the side, Adranis shook his head. "It's just as likely to chase us as them." The other dwarves quickly agreed.

"I've seen what them things can do to flesh an' blood," Rassun said. "I ain't goin' down there."

"We don't have a lot of time to mess about," Rohoh said.

Without warning, white-hot pain flooded Wick's ear. It took him a second to realize that the skink had bitten him, managing to hit one of the few nerves in the ear. Screaming with pain, he tried to knock the skink loose, but it only chomped down harder and tore at his ear. Before Wick knew it, he stepped over the side and fell.

Noooooooooo! Then he hit something hard and leathery, spongy like a melon gone bad. Panicked, totally afraid that he knew exactly where he was, he rolled from his back to his stomach. His torch lay farther down on the ground, burning against the stone floor and driving the four Burrowers away from it. They didn't like heat. He filed that away for future reference even as he plastered his face up against the hide of the Burrower he was currently on.

Then light from other torches flooded the pit as the dwarves and the goblinkin peered down at him. Wick looked around, feeling the Burrower shifting beneath him. He didn't know if he was on top of the creature or clinging to its belly. Maybe it didn't even make those kinds of distinctions.

One thing he became certain of: The Burrower didn't like him on it.

"What are ye a-doin' down there, halfer?" Bulokk demanded. "Ye're gonna get yerself killed! Get back up here!"

For the first time Wick noticed that most of the pain in

his ear was gone. The skink had stopped biting him, but it hadn't been lost in the fall. Rohoh clung tightly to his shoulder and hair again, digging his claws in deep.

"Come on, halfer!" the skink cried out. "Get up there and free this thing before the goblinkin kill those dwarves!"

Wick didn't think about freeing the Burrower or saving the dwarves. He only knew he wanted off the gigantic creature, and that the head was probably safer than anywhere else.

Grabbing fistfuls of the Burrower's leathery hide, the little Librarian pulled himself forward. If he reached the head, he was certain he could leap back to the ledge. Falling would no doubt mean instant death, crushed beneath the raw tonnage of the writhing creatures.

By the light of the torches held by the anxious dwarves, Wick reached the chain net that guarded the Burrower's maw. The creature felt him there then, and it gentled somewhat.

It thinks I'm its rider! Wick couldn't believe it, but he took advantage of his good fortune. He gripped the chain and prepared to leap to the ledge. Unfortunately, at that moment the Burrower chose to shift, maybe growing impatient. It shook its massive maw-end like a dog.

Wick tumbled down, scrabbling for a fresh hold, and caught the chain net again. Something clicked against his palm. When Wick looked up, he saw that he'd accidentally grabbed the locking mechanism. As he watched, the maw-net came loose.

"Move!" Rohoh yelled. "You're going to get us both eaten!"

Digging in with his bare toes, Wick climbed to the top of the Burrower again as the chain net fell away. The Burrower rose up immediately, twisting itself into a proud S shape and bugling like a moose—a very large, very angry moose. The sound filled the pit and the cavern.

Tensing like a bowstring, the Burrower lunged from the pit, sliding up the wall and over the ledge directly toward the doorway where the goblinkin were. Either it sensed the entrance or the goblinkin, or it remembered the direction. Wick had no clue. He clung on tightly, flattening himself against the Burrower's body, certain that he'd be scraped off on the entrance with every bone broken.

Instead, Wick sank down a little as the Burrower flattened its body and eased through the entrance. Goblinkin shouted in terror as the massive creature grabbed several of them with its maw and swallowed them whole. Immediately, the Burrower's teeth went to work, cutting and grinding, and its stomachs shivered into action.

Out in the main mineshaft, the Burrower took off in pursuit of the goblinkin fleeing down into the mine. Wick lost his hold and struggled to remain on top of the creature as it bounced and jarred beneath him. He finally gave up and wrapped an arm around his head and hoped he didn't have his brains bashed out or—Old Ones forbid!— end up *beneath* the Burrower.

Abruptly, Wick ran out of creature. He dropped off the posterior end and plopped to the floor. He landed in a pile of the foulest, gooiest mess he'd ever felt or smelled. As he tried to stand, his feet kept sliding out from under him.

The dwarves came out of the Burrowers' chamber with their axes and torches in hand.

"There he is!" Adranis shouted. "He's still alive!"

Wick finally got to his feet just as they arrived. Although they seemed happy enough to see that he was still alive, none of them wanted to touch him.

"That was a brave thing ye did, halfer," Bulokk said. "I don't think I coulda done that."

"Now you're a hero," Rohoh whispered into Wick's punctured ear.

Some hero, Wick thought sourly. *I'm battered and bruised, and have an ear that will probably never look right again, and I'm covered in—in—* He looked at the greenish paste that covered him from head to toe. Then he looked at Rassun.

"What is this?" Wick asked.

"Burrower leavin's," Rassun said solemnly.

Wick gazed back down at himself in disbelief.

"Goblinkin go right through 'em," Rassun said. "Told ye they digested fast. Goblinkin ain't no good for 'em nutritionally, but they do love to eat 'em. Like treats."

"Dung?" Wick cried. "I'm covered in goblinkin dung?" The foul stench nearly made him sick.

"It's not exactly goblinkin dung," Rassun said. "Though that's pretty foul, too. No, this here's Burrower dung. Usually it's rocks and suchlike. But this is, well, it's—"

"Right disgustin' is what it is," Adranis supplied.

Wick silently agreed. He wanted a hot bath with scented soap. He wanted a change of clothes. He wanted a book and a pipe, and to *never* be reminded that he'd once wallowed in Burrower poop made out of goblinkin.

The skink climbed down Wick, careful of where he trod. "If you don't mind," Rohoh said, "I'll manage on my own from here." The lizard was somehow miraculously clean of foulness.

"Come on," Bulokk said. "We've got an escape to attend." He trotted back up the mineshaft.

Wick took a moment and kicked as much of the dung from his feet as he could. He wished he had a stick to clean out between his toes, but he didn't. When he saw the dwarves leaving, he finally gave up and ran after them, avoiding the Burrower trail that had been left in the creature's wake.

Farther down the mineshaft, the goblinkin shrieked in terror, but the shrieks came less and less often.

They gained the front entrance without further incident, but there were ten goblinkin standing guard.

"Axes!" Bulokk yelled.

Immediately, Adranis, Hodnes, and Drinnick formed on Bulokk. The goblinkin tried to stand their ground, but they went down before the dwarven axes like wheat before a flail. The battle was short and vicious, with no mercy given to the goblinkin. Rassun and the other dwarf took on any that managed to escape the whirling death that was the dwarven axes. By the time they reached the entrance, all of them were covered in the blood of their foes.

Stumbling over the bodies of the fallen goblinkin, Wick peered outside. It took a moment for his eyes to adapt to the night.

"To the docks!" Bulokk roared, taking off at once. "They've made it around to the goblinkin ship!"

Glancing down, Wick saw that the escapees and the rest of Bulokk's warriors *had* made it around to the stone pier. A massive battle was taking place on the pier. Not all of the goblinkin had abandoned their posts to pursue the fleeing slaves.

Looking up, Wick saw that a number of dead goblinkin littered the stone steps leading up to the ridge. More of them had fallen to the hard-packed ground.

Wick followed the dwarves down the steps even though it meant running into the battle. He definitely didn't want to remain standing at the mine entrance by himself in case any goblinkin survived the Burrower's attack and decided to come out. Or if there were other groups that hadn't yet gone down before the Burrower.

Several of the loose rocks Wick had dumped down the steps remained and he had to be careful. Still, he slipped twice and ended up barely keeping himself from going over the edge, and he had new sets of bruises to show for his efforts.

When he reached the bottom of the steps, he was even with the dwarves. He was faster than they were, more sure-footed in spite of the falls he'd taken, and unburdened by armor.

Wick guessed that most of the prisoners had made good on their escape, because most of them appeared to be with Bulokk's warriors. They used weapons they'd taken along the way or picked up when they arrived at the harbor. Some of them threw rocks into the milled mass of goblinkin trying to keep the dwarves from reaching the anchored ships.

Within a few steps, the skink leaped onto Wick's leg and slithered up. At first Wick had started to beat the skink away, thinking that one of the dead goblinkin around him wasn't quite as dead as he'd looked. Then he recognized the lizard and relaxed a little.

"I guess maybe I don't stink so bad now," Wick said.

"I'm too short to wade through this makeshift battlefield," Rohoh replied. "I might get squished."

Maybe that wouldn't be a bad thing, Wick thought briefly, then chided himself for being so small-minded. Despite the skink's harsh nature, finding Master Oskarr's battle-axe would have been almost impossible without the creature given the logistics of the search.

Bulokk and his mineshaft team enjoyed a brief but telling advantage when they raced out of the darkness and slammed into the goblinkin warriors from behind without warning. The goblinkin went down in pieces, felled again and again by the dwarven battle-axes.

"Wick!" Bulokk roared, using his name for once instead of calling him *halfer*. "Get them women an' children to one of them ships! Adranis, you an' Drinnick give him a hand!" He was in the thick of the battle, standing

ankle-deep in the incoming tide, scattering dead goblinkin in all directions. But still they came. The dwarf
looked every inch the warrior, as at home on the battlefield as he would be at a blacksmith's anvil.

Wick looked around and spotted the women and children huddled in a mass on the other side of the stone pier.
He ran to them. "Quickly!" he cried. "We've got to get you
onto a ship! You have to hurry if you're going to have any
chance at all!"

"It's a halfer!" a woman grumbled. "I'm not going to
listen to a halfer!"

"Ye will!" Adranis thundered. "Elsewise we'll leave ye
here fer them goblinkin to lock up again!" He bristled angrily. "Now ye get on up here an' do as he says!"

The woman climbed to the top of the stone pier. Yelling
over the confusion, Wick organized a line that helped the
weaker adults and smaller children to the stone pier where
they were temporarily out of the way of the brunt of
the battle.

Looking over his shoulder, Wick saw that the goblinkin had already reorganized, taking a step back to put
both dwarven fronts ahead of them again. Now they were
once more pressing their superior numbers. Worse than
that, the human archers onboard the black ship had decided to weigh into the fight as well. Their shafts flew, but
they seemed to be indiscriminate about whether they hit
dwarves or goblinkin. Both were wounded and killed in
the fusillades, and confusion swept across the combatants.

Once he had the women and children behind him,
Wick led them to the goblinkin ship anchored on the
other side of the pier from the battle. Arrows sped toward
them as well, sometimes thunking into the stone pier and
sometimes hitting the goblinkin ship on the battle side.
Either way, the human archers from the black vessel were
aware of the attempted escape by ship.

What are they waiting on? Wick wondered as he helped the escapees on board. "Do any of you have sailing experience?" he yelled.

"Aye," an elderly human man said. He was long in years as humans went, with gray hair flowing down past his shoulders. Arthritis or old injury had rendered him largely infirm, and Wick knew the old man had probably only been days away from death by overwork or by execution once the goblinkin deemed his work wasn't enough to justify whatever meager amount they were feeding him to keep him barely alive. "I've sailed afore."

"You're the captain," Wick said, addressing the man like he would a Novice or a Third Level Librarian back at the Vault of All Known Knowledge. "Until you're relieved of command."

"Aye," the man replied, and immediately straightened his shoulders with the acceptance of the responsibility.

"Get a crew together and get us squared away," Wick called out. "I want to be able to leave as soon as we're able."

"You probably know as much about sailing as he does," Rohoh said.

"Probably," Wick admitted. "But most humans, dwarves, and elves would rather take orders from a human or a dwarf before they would an elf or a dweller." *Especially one covered in Burrower dung that had once been goblinkin.*

"Aye," the human replied enthusiastically. Instantly, he started separating the escapees into groups, those with sailing experience and those without.

When the last of the women, children, and elderly had been loaded aboard the ship, Wick glanced back at the dwarven front. Bulokk and his warriors were starting to crumble now. Two more of them were in the water, unmoving. Another had three arrows jutting from his chest but somehow still found the strength and courage to continue fighting.

"Bulokk!" Wick yelled.

Some of the human archers had quit the ship now, coming ashore in a longboat pulled by steady stroke. A tall man with a moon-white face under his bloodred cowl stood in the stern. He held a staff beside him.

That, Wick decided, *doesn't look good.* He scampered to the end of the stone pier, calling Bulokk's name again and again. But the dwarves couldn't disengage without exposing their backs to the goblinkin. Wick knew they would never make the distance to the ship.

The longboat with the humans landed.

"Back!" the man in the bloodred cowl roared.

Most of the goblinkin pulled away at the command, but there were some that didn't.

The man in the bloodred cowl waved. Instantly, the humans lifted their bows, drew, and fired in one smooth motion. The arrows cut through the goblinkin and dwarves alike. Seven goblinkin and two dwarves went down. Bulokk and two other dwarves remained standing, their bodies pierced by the arrows.

"Give me the axe," the man in the bloodred cowl ordered.

Bulokk drew a throwing knife from somewhere on his body and flicked it forward. The blade caught the moonslight as it whirled end over end.

The man in the bloodred cowl lifted a hand. The throwing knife stopped in midair less than an arm's length from the man. Casually, he flicked a hand and the knife shot back along the path it had come.

The blade took Bulokk high in the chest even as the dwarf strove to avoid the unexpected attack. Before he could recover, the man in the bloodred cowl gestured again, flinging his fingers wide as if flicking away a bothersome pest. In response, Bulokk went flying backward.

At another gesture, Master Oskarr's battle-axe suddenly flew upward. Bulokk tried to hang onto the weapon, blood streaming down him from his various wounds, but it was no use. Ultimately whatever magic the red-cowled man wielded was stronger than Bulokk's grip.

The battle-axe flew to the red-cowled man's hand. A grin split the moon-white face. Without a word, the wizard turned to go. The human archers closed ranks behind him and sent a few more shafts into the goblinkin and the dwarves.

Seeing that made Wick's heart sick as he took cover behind the stern of the goblinkin ship. But his keen vision also spied the identical tattoos under the right eyes of the archers: It was the black image of an unfolded straight razor overlaid with crimson lips.

No thieves' guild wears identifying marks, Wick thought. Then he remembered, from a book he'd borrowed from Hralbomm's Wing rather than a nonfiction source, that some thieves' guilds did mark their members. They were members of the elite, the special thieves that victims never saw and kings hired for clandestine missions or revenge.

But why would a thieves' guild be interested in Master Oskarr's battle-axe? How had they known where to find it? Questions tumbled through Wick's frantically jumping mind.

The goblinkin lay low while the thieves' guild members once more boarded their longboat and began rowing back to the black ship.

"C'mon, halfer," Adranis said at Wick's side. "We gotta go rescue them what's still alive."

Although he didn't want to, Wick went with Adranis and Drinnick. Hodnes brought up the rear. Wick couldn't sit idly by and watch the dwarves get killed even though he wanted to hide in fear for his own life.

They ran to the end of the stone pier and to the dwarves, humans, and elves that still stood and could wield weapons. Wick ran to Bulokk, who lay on his back with arrows and a knife sticking out of him. The little Librarian felt certain the dwarven leader would be dead.

Instead, Bulokk was in shock from his wounds and whatever mystical force had been used against him. His breath came in gasps as blood leaked out of him.

Even if we manage to get him out of here, Wick thought, *he's not going to live.* But Wick couldn't give up on Bulokk any more than the dwarf could quit laboring for his next breath.

Stepping behind the dwarf, Wick grabbed Bulokk's shirt and started trying to pull him toward the ship as arrows struck the ground around them. Having no other choice, Wick unhooked Bulokk's shield and stood guard over the fallen dwarf like any shieldmate would on a battlefield.

But Wick's thoughts were his own. *Please don't let me throw up,* he pleaded as his stomach swirled threateningly. *Heroes don't throw up on other heroes. I know I'm no hero, but I don't want to throw up on Bulokk. I'm already covered in Burrower dung—the worst kind of Burrower dung at that—and it just wouldn't be fair to be so inept.*

Slowly, inexorably, the goblinkin line advanced. Behind them, the black ship lifted its sails and raised anchor. It shifted, rolling on the tide, and got the wind behind it, heading into the fogbank that blew over the Rusting Sea.

Then, without warning, dwarven war horns trumpeted across the bay. The sound gave pause to the warriors battling on the beach.

Hunkered down behind Bulokk's shield, the wounded dwarf's breathing rasping in his ears, Wick gazed out to sea and saw the black ship slide right by *One-Eyed Peggie* as the pirate ship came into the harbor under full sail. The skull and crossbones fluttered under the topgallant.

"Pirates!" the goblinkin shouted.

Not just pirates, Wick thought with pride. *Those are*

*pirates of the Blood-Soaked Sea. They don't come any
more fierce!*

One-Eyed Peggie came about smartly, dropping anchor
and sail less than fifty paces away, evidently taking her
mark from the goblinkin ships floating at the pier. A longboat filled with dwarves smacked into the sea as a few of
the pirates with bow skills feathered the goblinkin with a
few shafts.

"Row!" Hallekk's lusty voice rolled across the sea.
"Row, ye seadogs, or by the Old Ones I'll dangle yer
corpses from the 'yards an' watch the gulls strip the flesh
from yer bones!"

Wick knew that the harsh words were more for benefit
of the onlookers than for the crew. Hallekk and the pirates wouldn't hesitate to give everything they had to rescue him.

Or maybe Master Oskarr's axe, Wick had to admit.

"Pirates?" Bulokk whispered weakly.

"Not pirates," Wick assured the dwarf. "You're among
friends, Bulokk. Hallekk and his bunch, why, they'll set
things to rights soon enough."

Bulokk's eyes closed, and for a moment Wick thought
he'd lost the dwarf. Then Bulokk whispered, "That man
took Master Oskarr's axe."

"I know," Wick said, watching as goblinkin dropped
from bowshots and tried to get reorganized. "But we're
not finished with that either, I'll wager." *Craugh won't let
this go*.

In the next moment, the two longboats bearing Hallekk
and the pirates arrived. The dwarven pirates jumped boat
at once and ripped their axes free, wading into the goblinkin with a ferocity that sparked a second wind from
those Bulokk had called in to battle.

Horrified but mesmerized at the same time, Wick
watched Hallekk walk into the thick of it. The big dwarf
whooped and hollered in a properly piratical fashion as

his axe lashed out again and again. The crew of *One-Eyed Peggie* hated slavers, too.

In a short time, the goblinkin line broke. Survivors ran screaming for the stone steps. Hallekk and the pirates pursued them all the way to the ridge, managing to catch a few of their opponents, killing them outright or sending them plunging into broken heaps at the bottom of the cliff.

"Just stay with me," Wick told Bulokk. "Everything's going to be all right." He took the dwarf's hand and held on tight, hoping for the best because his grip was stronger than Bulokk's. "Just stay with me."

epilogue

The Razor's Kiss

"W<small>ick.</small>"

Certain that he had to be dreaming that voice and that no one would be trying to wake him, Wick rolled over and nearly fell out of his hammock. He caught himself just in time, his heart threatening to explode in his chest. Angry and embarrassed, he turned to whoever had called for him.

"What do you think you're doing?" he demanded. "Don't you realize that I've nearly been killed several times in the last few days and—" He stopped at once when he saw who the offender was.

Scowling, Craugh stood in the small crew's room and looked at Wick.

I'm going to be a toad, Wick thought morosely. Still, he couldn't go down without pleading for his life. "I'm sorry. I didn't know it was you."

"Of course you didn't," Craugh said. "You've barely had enough sleep to know anything."

Wick looked at the wizard, waiting for the jaws of the trap to snap closed on tender flesh. What would it feel like to be turned into a toad? "I haven't. I didn't mean to—"

"Get out of bed," Craugh said, waving impatiently. "We need to talk."

Wait, Wick thought heatedly. *Just because you haven't turned me into a toad doesn't mean . . . doesn't mean . . .* He sighed and threw the blanket off. *Doesn't mean you won't if I make you angry enough.*

"Slops has a meal prepared, I believe," Craugh said. "Get dressed and let's go eat."

Holding the blanket tight around him, Wick took out a fresh set of clothes from the sea chest under his hammock. He looked at Craugh. "Uh, would you mind waiting outside?"

"Why?"

"I'm going to change clothes."

Exasperated, Craugh rolled his eyes up. "Old Ones help me. In addition to being a bungler, he's also modest." He let himself out and closed the door.

"I'm not a bungler," Wick called to the wizard's departing back.

"We didn't get Master Oskarr's axe," Craugh growled. "I'd say that was fairly bungled."

"I found the axe, though." Wick dressed quickly. "That's what you sent me there for."

"I didn't send you to find it so you could let the enemy have it," Craugh responded.

True, Wick told himself. "I didn't even know there *was* an enemy. If I'd known, I might have handled things differently." *Although I don't know how that would have been possible.*

"There is. And they're still out there. That's one of the things we have to talk about."

Wick opened the door and joined the wizard. Together, they went topside and entered the galley. The smell of fresh, warm biscuits and firepear jelly, sweet butter, bacon, sausage, pepper gravy, and journeycakes made Wick's mouth water in anticipation.

Few people were in the galley so they took seats by themselves. Wick piled his plate high, but discovered that his engineering lacked by comparison with Craugh. They dug in and ate without talking for several long, satisfying minutes.

When they were finished with their second helping, resting up before they rallied for a third attempt, Wick asked, "How is Bulokk?"

"Still alive," Craugh said. "That one is very tough. He comes from good stock. He's very disappointed to have lost his ancestor's battle-axe."

Wick sipped his razalistynberry wine. After the battle, Hallekk and the pirates had secured the shoreline and gathered all the scattered mine slaves. Instead of trying to get them out on one of the goblinkin ships, Cap'n Farok had ordered everyone aboard *One-Eyed Peggie*. There had been no chance of catching the mysterious black ship. Knowing the slave ships could never be made anything more than what they were, Hallekk had ordered them burned to their waterlines and sunk in the harbor.

They'd remained at anchor for nearly a full day, tending to the wounded and giving the dead a proper burial. Bulokk had also requested that Master Oskarr's anvil be rescued if at all possible. Cap'n Farok had ordered that done, and Hallekk and a group of the ship's crew had gone down into the mine and brought the anvil back up.

There'd been a brief set-to with the Burrower, but Wick let Hallekk know that Burrowers didn't much care for fire and it had given them a wide berth after they'd doused it with oil and set it aflame. In the end, though, Craugh had gone after the Burrowers and dispatched them all. Leaving the creatures to eat their way through the islands wasn't possible. There had been no sign of the fire elemental, Merjul.

"I'm not a bungler," Wick said, when he could no longer stand the guilt the wizard had heaped upon him. "There was a lot I didn't know. Mostly things you didn't tell me. And you should have."

"I'm aware of that." Craugh reached into his robe and took out Wick's journal.

Only then did Wick realize that he hadn't switched the journal out of his other clothes back in his room. "Did you read that?"

"I did." Craugh nodded.

"That's not my best work," Wick said defensively. When he hadn't been helping with the wounded, Wick had climbed up to the crow's nest and worked on the journal. As a result, his work at recording the events that had taken place after he'd reached the Cinder Clouds Islands was hurried, more in the form of notes than in anything presentable.

"It isn't," Craugh agreed. "But I know it's an unpolished first draft. You'll get it right as you work on it. I just wanted to get an idea of what you'd been through."

Wick flipped through the pages, making certain everything was there. Every time he started a new journal, he always numbered the pages ahead of time, so he would know if anything had ever been removed.

"It's all there," Craugh grumbled. He tossed the protective oilskin pouch and writing supplies onto the table as well.

"Wizards have a habit of making things disappear," Wick returned. "They don't always put those things back where they belong."

"We have to get Master Oskarr's axe back," Craugh declared.

"How?" Wick asked. "We don't even know who took it."

Craugh snatched the journal from Wick's hands, then opened it to a page displaying the thieves' guild symbol of the straight razor and lips. "We do." He tapped the tattoo on the drawing Wick had made for reference. "The thieves were members of the Razor's Kiss, a thieves' guild that operates out of Wharf Rat's Warren."

Wick thought about that. He'd never been to Wharf Rat's Warren. Nor had he ever wanted to go. The port city was in the Deep Frozen North and was said to be one of the most lawless around. Only thieves and murderers lived there, safe from the vengeful arm of anyone who tried to make them pay for their crimes.

"You recognize the tattoo?" Wick asked.

"I do."

"How?"

"I've been there and seen it."

Wick resisted the impulse to ask what business had taken Craugh there. No doubt it wasn't good business. Craugh wasn't exactly a good person. The wizard tended to chase after his desires and seldom addressed the needs of others.

"That being the case," Craugh went on, "you'll have to go search for the thieves' guild." He sipped his wine.

At first, Wick couldn't believe he'd heard correctly. "No," he said, folding his arms across his chest. "I'm not going."

"Second Level Librarian Lamplighter," Craugh said in tones that sent a shiver through Wick just as surely as though they'd been uttered by Grandmagister Frollo, "you have a duty to protect the Vault of All Known Knowledge."

"I don't see how going into Wharf Rat's Warren is going to accomplish that."

"That's because you have limited scope of vision."

"My vision," Wick insisted, perhaps a bit emboldened by the razalistynberry wine, "is perfectly fine."

Craugh looked at him.

For a moment, Wick felt certain he was about to be threatened with toadification, and he wasn't certain how he was going to react to that. But for the moment he held onto his newfound belligerence.

"We still need to know what happened at the Battle of Fell's Keep," Craugh said.

"We know that Master Oskarr didn't betray anyone," Wick countered.

"Do we? Aren't some of those books in the Vault of All Known Knowledge sometimes in conflict with each other about events?"

Grudgingly, Wick had to admit that was true.

"Someone's lying then," Craugh said.

"Not necessarily," Wick replied. "It just depends on when the account took place."

"The victors always write the histories."

Sitting there looking at the wizard, Wick felt torn. He didn't know if it was better to argue with someone who didn't acknowledge books or the information in them, or with someone who was suitably educated. *And opinionated*, he added unkindly.

"Do you have Master Oskarr's stone table in which he writes he was betrayed?" Craugh asked.

"No. You know we don't." Wick hadn't even thought to bring it. "I have the rubbings I took of his statement, though. They're legible. And if we need to, we could go back for Master Oskarr's table."

"How many people can read that statement, Second Level Librarian Lamplighter?"

Wick drummed his fingers on the tabletop irritably. *Okay. Point taken.* He sighed. "No one who doesn't work at the Vault of All Known Knowledge. Even of those there, only a few can read it."

"I see. So can you prove your claim?"

"No."

Craugh nodded. "Then there's the red-cowled wizard who was with the black ship."

Wick looked at Craugh in surprise. "You knew him!"

"I know *of* him," Craugh corrected. "He's a very dangerous man. A wizard-for-hire to the highest bidder."

Unconsciously, Wick turned to the page where he'd drawn the red-cowled wizard's face. Wick had drawn the man four different times, using his memory of the wizard to remember how he'd looked and moved. Even rendered in charcoal, the man looked dangerous.

"His name is Ryman Bey," Craugh said.

Automatically, Wick asked for the spelling and inscribed it at the bottom of the page.

"He's an albino," Craugh said.

That explains the coloration I saw, Wick thought.

"As such, you don't find Ryman Bey often out in the daylight hours," Craugh went on.

"Is he part of the Razor's Kiss?"

"Not to my knowledge."

"Why would Ryman Bey be with them?"

"That's one of the questions we'd like answered, isn't it?"

Not we, Wick wanted to reply. But he couldn't. Not simply because he didn't want to anger Craugh, but because he was curious, too.

"The Razor's Kiss is for hire as well," Craugh said.

"You believe someone hired them to look for Boneslicer."

Craugh nodded. "I do."

"Why?"

"Because someone doesn't want the truth of what happened at the Battle of Fell's Keep to come out."

"Who?"

Craugh smiled. "If I knew the answer to that, we might not have to go to Wharf Rat's Warren."

Wick looked into Craugh's green eyes. "What if I choose not to go there?"

Craugh started to speak, then Cap'n Farok's rough voice blared through the galley.

"If'n ye chooses not to go," the dwarven captain said from the doorway, "then ye'll not go."

"What if I want to go back to Greydawn Moors?" Wick asked.

"Then I'll take ye there, Librarian." Farok glared at Craugh. "I've had me fill of slave ships. I'll not abide bein' made part of one."

Craugh was silent for a moment, then gave a tight nod. "All right then, Second Level Librarian Lamplighter. The choice is yours." Without another word, the wizard got up from the table and stalked outside.

For some reason that he couldn't explain, Wick felt ashamed, like he'd somehow let the wizard down. *That's stupid*, he told himself. *You don't owe him anything. You've already risked your life several times for him.* But he couldn't shake the feeling.

"Are ye all right, Librarian?" Cap'n Farok asked.

"I am," Wick answered. *I will be.*

"Will ye be wantin' to go back to Greydawn Moors, then?"

"I'd be safer there," Wick said, hoping the old pirate captain would understand.

"Aye." Farok nodded. "Ye would be. An' it's a more fittin' place for ye than out here on the sea or on the mainland."

Somehow, though, even though Farok said that, Wick still felt guilty.

"I'm gonna see them we rescued to home first," Farok said. "They's closer an' we could use a few supplies afore we cross the Blood-Soaked Sea again. All these extra mouths we took on to feed ain't doin' our supplies any good." He clapped Wick on the shoulder. "Just let me know what ye've a mind to do."

"I will. Thank you."

Hours later, Wick sat up in the crow's nest with a fresh journal, the one he'd taken notes in, and his writing supplies. After the time he'd spent in the Cinder Clouds Islands, he enjoyed the simple and familiar task of rendering his notes into properly stated text.

He used one of the codes he'd invented to record his adventures and the events that had propelled him into them. Even as he reworked the argument in Paunsel's Tavern, beginning with how Paunsel had dragged him away from the adventure of Taurak Bleiyz, a vague wave of discontent filled Wick.

He hated unfinished things.

Since he'd been back on *One-Eyed Peggie*, he'd tried to focus on the book. He hadn't even been able to get the intrepid dweller hero across the spiderweb spanning the Rushing River high in the Death Thorn Forest. Swinging Toadthumper with Taurak just hadn't seemed . . . right.

So many things about the Battle of Fell's Keep remained undone.

It's not yours to do, Wick told himself. *You're a Librarian, not some larger-than-life dweller hero from a romance on the shelves of Hralbomm's Wing.* He watched the sun slowly sinking into the west, painting the sky fiery orange and red above the silvery water. *You don't even want to be a hero.*

Still, he knew that Taurak Bleiyz would have been able to slip unnoticed into Wharf Rat's Warren and spy on a thieves' guild.

And that was what Craugh was proposing. It was the only strategy that made sense.

It's also the strategy that could get you strung up from a net for the birds to eat, Wick reminded himself. *Or tossed to the sharks.*

He looked down at the page he'd been working on. It was an image of the Battle of Fell's Keep, pulled from the few pictures he'd seen drawn of it and from the descriptions he'd read. His picture centered on Master Oskarr standing atop a boulder in the heart of the Painted

Canyon, swinging Boneslicer at goblinkin and the trolls that accompanied them.

Master Oskarr gave his life, Wick thought sadly, *maybe not then, but eventually all the same. And he was branded a traitor for that.* The realization didn't set easily with the little Librarian. He'd seen in Bulokk how those hurts from the past could still wound. *How long will they continue to do so?*

In the end, Wick knew he had no choice. What if he went back to Greydawn Moors, to the Vault of All Known Knowledge, and couldn't find peace to do his work or enjoy a good book?

It could happen. It was happening now. He could only imagine Grandmagister Frollo haranguing him for his absence, then for his inattention to the tasks before him. If he couldn't find it within himself to finish the Taurak Bleiyz adventure, how could he ever return home?

When it was almost dark, Wick packed the two journals away. He was too unsettled to work anymore, and it was even more unsettling realizing he knew what he had to do about it. He folded up his writing supplies and made his way down the rigging.

Critter and Rohoh were involved in some argument on one of the 'yards. It was evident from the ungainly way they were swinging upside down from their claws that they'd been raiding Slops's cooking brandy.

Once he reached the deck, Wick made his way to Craugh's room. Before he even knocked on the door, the wizard called, "Enter."

Sighing, Wick thought, *I hate when he does that.* Craugh had a habit of laying wards on the doors of rooms where he slept.

Inside the small room, Craugh sat cross-legged on the narrow bed.

"Why did you get a bed?" Wick asked, thinking of the

hammock he'd been sleeping in. He'd never visited Craugh's room.

"Because I asked," Craugh answered. He closed the book he'd been reading and tried to hide it from sight.

Before he could stop himself, driven by curiosity, Wick grabbed the book. Craugh didn't let it go. Green sparks leapt from the wizard's baleful gaze. Wick saw the title anyway. He released the book.

Craugh tucked it into his traveler's pack. "Well?"

"That book was one I wrote," Wick said in surprise.

"You gave it to me."

"I know. As a gift." Wick shook his head. "I didn't think you'd still have it."

"I just found it in my pack," Craugh said. "Obviously I forgot to remove it."

Wick knew that wasn't true. The book had shown a lot of careful attention, but it also looked decidedly well read. Like a favorite book should. Wick had written it about his adventures with Craugh down in the Seltonian Bogs when they'd gone in search of Ralkir's hidden library.

"Was there something you wanted?" Craugh demanded.

Wick squinted up at him. "Some days, Craugh, you're a miserable excuse for a person."

Craugh glared at him.

"If it wasn't for the whole toad thing you do," Wick said, "I think more people would tell you that."

"Hmmmph," Craugh responded. "And more people would be toads."

"You know why I'm here, don't you?"

To his credit, Craugh didn't gloat.

"I can't leave this unfinished," Wick said, realizing the wizard was going to make him say it.

"I know," Craugh said.

"There are too many questions that need to be answered. And I've started taking some of them personally. During the last few days, I've gotten to know Bulokk. He's a good person. He shouldn't have to suffer under the weight of the accusation of Master Oskarr."

"I agree."

Wick regarded Craugh suspiciously. "But there's more to this, isn't there?"

"Yes."

Wick waited, then sighed as he gave up. "You're not going to tell me, are you?"

"No."

"Why?"

"Because I know too much to be neutral the way a good investigator should be. I have too many preformed suspicions."

"Do you know who hired the Razor's Kiss?"

"Perhaps."

"Then why should I go there?"

"Because we need proof before I start making accusations."

"I could get killed in Wharf Rat's Warren."

"I sincerely hope not. But it is a distinct possibility. I never said any of this was going to be easy."

At least that, Wick thought, *is the truth.*

A Note from Grandmagister
Edgewick Lamplighter

I look back on this document after so many years have elapsed and it seems like only yesterday. The task that Craugh and Cap'n Farok set before me on that day was far more perilous than even they believed.

Well, I think that Craugh knew more than he was telling. He usually does.

As you can plainly see from this note, I lived through it all. But many didn't. And even now if all the truths come spilling out that we left hidden, more people will die.

"Secrets are such hard things to manage when you're not the only one who knows." Of course, as any Librarian worth his salt would recognize, that's a quote from Gart Makmornan's Cashing In on Secrets: A History of Blackmail in the Higher Elven Courts.

In all, there are three of these books, these journals of my travels during this time of trouble. I have divided them up to forestall any inadvertent discovery of them before their time. Timing is, as they say, everything. And it was never truer than now. The trouble I was witness to, the discovery of Lord Kharrion's Wrath so long after the Cataclysm, was not ended. I knew that when I walked out of the Forest of Fangs and Shadows.

But it was finished enough for the time. The danger was put aside.

The second book details what happened to me during my travails at Wharf Rat's Warren, of how I tracked down the Razor's Kiss, Ryman Bey, and the person who hired them to search for Master Blacksmith Oskarr's battle-axe, Boneslicer.

That journal, as with the third, will not be found with this one. Only one person knows where this journal may be found. And I will teach only one other Librarian—an apprentice I know whose heart and mind I can trust—the trick of the code I have used to record this narrative.

Only you, my apprentice, know the code to these books. And I will have taught you the way to find them. But know that the secrets they guard are dangerous things. I cannot impress that strongly enough upon you.

To find the second book, you must first find Ordal the Minstrel, who is as eternal as the wind. When you find him, ask him, "What rides in on four legs, stands on two legs, and stumbles away on three legs?"

Ordal doesn't know anything of the book that has been hidden, but his answer will give you a clue as to where you should look for the second book.

May your journey be successful, apprentice, and may your search be compelled out of curiosity rather than need.

> *Sincerely,*
> *Edgewick Lamplighter*
> *Grandmagister*
> *Vault of All Known Knowledge*
> *Greydawn Moors*

afterword

Worn and bleary-eyed from working by lantern light aboard *Moonsdreamer*, Juhg pushed up from the small table in the cabin Raisho had given him. He'd been sitting so long that his sea legs had evidently swum without him because he found the ship's deck seemed to be tilting beneath him.

Suddenly aware of the hunger that consumed him, Juhg lurched out into the corridor and made his way up onto the deck. He was surprised to find that it was night and that *Moonsdreamer* was rolling in the clutches of a storm.

He'd been so consumed by Grandmagister Lamp-lighter's narrative that he hadn't even noticed the storm's descent on the ship.

Fierce rain raked the deck, deep enough to slosh small tides back and forth as the ship rocked. Lightning blazed across the sky, burning through the dark masses of clouds swirling overhead. The hollow booms were so close and so loud they shivered through *Moonsdreamer*.

Looking back at the stern, Juhg found Raisho standing near the pilot. When a storm was on, there was nowhere else Raisho would be.

"When did this start?" Juhg asked his friend as he joined him.

Raisho stood dressed in a dark cloak, his face concealed in the shadows except for when the lightning struck. "Right before dusk. We're hours into it now." He squinted and turned his face up against the rain. "Thought it'd be played out by now, but it just keeps comin'." He shook his head and looked back at Juhg. "Don't care none for this storm, I tell you. It's got a bad feel 'bout it. Like it ain't natural."

Juhg remembered the bog beasts they'd fought back in Shark's Maw Cove. Someone had sent those creatures. Could a storm have been sent as well?

A wave caught *Moonsdreamer* broadside and twisted her. The helmsman struggled to hold onto the large wheel. Crossing over to the man, Raisho threw his strength into the task as well.

Stumbling, Juhg managed to grab onto the railing and keep his feet. But only just.

"Been thinkin' maybe we should 'ead into port somewhere," Raisho shouted. "But didn't know which way we should make for."

"Calmpoint," Juhg said.

Raisho looked at him. "Ye finished translatin' that book?"

Juhg nodded. "I did."

"Does Craugh know?"

"I just came up," Juhg said. "I thought he'd be up here."

Shaking his head, Raisho said, "I haven't seen 'im since before the storm 'it."

Juhg didn't much care for the coincidence of the two events. "Make for Calmpoint."

"What are we gonna find there?"

"Not at Calmpoint," Juhg said. "We'll have to go up Steadfast River to Deldal's Mills."

"Why?"

"There are three books in all," Juhg said. "The book that Craugh brought me told me how to find the second."

"Where's the third?"

"I don't know. Perhaps the second book will tell us that."

Another wave slammed *Moonsdreamer*. Raisho fought with the wheel as a deluge of water slapped over him. The helmsman lost his footing and started to slip away. Moving with surprising quickness, Raisho managed to grab the younger sailor and haul him to safety with one hand.

Then Raisho lifted his voice and started calling out orders to bring the ship around on the correct bearing.

Feeling a little panicky but trusting his friend's instincts when it came to sailing, Juhg went belowdecks. He lurched through the companionway using his hands. The lanterns swung and batted against the walls, the flames flickering from the abuse.

At Craugh's door, Juhg knocked and waited. When there was no response, he knocked again, louder this time. "Craugh!"

No response.

Opening the door, Juhg stepped inside. Darkness filled the small room. A coppery scent was on the air, and it seemed disturbingly familiar.

Juhg stepped back into the companionway and took down one of the lanterns. He returned to the room.

Craugh wasn't there. But the coppery stink came from the pool of blood on the floor. Beside it, using the same blood, someone had written BEWARE.

Standing there in the room, feeling Craugh's absence, Juhg knew that even out on the Blood-Soaked Sea they weren't out of reach of the mysterious enemy who pursued them.

from the annals of
the vault
of all
known
knowledge

1

Drathnon and the Dragon's Tooth

A Tale of the Ringing Anvil Dwarves

𝕬 fight brewed among the patrons of the Twisted Horn that night as surely as wine aged in the casks in the venerable tavern's basement.

As he sat at one of the back tables in the tavern, Drathnon swore to himself that he'd have none of it, though the braggart's quick tongue and unpardonable claims marked him for a swift comeuppance. Worse than that, Drathnon had sworn to his da that he'd take no part in fighting while they were in Blarrick's Falls.

But ignoring the cock's crows of the insufferable Thunderblow dwarves while trying to enjoy quiet conversation among companions was nigh impossible. Drathnon tried to pay more attention to his ale and not so much to the constant chattering of the other dwarves. His da had been adamant about them getting into Blarrick's Falls and getting out again without collecting bruises and knots, along with the ill will of the local merchants. Several of Naklegong's older smiths had grimaced and grumbled at the orders they'd received.

That hadn't always happened, but Drathnon hadn't always been the one responsible. Those slugfests had started long before Drathnon had been born.

With all the dwarven smithies in the Seared

Mountains—so named because legend had it the local dragon, Kallenmarsdale, had for years shorn the mountains of all wildlife and vegetation with his fiery breath before he'd grown bored—there was always some confrontation or another between clans while in the town.

Blarrick's Falls was a clearinghouse for iron ore. All the local smithies had exhausted the once-rich iron veins that had run deep in the Seared Mountains. Too many dwarves had collected the ore to make armor and steel for the burgeoning human cities farther down Slither River, which was named for the way it switched back and forth through rough terrain and sprang from cliffs.

As a result, some of the younger dwarven clans had gone upriver and mined iron ore there. Part of their payment was getting to send young blacksmiths to the other clans to be trained. There was talk that one day those clans might be intense rivals, but it took generations for a dwarven smithy clan to become a household name.

Mayhap some day they would become fierce competitors, but for now they were only upstarts who had access to a lot of iron mines. The established clans were only now sending younger dwarves out to stake mines of their own.

But most of the dwarven clans were certain they could outlast the other clans. None of them wanted to give up their homes or have to rebuild their forges because then they would fall behind in the business the humans provided.

So they stayed and tried to get along, for there was almost enough work to keep them all busy. But sometimes, when they were in their cups and collected in Blarrick's Falls, they didn't try as hard as others to get along. It was a dwarven smithy clan's nature to be greedy for business and prideful about the work that they did.

The Ringing Anvil dwarves had come down the Boar Snout Mountains with Naklegong to buy iron ore and transport it back to the forge. They had to make the three-day trip five or six times a year to keep enough ore on hand for their orders.

Drathnon had only started making the trip with his da two years ago. As dwarves went, he was still young and prideful. He was built wide and powerful, and his hands, wrists, and forearms were strong enough—some said, even in those days—to tear trees from the ground.

He wore good breeches and a shirt his ma had only just made him because he was still coming into his full growth. His war hammer, which he and his da had forged when Drathnon had gotten near adult-sized, sat on the floor within easy reach. His dark brown hair ran into his full beard.

"They ain't a dwarf in these mountains can hold a candle to the Thunderblow dwarves," one of the most offensive dwarves declared. "Why, if we could keep iron ore up to our forges, no one would ever buy anything from any other clan in the area. There wouldn't be any need."

"So says ye," another dwarf snarled back. He was one of the Glass Mountain dwarves. Their homeland had once had another name, but they'd so riddled the mountains with tunnels that summer thunder and earth quivers from the nearby volcanoes sometimes caused them to collapse. Rumor was they were already scouting for mines.

Other dwarves thumped their metal cups on the tables in support of the second dwarf. A few catcalls also issued forth.

The Thunderblow dwarf drew himself up to his full height and tried to look calm. His flushed face gave away his emotions, and the fact that he'd been drinking steadily. Not even his ferocious beard could cover that.

"I am Vahdrok, son of Bleddo, who was son of Charnagor, all of 'em fine smiths of the Thunderblow Clan," the dwarf roared. "And if it's me honor or that of me clan, I'll fight ye to the death, I will."

"Ye come in here looking for a fight," another dwarf

roared back at him. "And here ye'd pick on Wylaad, and
him so drunk he can scarce stand up. That's not what I'd
call a testimony to bravery."

Drathnon bridled at the big-mouthed ways Vahdrok
had. They'd known each other for years, and never been a
friend a single day of that time. Vahdrok was older, and
Drathnon used to endure his ire while in Blarrick's Falls.

"It's okay," Wylaad declared as he pushed himself to
his feet. He was unable to stand on his own two feet,
though. He was also so young that he had only wisps
where a beard should be.

One of the dwarves at his table had to grab his shirt to
keep him standing.

"No, ye won't," the other dwarf said. "Ye're a-goin' to
bed is what ye're a-goin' to do." He stood and pulled the
young dwarf toward the door.

"By the Old Ones," Vahdrok snarled, "I'll not be cheated
of me right to avenge me honor!"

The dwarf holding onto the younger dwarf looked
around the tavern. Evidently they'd outstayed their clans-
men.

Drathnon was certain Vahdrok had known that. The
foul-tempered dwarf had a keen eye for such things.

The tavern patrons seemed to draw a collective breath.
The human tending the bar stepped back toward the door
behind him. The young dwarven maid on the small stage
vacated her chair.

"Mayhap in the morning then," the older dwarf said.

Evidently even Wylaad had had second thoughts, because he kept his mouth shut and looked slightly pale.

"That's the way of it, is it?" Vahdrok shook his shaggy
head. "Well ye'll not be gettin' out of this so easy." With a
casual economy of motion, he plucked the small throwing mace from his side and heaved it at the two dwarves.

2

*Q*uick as a trader's smile at the end of a long and successful bartering, Drathnon swung his war hammer out to intercept the thrown mace. His eye and his hand, trained together for years laboring over an anvil in his da's foundry, were certain and true.

The mace *clanked* mightily against the war hammer's head. Drathnon felt the force quiver along his outstretched arm. He had no doubt that if the mace had hit its intended target it would have killed the dwarf. Then the mace thumped to the floor.

To make matters worse, the mace shattered, obviously not standing up to Drathnon's hammer.

Every eye in the room turned to Drathnon.

"Ye picked the wrong fight to interfere in," Vahdrok growled.

Drathnon, ever one to deliver a cutting phrase when he could think of one, said, "Well, I didn't have much choice, ye see. Wasn't but one unfair fight going on at the moment."

Vahdrok plucked his hammer from the floor. "Ye've had this comin' for a long time, whelp."

Despite his da's admonition, and certain knowledge that if Vahdrok didn't kill or cripple him his da might very well do it himself, Drathnon felt that old familiar grin pull at his lips.

"By the beard of my da," Drathnon answered, "now there's an invitation I've been waiting some years on."

"Ye lunkheads just hold up," an old dwarf said. "There's too much drinking what's been goin' on to be makin' decisions like this. Ye'd best sober up and think it over till mornin'." Pipeweed smoke wreathed his hoary head. Scars showed on his face from battle and circumstance. He held a cane in one hand and favored his right leg.

Drathnon knew the old dwarf. His name was Keldd, and he was one of the Molten Rock Forge dwarves who had been in the area the longest. The Molten Rock Forge sold a lot of goods to everyone that had the price. Their creations never went down in value, only up.

Keldd had been one of those dwarves given to the art of war. He'd been too restless to labor all his days at a forge. Instead, he'd walked off as a young dwarf and been a mercenary for a time in far-off lands, then returned to his clan to help fight in some of the bloodiest Clan Wars ever fought in the Seared Mountains. Legend had it that he and a group of warriors had fought Kallenmarsdale to a standstill while defending a village. Keldd never talked about that, though.

"Ye best stay out of this, ye old fool," Vahdrok snarled. "Otherwise I'll take away that stick ye're a-leanin' on an' use it to pick my teeth."

Keldd scowled and his face darkened. He turned his attention to Drathnon.

"Flatten those ugly ears for him, Drathnon. Pin 'em right up against that disgusting lump he uses for a head."

The dwarves in the tavern cheered, because it really wasn't an evening of drinking and carousing unless there was one good fight.

"But ye'll not be fightin' in here," Keldd stated. "Ye'll do it outside."

Despite his outward demeanor, Drathnon was nervous. Vahdrok was larger than he was, stronger and older. Those things meant something in a fight. Still, he made his way through the tavern's door and out into the rutted street.

Night had fallen over Blarrick's Falls hours ago. The Twisted Horn sat atop the gentle slope that led down to the Slither River. Silvery fog ghosted along the banks and partially concealed the riverboats sitting at anchorage among the stone docks. Other taverns, and shops that featured sail makers, coopers, leatherworkers, and other enterprises lined the street on the other side of the riverbank.

Several dwarves brought lanterns from the tavern to light the dark street. In short time, several dwarves from across the street had come running.

"Yer da isn't gonna like this at all," Mardin told Drathnon as he helped cinch up the younger dwarf's chainmail shirt. Mardin was one of Drathnon's shield mates. They trained at Axes and Anvils, the fighting system the dwarves had worked out for small groups of four warriors.

"Let's hope he doesn't find out about it," Drathnon suggested. "I don't plan on telling him."

"Me neither." Mardin smiled. "He's gonna blame me for this, too. He told me to look out for ye."

"Not like ye could stop this," Drathnon said, eyeing Vahdrok as his seconds squeezed him into his own banded armor.

"No, an' Vahdrok's had this comin' for some time." Mardin put Drathnon's helmet on and slammed it into place with the palm of his hand. "Are ye good?"

"I am." Drathnon watched Vahdrok taking practice swings with his hammer. The other dwarf was a fierce fighter in his own right. His polished skill showed immediately at the effortless way he swung his hammer.

"Stop stallin'," Vahdrok bellowed. "I don't have all night."

"Gettin' too old to stay up late, Vahdrok?" someone shouted from the crowd ringing the fighters.

Vahdrok loosed a foul curse and scoured the crowd for the offender. During that time, Drathnon walked to the center of the impromptu circle. He held his hammer in front of him across his thighs.

With lightning speed, Vahdrok pulled a small throwing knife from his sleeve and flung it at Drathnon. If he'd had only moonlight to see by, Drathnon was certain he'd never have seen the blade until it was too late. With the lanterns, though, the edged steel glowed golden in flickers as it spun.

Drathnon swung the bottom of the war hammer around in a short, quick arc. The hammer haft caught the throwing knife and knocked it aside. The blade floated through the air like a dying bird.

With surprising grace, Keldd flicked a hand out and caught the knife almost effortlessly. He broke it in his calloused hands and dropped the pieces onto the rutted street. Breaking something made by a dwarven smith was a huge insult.

Vahdrok launched his attack immediately after throwing the knife. After taking three quick strides forward, Vahdrok brought his hammer down in an effort to smash Drathnon's skull. Drathnon was certain the blow would have caved in his head if it had landed.

Instead, he blocked the blow with his hammer haft, slanting the iron-reinforced wood so the angle took Vahdrok's hammer away from him instead of trying to stop it. Even if the haft had held, it would have left deep bruises in Drathnon's hands. Before Vahdrok could move back, Drathnon kicked him in the ribs hard enough to make the banded armor clank.

Air and spittle rushed from Vahdrok's mouth. He stumbled just for an instant. Drathnon tried to press his advantage, but the other dwarf blocked his hammer, expertly catching it. Vahdrok yanked and pulled Drathnon off balance. Unwilling to let go his hammer, Drathnon stepped forward. Vahdrok punched him in the throat and almost succeeded in crushing his windpipe.

drathnon staggered back and tried to breathe. Panic
shivered through him when he couldn't take in any air.
He gave ground before Vahdrok, barely escaping blows
that would have maimed or killed. Even though Vahdrok
wasn't supposed to kill in a fight like this, Drathnon had
no doubt that his enemy would if he had the chance.
Black spots whirled at the edges of Drathnon's vision.

The impacts the hammers made against each other
sounded dulled and far away. Drathnon's grip loosened.

Then Drathnon's throat finally relaxed and he took a
breath. When he could manage a full breath of air that
burned the back of his throat and took away most of the
blackness that had swallowed his eyesight, Drathnon set
himself.

Strength flowed back into his arms. He felt it. Vahdrok
saw what was happening and tried to increase his offense.
His blows came faster.

Drathnon gave himself to the pleasure of the battle.
His da drilled him every day. Drathnon and Mardin had
been paired for Axes and Anvils since they both could
walk. They fought with each other as well. And Naklegong was a harsh taskmaster when it came to the forge.
He didn't allow Drathnon to practice combat till after all

the smithwork was finished. As a result, Drathnon had a large reservoir of strength to draw from.

At first, he struggled to match Vahdrok's speed with the hammer. Then he met him blow for blow. When Drathnon began to pass Vahdrok, the latter grew concerned. Behind his faceplate, his features knotted up in worry.

With a sudden shift, Vahdrok tried catching Drathnon's hammer haft again. Only this time Drathnon saw the maneuver coming. He bumped his weapon's haft against Vahdrok's to throw the other dwarf's timing off, then pulled back and spun around. For a moment, Drathnon was left defenseless as he turned completely around. Then his hammer head hooked Vahdrok's haft. With a vicious surge Drathnon yanked his opponent's weapon from his hands.

Panicked for certain then, Vahdrok tried to fling himself at Drathnon. Instead of backing away, Drathnon stepped forward and brought his hammer haft up in a vicious blow that caught Vahdrok under the jaw.

Vahdrok stumbled back. His eyes unfocused and he shook his head. Then he sat heavily upon the ground. Almost as graceful as an elven dancer, Drathnon whirled again and brought the hammer streaking toward Vahdrok's head.

"Drathnon!"

The voice was immediately recognizable. Drathnon had heard it nearly every day for all of his years. Although he hadn't planned to harm Vahdrok any more than was necessary, Drathnon pulled up at once and stepped away from his vanquished foe.

The dwarves immediately made way for Naklegong to walk to the center of the circle. Drathnon, chest heaving and covered in sweat, stepped back as well. Part of him, that child he had not quite shed, wanted to break and run.

"After I told ye there'd be none of this foolishness," Naklegong said in that terrible voice that had commanded dwarves in the forge and in battle against the goblinkin, "here I find ye. In the middle of the street trying to get your head bashed in."

Drathnon wanted to object and point out that he wasn't the one sprawled in the street at the moment. He'd won!

"To set things a-right," Keldd spoke up, "wasn't yer pup's fault, this set-to what happened."

Angrily, Naklegong turned to the old warrior. "It's only out of respect for ye and what ye've done with yer life that I don't beat ye down where ye stand for interfering in a man's private words to his son."

Keldd folded his gnarled hands atop his crutch. "Ye'd do what ye're telling yer son not to do?" The old dwarf's face showed nothing but polite curiosity.

"That's not what I said."

"It's exactly what ye said." Keldd nodded to Drathnon. "An' I'm thinkin' that's not such a good example to be a-settin' for yer pup."

Before Drathnon knew it, a smile spread across his face. His da, who had an amazing sense of when Drathnon was taking pleasure at his embarrassments—most notably with his wife—turned toward his son at once.

Drathnon just had time to lose the smile before his da caught sight of him. He looked as innocent as he could, but he knew that effort would never work on his father.

"Vahdrok was the one what started it all," Keldd said. "In the tavern, Drathnon stopped Vahdrok's cowardly attack against one of the young dwarves that wouldn't have been able to fend for himself. For his troubles, Vahdrok made fun of him an' invited him out into the street." He paused. "Now I don't know about ye, but I wouldn't want to raise a pup what wouldn't stand up for himself and his clan when honor is questioned."

For a moment, Drathnon feared the old dwarf had been too bold. Naklegong wasn't one to take overmuch from someone else. Instead, he turned to Vahdrok.

"Is that what ye did?" Naklegong roared. "Did ye question the honor of me son and me clan?"

Vahdrok wouldn't meet Naklegong's gaze.

"Is yer *honor* satisfied then, ye great lump of guts?" Naklegong demanded. "Or would ye rather get back to the beatin' ye was bein' handed?"

"He—" Vahdrok stopped.

Drathnon knew that Vahdrok had been on the verge of telling Naklegong that Drathnon had cheated. When they'd been younger, Vahdrok had often accused everyone smaller than him of that. When fights started over honor, Vahdrok would beat his younger opponents to a pulp.

"Well?" Naklegong asked.

"No," Vahdrok said in a quiet voice. "Me honor is satisfied."

Naklegong shifted his gaze to Drathnon. "What about you?"

That surprised Drathnon. He wasn't used to being given a choice by his da. But truthfully as he looked at Vahdrok, although part of him wished to continue administering a beating, he couldn't bring himself to feel good about what he'd do to the other dwarf.

"Me honor is satisfied," Drathnon answered. "Thank ye for the opportunity to speak me mind."

"Good. Then you need to get back to the inn. We've a long ride ahead of us in the morning."

"Yes, sir." Drathnon let his grip on his hammer slip from the haft to the head.

"Then get to it."

"Yes, sir." Drathnon stepped out of the ring and walked east along the river back in the direction of their inn.

Mardin walked along at his side. "Well," the other dwarf said, "that certainly went better than it could have."

Drathnon felt a little apprehensive. His da had chosen not to punish him then, but that didn't mean it wasn't going to happen.

4

The next morning arrived as its own punishment. Dawn came early and Drathnon quickly discovered that he'd drunk far too much the night before. His head pounded and he felt sick. He was certain his da had taunted him with the prospect of breakfast as a cruel revenge.

Bright sunlight filled the air as Drathnon helped hitch the oxen to the ore wagons. The oxen, trained by humans instead of elves and traded for with goods the dwarves made, shifted nervously in their traces.

Drathnon walked on the other side of the wagons than his da. Both of them inspected the ironbound wheels and the wooden spokes. The load was heavy and the way would be hard. They'd already changed out three wheels after seeing what the cargoes did to the wagons.

The ore, great and raw masses of broken stone, was stacked as neatly as could be in the back of those wagons. Canvas and rope held the ore in place, but some shifting could still occur and that was dangerous.

Drathnon ran his hands over the chunks, marveling at the feel of the good metal within the rock. Iron was the heart of the world, and like blood through the body, it was pumped throughout the rest of the land.

At the last wagon, he looked up at his da.

"Everything's satisfactory?" Naklegong asked.

Drathnon nodded, then regretted it at once. He was surprised that his head didn't tumble to the ground.

"We'll be leaving in a short while," his da said. "We're going to be traveling with some merchants from Teldane's Bounty."

Drathnon was ready to be on the road. He knew from experience, hungover or not, that he could sleep while sitting in a wagon. But there was safety in numbers.

He was also interested in Teldane's Bounty. Although he'd never been to that area near the Gentlewind Sea, he'd heard much about it. The goblinkin were massing down in the south, encroaching even on the city of Dream, where humans, elves, and dwarves lived among each other. All the other races were steadily being driven north into the frozen lands. Teldane's Bounty, filled with pasture and farmland, with orchards and berry patches, remained a wondrous place to live.

Merchants were generally storytellers. People that traveled regularly tended to like to talk. Drathnon looked forward to the stories he would doubtless hear.

A little longer than a short while later, but that may have been only due to Drathnon's impatience and foul mood, the merchants' wagons—brightly colored as if going to a fair and worn to the point of falling apart—joined the dwarven ore wagon convoy. The merchants were mostly human, but they'd hired elven warders as guides and there were a few dwarves journeying back to clan territories after fighting goblinkin and territorial wars in faraway places.

Drathnon was excited. The nights looked to be wonderful entertainments. Each campfire would have its own tales to tell. They had at least five nights on the trail together.

"What are ye thinkin', pup?"

Startled, Drathnon looked over and saw Keldd limping toward him. "Good morning, sir," Drathnon greeted.

Keldd waved that away as he stopped at Drathnon's side. "Well?"

"Well what?"

Keldd snorted impatiently. "What's on yer mind? When I walked up, ye were grinnin' like a loon."

"I was just admiring our companions of the road," Drathnon admitted. "They probably have a lot of stories to tell."

Keldd looked at the gathering of wagons and frowned a little. "Just ye remember, pup, not all of them stories will be true. Some of them folks will try to fill yer head with nonsense an' such."

"Yes sir," Drathnon said, but he didn't feel as jaded as the old dwarf apparently was.

Hours later, Drathnon sat on the swaying wagon seat and occasionally spent time trying to get more out of the oxen. He'd also spent considerable time trying to figure out which wagon camp he'd "happen" to walk by that night.

He'd been tempted by the clothiers because fine clothes sometimes caught his eye. But he knew that buying something that would look good on a dwarf was next to impossible. And haggling was an art he'd not yet developed, and didn't care to spend any time at. Everything he'd seen in the wagon looked expensive.

He'd almost settled on the vendors that sold magical items. They were charms, mostly, for luck and for love.

Most dwarves didn't care for magic. It went against the things that dwarves knew about the world. Dwarves loved natural things, things that could be held in the hand and were constant. Magic was a wild thing that couldn't always be controlled or summoned. When a dwarf worked with molten metal or a piece of red-hot steel caressed by the forge, he knew what he could do with that metal.

Drathnon supposed that was true of powerful wizards and the forces they used as well. He'd heard of a few that could control the weather and summon fireballs, and there were a few others that could even control the sea. Drathnon had no intention of being out on the sea in a ship, but if that ever happened he thought having a sea wizard along for the trip would probably be a good thing.

The thing that interested him most were the tales of magical metal that was used in the creation of powerful weapons and items that would never rust or be harmed by acid. If a dwarf could learn the secret of pounding some of that magic into things he forged, just enough to insure that whatever was made was at least sturdier than normal iron allowed, Drathnon was certain that dwarven blacksmith's weapons and armor would be prized above all others.

Dwarves had gotten their hands on some of that kind of metal over the years. There were nearly always dribs and drabs of special metal in stars that plummeted from the sky, and from dragon's breath after an attack. Those had nearly always arrived with some magic about them. They were also harder to work with in the forge and on the anvil.

Although dwarves had studied the metals they'd found in craters and left from a dragon's attack, they hadn't gotten any satisfactory information about what caused the affinity for magic. Weapons that came out of the metal forged during those times would never rust, had edges that would never go dull, and somehow dealt more damage when they were used in battle.

Drathnon looked forward to the evening, and he hoped the humans dealing in magic would be amenable to his

questions. After he'd found out they would be traveling
with traders, Drathnon had purchased a sackful of honey-
cakes to garner goodwill. They had never failed when
he'd come along on these trips with his da.

He gazed at the deep forests that lined the valley they
traveled through. They were safe here, but the forest gave
up the higher they climbed into the mountains. The Boar's
Snout, where the Ringing Anvil dwarves lived, was almost
completely barren of vegetation. Still, the rock was solid
and mostly impenetrable, and enemies couldn't easily in-
vade clan holdings.

Drathnon glanced at the fading sun and knew there
couldn't be much more than a few more hours of travel
before they put up for the night.

At that moment, though, Galaug—one of the scouts
sent on ahead of the caravan—squalled out in alarm.

5

drathnon grabbed his war hammer and bailed from the wagon seat. He held onto the harness traces and ran into the bush at the side of the narrow trail road. He tied the traces to the nearest tree to keep the oxen from wandering away, or spooking if it came to that. Then he walked slowly through the forest toward Galaug.

All the other dwarven warriors did the same.

"What do ye suppose it is?" Mardin asked. He flanked Drathnon, as he always did when they headed into trouble.

"Galaug didn't say, did he?" Drathnon asked irritably. Mardin was always expecting him to know the answers about things.

"No."

"Then I suppose we'll be finding out soon." Drathnon kept walking. He glanced forward and saw his da leading the pack of dwarves. There was no other place Naklegong would be at that moment. He carried a large battle-axe and looked ready but not overly concerned.

The trail curved around a thick copse of birch trees and a rocky outcrop. After that, the land fell away into a bowl sprinkled with underground spring-fed pools. Drathnon had been through the area several times.

It wasn't really a valley, more like a hollow in the

earth. Abandoned mines on the sides of the flanking hills showed dwarves had quarried in the area but obviously hadn't gotten much for their trouble. Most of the paths that had wound through the hills had almost vanished, reclaimed by the dense forest.

As he got closer, Drathnon saw the thin rivers of smoke that poured up from the wreckage that lay at the bottom of the hollow. Several overturned and broken wagons and carts covered the forest floor. Arrows jutted from them as well as from the bodies of the dwarves and humans scattered across the torn ground.

Even more telling were the great charred places filled with burnt timber and blackened grass. In areas of direct contact, the heat had turned the ground to irregular pools of glass and shattered rocks.

"Only one thing could do something like that," Mardin whispered, as if he were afraid of mentioning what it was might draw down the same doom upon them.

Drathnon gripped his war hammer more tightly and peered at the open blue sky above the hollow. Nothing flew there, but he knew that didn't mean that they were safe.

Even though most of those traveling with the caravan had heard about a dragon's attack and how little chance there was of survival, they went through the motions of sorting the quick from the dead all the same.

Drathnon found himself getting sick of all the dead lying around him. There were females and young among them. More than anything at the moment, he wished that he could face the dragon that did this.

"That would be a foolhardy wish," his da's quiet voice stated.

Feeling guilty, knowing his thoughts were apparent to Naklegong, Drathnon glanced at his da.

Naklegong's face was hard as granite as he walked with Drathnon. "Better ye should wish Kallenmarsdale never catches another caravan out like this."

"This isn't right," Drathnon croaked. He was embarrassed at how weak his voice was. He'd trained himself to be able to shout down in a mine tunnel and alert everyone.

"No," Naklegong sighed. "But this is the way of the world. Dragons hunt, and we are prey."

"Dragons can be hunted too," Drathnon replied fiercely.

Naklegong clapped his son on the shoulder. There was fierce pride and love in his flinty eyes.

"We're smiths, Drathnon. Not dragon hunters. And the days of dragon hunters are over. In those days, the dragons hadn't made any bargains with the goblinkin, nor with their master Lord Kharrion."

The name sent a chill through Drathnon. Lord Kharrion's name was an evil thing. No one knew much about him, save that he was uniting the goblinkin and forging peace with the dragons. There were some reports of his activity among the goblinkin and how Lord Kharrion had ordered his goblinkin troops to destroy all the libraries of the world as they encountered dwelling places of men, elves, and dwarves.

"But a wizard might slay a dragon," Drathnon pointed out.

"Wizards tend not to want to risk their lives any more than most," Naklegong replied. "The only time they took on the dragons was when they could raise an army of dwarves to fight with them." He shrugged. "Or humans or elves if they had to make do. But you won't see much of that anymore. The wizards fight among themselves these days, and they've taken to living far from the dragons."

Still, the idea nagged at Drathnon as he bent down and pulled the burned form of a dead child from the wreckage of a shattered wagon. The creature that had done this deserved to pay with its life.

That night, after laborious hours of hauling out the dead and laying them to rest in a common grave in some of the abandoned mines in the hillside, supper was quiet and solemn. Not even Drathnon chose to abandon the small campfire beside his wagon. He and Mardin ate in silence after feeding and watering the oxen.

"Ye know we didn't bury all of them," Mardin said. "Some of them lived. At least for a while."

"I know." Thinking about that almost cost Drathnon his appetite. If the day hadn't been so long and so hard, he might not have eaten at all. But his da had always insisted he keep his strength up.

"The goblinkin that came among the caravan took away those that lived."

Drathnon thought about the illustrations in the books he'd seen, and the images his mind had created when he'd sat around a campfire and listened to stories. The goblinkin would have tied the survivors together, arms behind their backs so they couldn't do anything, and leather loops around their necks to bind them all together. Then they would be marched off to Kallenmarsdale's lair to be eaten at the dragon's convenience.

It was a horrible fate.

"Mardin, I'd rather not talk of this," Drathnon said.

Mardin sighed. "I know. I'd rather not *think* on it. But I do."

Fear gripped the caravan for the next two days. The camaraderie and easygoing ways were slow to return. None felt safe. During the open patches of the forest trail, every eye turned toward the sky to search for the great dragon. Thankfully, the route they traveled had few such open places.

Drathnon kept his war hammer close. He had fought against goblinkin, brigands, and some of the fierce bears and wolves that lived in the forest. There'd even been an encounter or three with the giant spiders that occasionally dwelt there, too. Despite coming out of those confrontations the worse for wear at times, he'd still made it out on his own two feet.

It was something to be proud of.

But he'd never fought a dragon.

6

$\mathfrak{A}$ short time later, they stopped at a low stream to fill the water barrels and let the oxen drink their fill. The afternoon sun blazed down on them.

Drathnon felt overly warm in his chain mail, but he didn't take it off. None of them did, and he could tell by the gleam of fear in the eyes of some of the merchants that they were wishful of armor at that time.

"If we had armor to sell," his da said quietly, "we could turn a pretty profit today."

Drathnon nodded in agreement. Then movement among the rushes upstream caught his eye. He reached for his hammer even before he found his voice.

"Da," he said quietly. "There among the rushes." He pointed with his chin. "Do ye see it?"

Naklegong casually peered upstream for a moment. "No. But ye've always had better eyes than I have. What do ye see?"

"Someone's there."

"Brigands?"

Several brigand crews worked the trail. As quickly as one was snuffed out, another seemed to move in. With all the arms and armor the dwarves traveled with on a regular basis, plus the goods that could be gotten from the overland merchants, the brigands had a lot of reasons to haunt the Seared Mountains.

"I'm not sure," Drathnon said.

With wild frenzied yells that chilled the blood, the skulkers broke cover. Dozens of goblinkin raced for the caravan. Their gray-green bodies stood out falsely against the verdant green of the forest. They were thin and thick, muscular and wiry, with long black hair, eyes set far too close together, and wide jaws with crooked teeth. They wore animal skins and clothing they'd taken from humans that would fit their lumpy and misshapen bodies.

"'Ware!" Naklegong thundered in his powerful voice. "To arms! Make a line! Axes and Anvils!"

Only a step behind his da, his blood already singing with the coming battle, Drathnon spied Mardin and ran to join him. Their two shield mates fell into place beside them and they formed the core of the dwarven army.

"Axes!" Drathnon yelled, and immediately took point in the formation. Mardin and one other dwarf stood to the sides and slightly behind him, offering supporting positions as they advanced at a trot toward the goblinkin. The fourth dwarf flanked them all to cover their backs.

Drathnon met the first of the goblinkin with viciousness. He fed his outrage of the sight of the last caravan into his anger and whirled the hammer expertly. An overhand strike crushed the skull of the goblinkin in front of him. He pulled his weapon free, stepped over the falling corpse, and slammed the haft into the teeth of the next goblin, breaking them to bloody stumps.

In axe formation, the dwarven fighting units were terrible things to behold. They were designed to shatter enemy charges and poke holes in defenses.

Drathnon fought until his arms grew weary. He blocked sword and axe blows, even a few hammers, with the haft of his weapon, and returned those blows with interest.

Although he no longer made any headway against their foes, the ground ran green with goblinkin blood.

"Archers!" someone cried in warning.

Gazing ahead, Drathnon saw that the goblinkin were backed by a ragged line of archers. As a general rule, goblinkin weren't overly talented with bows, but when presented with a tightly packed enemy and plenty of arrows, luck could be deadly.

"Anvils!" Drathnon ordered. He stepped back and to his left, allowing Mardin to come up from the right wing position. They matched each other and made a two-by-two formation with the others in their group.

Filled with bloodlust, the goblinkin surged forward and didn't realize they were stepping into the way of their own archers. Drathnon and his shield mates held their positions, only blocking attacks now instead of chewing through their enemies. The goblinkin massed before them and even drove them back a few feet.

Almost immediately, the goblinkin archers loosed their shafts. Struck from behind, the goblinkin facing the dwarves went down in waves. The rearmost fell into the foremost and created havoc in their attack.

"Axes!" Drathnon roared, and dropped into the left wing position as Mardin rotated to the lead position. Mardin battered the goblinkin mercilessly, breaking their line and shearing them off.

Drathnon's heart filled with pride as he saw all the damage that his friend could do. They had all trained hard to be warriors. With swift movements, Drathnon took advantage of those left broken or confused by Mardin's attacks. Goblinkin died beneath the hammer, pounded brainless by the flat end or pierced by the cruelly curved hook on the other side. Drathnon flipped the hammer effortlessly as he needed it. His body had been strengthened by long hours at the forge with a hammer in his hand. The only thing the goblinkin had in their favor was numbers.

Mardin led the way across the marshy ground toward the goblinkin archers as they nocked fresh arrows to string. If the dwarves were caught out in the open, their lives might be forfeit.

Holding in the wing position, Drathnon planted his hobnailed boots with care and crushed the skulls of goblinkin wounded as he ran after Mardin. Then they met the line of goblinkin archers and decimated it. Other dwarven fighting groups did the same.

A horn blasted two short notes.

As one, the goblinkin disengaged and ran back upstream along the banks.

Drathnon's chest heaved as he watched their foes turn tail.

"Do ye think it was the signal to retreat?" Mardin asked.

"That's what they're doin'," Kayrob growled, then spat blood. "They left plenty of dead behind them."

When he gazed back over the battlefield, Drathnon saw that was true. The sight of dwarves lying wounded and dead across the landscape bothered him even more. Some of the wagons were on fire from flaming arrows the goblinkin archers had used. Merchants scrambled among their wares, yelling to each other to help extinguish the blazes.

Then a great shadow sped across the ground and blocked the sun for a moment.

Dread filled Drathnon as he gazed upward. Even though he knew what he would find, fear still shivered through him.

Then someone gave a name to the terror that flew through the bright blue sky.

"Kallenmarsdale! *Kallenmarsdale!*"

7

Salty perspiration burned Drathnon's eyes as he stared at the great beast above them. "Old Ones preserve us," he whispered in a dry voice.

The dragon was forty feet long from nose to the tip of its spiked tail. The wingspread had to be at least eighty feet, and the leathery membranes held curves like that of a bat. The scales glittered and shimmered like jewels in the sunlight. Kallenmarsdale was primarily indigo and dark green, but splashes of red colored his hide. His head was massive, and the huge mouth was filled with serrated teeth as long as Drathnon's hand and forearm.

With a flick of his wings, Kallenmarsdale changed direction, heeling over to plunge without warning toward the dwarven blacksmiths and the caravan. Only then did Drathnon realize that they stood in the open.

He turned and bawled, "Run for the trees!"

But it was already too late.

The dragon opened its massive jaws and belched liquid fire and flames in a wide arc. Before Drathnon's horrified eyes, he saw dwarves catch on fire and burn as the earth exploded from the sudden change in temperature. Only a few of those stricken had time to scream in pain and terror.

They ran a short distance, then the flames stole their breath away and filled their lungs with fire.

Beside Drathnon, Kayrob got hit by a glob of dragon-fire that smacked into his head and shoulders. He stood for a moment and flailed at his burning face as his features melted from the bone underneath, then he succumbed and dropped face-first without a sound.

Drathnon ran. There was nothing else to be done. He carried his hammer in both hands and it bumped against his chest as he pumped his legs. The dragon's shadow slid over him again as it returned for another attack. A moment later he felt the heat of a new fiery blast scorch the earth.

The resulting explosion knocked him from his feet. He rolled and bounced, picking up lumps and bumps and bruises by the score. His face slammed into the ground and left him dazed and disoriented.

Mardin pulled him up by one arm. "Come on! To the wagons!"

Blearily, Drathnon saw that the wagonmasters had the wagons in motion. The surviving dwarves, men, and elves ran and staggered toward them. Frightened by the death and destruction around them, as well as the great dragon circling in the sky, the oxen fought the traces and became unmanageable.

Stumbling at Mardin's side, Drathnon barely managed to reach one of the ore wagons. Two dwarves knocked the pins holding the rear gate section loose and ore fell freely to the ground as the wagon lurched forward. Drathnon avoided the ore and caught hold of the wagon's side and hauled himself forward. Hands grabbed him and pulled him inside. He tumbled unceremoniously among the ore debris.

Weakly—unable to catch his breath, partially due to the sulfurous stench that filled the air—Drathnon pushed himself over onto his back. He peered up at the dragon as Kallenmarsdale came around for another assault, then the trees hid the great creature from view. A moment after that, fire engulfed the treetops, but thankfully didn't penetrate.

"Yer da isn't here, Drathnon," Mardin said.

Even though he'd been prepared to hear that news, Drathnon still denied it. "Ye've missed him. Go back and search again."

"Drathnon," Mardin said softly, "I've been three times. So have ye."

Drathnon had actually been four times. Each time he'd gone, he'd had less hope than the last.

"He's not here," Mardin said.

"Then he'll be here," Drathnon said defiantly. "Dwarves are still coming."

That was true. They'd come through the forest on foot, straggling in from the battleground. Naklegong, however, wasn't among them.

They'd lost almost half their number in the attack. Over half the wagons had been left. A fortune in iron ore was lost, and the Ringing Anvil clan was going to be hard-pressed to recover their losses to buy another shipment.

But Drathnon knew that was a fool's dream. All of the dwarves that had been lost were blacksmiths. The forge had lost a sizeable portion of their workforce.

In quiet fear, Drathnon waited and helped tend the wounded. There were a lot of those as well. They'd hidden more than four miles from the battlefield, near a stream they'd passed only that morning.

Even at that distance, the stench of sulfur and burned meat filled the air. Patches of smoke still drifted among the trees, and it only turned from gray to thin silver as the sun dropped below the horizon and night filled the forest.

And still Naklegong didn't come.

Drathnon searched among the dead when they returned to the battlefield the next morning. He found many friends and companions, dwarves he'd lived with for all of his life in the Boar Snout Mountains. He also found merchants he'd noticed along the way as they'd traveled.

But he didn't find his da.

"There are a lot of them missing," Keldd said as he limped up to stand by Drathnon.

"I know," Drathnon whispered. His heart felt dead inside him, like a forge that had gone untended too long and lost the perpetual flame that gave it life. "There are at least thirty of us unaccounted for."

"The elven warders counted eleven of their own among the missing," Keldd said. "They know what this means."

Drathnon did too. Somewhere in the nearby mountains, the goblinkin forces would be taking their prisoners to the grim fates awaiting them in Kallenmarsdale's belly.

His da would be one of them.

It was unacceptable.

"What are ye going to do?" Keldd asked.

"Me?" Drathnon looked at the old warrior in surprise.

"They look to ye for leadership," Keldd said. "Haven't ye noticed that?"

Drathnon had, and the role of being the leader hadn't set well with him. He knew the task wore on his da, but he hadn't known how wearing it could be.

"Ye should be leading this," Drathnon said.

"Not me," Keldd said.

"Why?"

"Because I'm too old. They won't believe in me."

"Ye're . . . *ye're* Keldd, by the Old Ones. They won't disrespect ye."

"They won't believe in me either." Keldd stared at Drathnon. "But they believe in ye."

Anger pushed Drathnon past all point of control. "They can believe in me all they want, but what am I to do?"

Keldd ignored the outburst. "Ye can lead them home, or ye can lead them after their comrades."

"They won't follow me after Kallenmarsdale." Drathnon waved to the mass of burned bodies they intended to bury.

"Do ye wish for yer da to get et by the dragon?"

"No. Of course not." The thought alone made Drathnon sick.

"I think ye'll find the dwarves and them elves are of a like mind."

8

We don't want to lose our people to the dragon either," Shamalis said. The lean elf with bronze hair and deep green eyes was the leader of the elven warders. His pointed ears stood tall and proud. Scars offered mute testimony that he'd fought for his life on several occasions. "But chasing after the dragon is tantamount to suicide."

Drathnon sat with all of the caravan's survivors under the cool shade of the trees that ringed the battlefield. The nearby stream babbled as it spilled over stones. But the stink of death and burned meat hadn't departed the immediate vicinity. Carrion feeders had fallen upon the dead goblinkin left lying where they'd fallen. No one would bury them.

"We've got a chance," Drathnon said. "It's not much of one, but it's a chance."

"What chance?" Kilvas demanded. He was an older dwarf, and one that Naklegong sometimes had problems with in the forge.

"We can make weapons," Drathnon said.

Kilvas snorted. "Out here?"

"We have anvils," Drathnon said. They carried a few on the ore wagons in case they had to repair the iron-bound wheels. "They aren't our best."

"Even if they were our best," Kilvas said, "we wouldn't be able to make much in the way of weapons."

Never taking his eyes from those of the elf because he knew Shamalis was the one he had to convince above all others, Drathnon said, "We can make magic weapons."

That started a hubbub among dwarves and elves alike.

"I've always been told that dwarves don't much care for magic," Shamalis said.

"We don't trust spells and such," Drathnon said, "that's true. But we believe in metal that holds magic. We just can't ever get enough of it to do more than a few things."

"Where are you going to get such metal?"

Drathnon picked up one of the ore lumps he'd found earlier. The dragon's flames had slagged it, causing it to melt and harden again. "Here. Kallenmarsdale gave it to us. This ore, fired by the dragon's breath, has become magical. There's only two ways we get ore like this."

"From falling stars and dragon's breath," Shamalis said quietly.

Drathnon nodded. "So you see."

"I do." The elven warder reached for the ore. When he touched it, green sparks crackled in the air.

Drathnon almost jerked back in surprise. The elf must have had some magic in him in order to cause such a reaction.

Shamalis smiled. "Metal doesn't always pick up the magic from a dragon. This did."

"And what are ye gonna make out of a lump like that?" Kilvas demanded. "A knife? Mayhap two? For ye surely don't have enough there to attempt a sword. And one sword wouldn't be enough to do much."

"He has a point," the elven warder said.

Drathnon met Shamalis's gaze. "I've been told that an elven archer, properly trained, can pin the wings of a gnat at fifty paces."

Shamalis smiled. "That's true. If you've got a properly trained archer."

"Do you have any such archers?"

"I don't," Shamalis admitted. "But a dragon is much larger than a gnat, isn't it?"

"It is." Drathnon grinned. "So ye see my point, Shamalis?"

"I do, smith." The elf nodded toward the lump of magic-imbued metal. "Are you as fine an arrowhead maker as you are talker?"

Drathnon bared his teeth. "With a hammer in my hands and a cold-fired anvil, I'm a poet. Ye can bet on that."

"We will be," Shamalis said. "Make your arrowheads then. We'll put 'em in the dragon when you've finished with them."

Crafting an oven to heat the metal was the hardest part. Drathnon built it from stone, barely as tall as his waist, and he used coal they'd mined from the Boar Snout Mountains and brought with them. Shamalis added a charm of his own to heat the fire even more. The charm wouldn't have worked on a full-sized forge, but it served quite well on the small one.

Once he had the metal heated, Drathnon worked it with his hammer. The hammerblows rang out across the bowl beside the battlefield.

Shamalis had stationed his warriors to stand guard around the perimeter while Drathnon worked. If any goblinkin came to investigate the noise, they'd give warning.

The work took away most of Drathnon's worries and fears. He still thought of his da, but he consoled himself with the thought that what he was doing right then would help his da much more than fretting over what might have happened already or what might happen in the next few hours.

His arm rose and fell in rhythmic cadence. As he finished each arrowhead, he cooled it in the stream. The hot metal hissed when it touched the water, and tendrils of steam curled up.

After the arrowheads were cooled, the elven warders took them and fitted them to rowan shafts. They'd found a tree in the forest. Although unable to work any magic on the metal, the elves were perfectly able to work magic on the rowan wood.

When the arrows were fletched and pronounced finished by Shamalis, they were passed out among the seven best archers. Each of those elves took special care to learn the difference between those arrows and the normal ones in their quivers. In the heat of the coming battle, they didn't want to lose track of which was which.

Drathnon worked through the night. It was all the time they figured they could allow for the effort. Having prisoners would slow the goblinkin, but no one knew how far they had to travel to get back to Kallenmarsdale's lair.

If the dragon got back to its lair, there would be no chance at all of rescue.

Finally, as the sun was rising in the east, Drathnon straightened up a final time and cooled the last arrowhead he'd made. All in all, he'd fashioned thirty-seven of them, all of them cruelly curved to slice into the dragon's body.

Shamalis had stayed awake throughout the night. He'd sat with his back to a tree, his bow across his thighs. When he saw Drathnon stand, he stood as well.

"Are you done then, smith?" the elven warder asked.

"I am."

"Do you think you still yet have the strength to do this?"

Drathnon picked up his war hammer. "That creature has my da. I'll do what I need to." Then he took out the device he'd made for himself: a foot-long spike that fit cunningly into the hollow of his hammer haft. It slid into place smoothly, then clicked as it locked.

"That looks to be made for close-in fighting," Shamalis said.

"It is."

"I wouldn't want to be that close to the dragon."

"I don't, but if it comes to that, I want to be able to hurt it."

9

The elven warders easily found the trail left by the goblinkin and their prisoners. In the still dawn hours, Drathnon strode behind the elves. He didn't think the goblinkin would be early to rise, but they had no way of knowing how far they'd have to travel to overtake them.

By early afternoon, one of the elven warders came back with the news.

"They're just over that hill," the elf said.

Drathnon stared at the jagged line of trees that crested the foothill nearly half a mile away.

"There's a valley at the bottom," the scout informed them. "They're in the open."

Shamalis grimaced, obviously not happy about that. Drathnon wasn't either. Being in the open would play to the dragon's aerial superiority.

"How many?" the elven leader asked.

The scout grinned. "Enough to make saving our people difficult, but not so much as to make the task impossible."

A mile ahead of the advancing goblinkin, Drathnon worked with the other dwarves to fell trees across the narrow throat of the valley. The elves had been through the area several times and knew about the bottleneck. Choking that opening with trees only took the work of a few minutes, though none of the elves were happy about the loss of the trees.

"When we have time," Shamalis said to the forest, "we will come back this way and return what we have taken this day."

Then they set up to wait.

Only a few minutes later, Drathnon stood in front of the hastily erected barricade and waited. An elven horn bleated, signaling the attack of the archers on the goblinkin. The way he, Shamalis, and Keldd had discussed it was to take out as many of the goblinkin as they could in the initial skirmish, then drive the survivors into the teeth of the dwarves waiting at the bottleneck.

Drathnon felt the drumming of goblinkin feet on the ground through the soles of his hobnailed boots. He took a fresh grip on his war hammer.

"Ready," he called out. "Wait until my signal." He focused on the top of the rise that led to the bottleneck. Then he saw the goblinkin running, urging their prisoners on with spears and swords.

As Drathnon watched, the elven archers brought down more of the goblinkin and spread panic through them. Their bleats of fear and savage threat filled the air.

"Steady," Drathnon said as he remained concealed in the branches of the fallen tree. "Wait for them."

If the goblinkin noticed the fallen trees, they gave no indication. They knew only that the trees on either side of the valley harbored enemy archers that killed them mercilessly.

"Now!" Drathnon ordered as the goblinkin raced to

within fifty paces of the barricade. "Kill them all!" He stepped forward and raised the war hammer.

The goblinkin saw the dwarves too late to stop. And the few that did try to stop were cut down by the elven archers. The goblinkin suddenly milled around in confusion and didn't know what to do.

Drathnon met them with Mardin, his other shield mate, and a warrior they'd picked up to fill in for the warrior that had fallen two days ago.

"Axes!" Drathnon shouted, and took point. His war hammer rose and fell, and goblinkin fell to the ground around his brutal attack. There was hardly any finesse to what he was doing. But there didn't have to be. Their enemies were massed too closely together to allow much skill. This close up, everything was based on strength and speed, and the dwarves were the undisputed masters of face-to-face warefare.

The prisoners took heart in the attack and began kicking and headbutting the goblinkin, adding even more madness to their battle because the center fell apart. In seconds, the goblinkin were harried from within as much as they were harried from without.

Drathnon fought with the same unfailing rhythm as he did when working metal on his anvil. If goblinkin heads and appendages could ring when struck, a fatal melody would have issued forth from his efforts. Dead foes dropped at Drathnon's feet till he battled his way over them and pushed the goblinkin farther and farther back.

Then stillness rode the wind over the valley. The dragon's great shadow coasted across the ground.

Despite his efforts not to be afraid, terror filled Drathnon. He pushed the dead goblinkin from him and looked up as Shamalis called out orders to his archers in the elven tongue.

When Kallenmarsdale turned to come back around, the

archers loosed their shafts. To their tribute, all of the arrows found a home in the dragon's sinewy body.

The dwarves cheered as they saw that the arrows had pierced the dragon's flesh. Most normal arrows wouldn't, but the magic in the dragon-fired metal did. They didn't stay there long, though. Within the space of a drawn breath, the arrows erupted into bright green flames.

Kallenmarsdale writhed in pain.

Another glad cheer arose from the dwarves, and it scared the goblinkin even more than they had been.

"Free the prisoners!" Drathnon shouted. He went forward, still in axe formation, and chopped through the goblinkin.

"Drathnon!" a familiar voice called out. "Over here!"

Relief flooded Drathnon when he saw Naklegong standing to his right. "Da!"

Naklegong looked worse for the wear, bruised and bloodied and burned here and there, but he was healthy and standing on his own two feet.

Drathnon fought his way to his da's side as Naklegong battled the nearby goblinkin. The dwarf next in line to him was dead, though, and trapped the prisoners there. Drathnon used a small knife to slice through the ropes that held his da, then pressed the knife into his hands.

Naklegong fiercely hugged his son for a moment, then buried the knife blade in the throat of a goblinkin that tried to skewer them with a short sword. As the goblinkin perished, Naklegong snatched the sword from the goblinkin's fist and made it his own.

"Watch out!" someone yelled. "The dragon is back!"

Drathnon broke free of the press of bodies around him. In the sky, the dragon flew toward the mass of combatants.

10

Shamalis!" Drathnon yelled.

Instantly, the elven archers came to bear again. More arrows struck the dragon and blazed green fire. Kallenmarsdale shuddered in displeasure, but stayed the course this time. Evidently the dragon had decided that the arrows might be painful, but they weren't going to kill him.

In the open now, Drathnon took his war hammer in both hands and set himself behind the writhing mass of struggling bodies that fought on. The elven archers continued shooting the dragon, but Kallenmarsdale wasn't going to pull up this time.

Drathnon spun around and around, then let go his hammer. The weapon flew through the air but flipped end over end just as he'd hoped it would. But it was as much luck as it was skill when the sharp spike at the hammer's end sank into the dragon's throat.

Squalling in disbelief, Kallenmarsdale lost control over his wings and fell to the ground with an impact so hard that it caused the ground to quake. Drathnon lost his footing and fell to one knee. As he watched, the dragon bounced on the ground, then skidded through the grass and brush with his legs and wings flailing.

Kallenmarsdale was nowhere near as graceful on the ground as he was in the air.

As the dragon slid toward him, still squalling in fury, Drathnon ran forward and caught his war hammer. His intention had been to plunge the spike even more deeply into the dragon's neck. Instead, Kallenmarsdale's uncontrolled slide knocked Drathnon from his feet and sent him ricocheting from the creature's massive chest. He kept hold of the hammer and yanked it from the dragon's flesh.

Dazed, the wind knocked from him, Drathnon used the hammer to push himself to his feet. He stepped forward, found it was in the wrong direction, and took another step. This one was toward the dragon.

The elven archers didn't pause in their assault, but Drathnon knew they must be close to using up their stock of arrows. And there was no sign of a mortal wound on the dragon.

Kallenmarsdale spat a great gout of flames. The fireball smashed into the nearby treeline and set it ablaze. But in that moment, Drathnon saw something he'd never seen before, or ever heard anyone mention.

Just before the dragon had unleashed his fiery breath, the huge teeth glowed cherry red like coals. Kallenmarsdale's breath ignited as it passed over them.

Then the dragon curled his neck and tried to right himself. He focused on Drathnon.

"Who are you, dwarf?" the dragon demanded.

"The death of ye if the Old Ones favor me this day," Drathnon promised. He brandished the war hammer. "I've made something to do the job out of what ye done spat out."

Kallenmarsdale flailed his wings and managed to roll over. Then he hissed wetly and belched fire. Just before the superheated mass descended on Drathnon, and he too slow to get away from it, Shamalis crashed into him and knocked them both from the path.

The dragon's breath ignited forty yards of grass and brush less than an arm's reach from where Drathnon came to a stop.

"Now is not the time for speeches." Shamalis stood and put an arrow to string.

Drathnon shoved himself to his feet as the elven warder loosed the shaft. The arrow sped true and plunged deeply into Kallenmarsdale's obsidian left eye. Almost immediately, green flames boiled from the orb.

The dragon howled in pain and shook his head like a dog. He clawed at his face in an effort to extinguish the flames.

Taking advantage of the wounded dragon, Drathnon raced forward. He'd intended to shove the spike into the underside of the dragon's chin in an effort to pierce its brain, or perhaps slit his throat. Drathnon would have been happy with either outcome.

Instead, the dragon turned his head and focused his one good eye on him. "You're going to die," he growled. Then he opened his jaws wide.

Knowing he'd never get away in time, Drathnon set himself and swung the hammer. The head collided with Kallenmarsdale's jaw so hard that Drathnon felt the impact shiver all through his body and reignite the pain throbbing in his head.

The dragon's breath blasted harmlessly skyward instead of over Drathnon and Shamalis.

"The eye!" Shamalis yelled to his archers. "Shoot him in the eye! Blind him!"

Drathnon reversed his war hammer and ran at the dragon with the spike pointed. Before he reached Kallenmarsdale, though, the dragon pushed himself up. More arrows turned to fire in his body, a handful of them along his face, and he beat the air with his wings.

Wobbly and dazed, Drathnon couldn't stand against

the wind that whipped over him. He fell heavily and watched as the dragon flew away.

Something gleamed in the grass nearby.

Breathing hard, Drathnon walked over to it and recognized what it was: a dragon's tooth.

"At least you've got a souvenir," Shamalis said. "That will be something to talk about."

Drathnon felt the heat from the tooth and didn't attempt to pick it up. "Actually, I'm hoping for more than a souvenir. Can you see if that tooth is magical?"

Shamalis joined him, then put his hand out over the tooth. Green sparks danced in the air.

Days later, after the Ringing Anvil dwarves salvaged what they could of the iron ore and got new wagons, Drathnon stood in front of the hearth where he spent most of his days. He carried the dragon's tooth in tongs that were starting to melt from the constant heat.

Traveling with the tooth had been problematic. Wooden crates burst into flames when they were in contact with it. Cloth burned. Metal melted. In the end, he'd kept the tooth in a stone container, but the heat had fused it and made it as fragile as glass.

Drathnon poised to throw the tooth into the lava forge the Ringing Anvil dwarves had created to smelt the ore. He glanced at his da.

"I've no way of knowing if this will work," he admitted.

"If it doesn't, we'll at least have additional heat as long as the tooth lasts."

"Scales from a dragon's back last forever," Shamalis said. "There's no reason to think a tooth won't do the same."

Knowing there was no other way to find out, Drathnon heaved the tooth into the lava pit. The bubbling lava instantly churned and exploded, throwing gouts out into the foundry. The heat was appreciably hotter.

No one spoke as Drathnon put an iron bar into the forge. When the metal turned cherry red, he took it out and held it for Shamalis to inspect.

When the elf held his hand over the metal, green sparks swirled around his hand. "The magic is there."

Excited, Drathnon took the bar to the anvil and began to work it. After a short time, when the metal had lost much of its heat and all of its color, he asked the elf to inspect it again.

The green sparks swirled again.

"The magic is still there," Shamalis said. He grinned. "I'd say you've found a way to re-create what only nature and dragons have given before."

Drathnon gazed at his da. "We have this, and it will be the secret of the Ringing Anvil clan. Only we will know how to beat magic into metal to make armor and weapons."

"I don't think we have much to worry about when it comes to keeping that secret," Naklegong said. "I don't know of any that are going to be willing to hunt a dragon for its teeth."

Drathnon knew that was true. No longer would they be limited, as other dwarven blacksmiths were, to chancing upon magic metal or bargaining for it. They could make their own.

Despite all the losses they'd endured, the Ringing Anvil dwarves had gotten something back that was priceless. Even with their fewer numbers, they were going to make things that would ensure their survival throughout all of time.